DEATH SHALL BOW

GEMMA ASHBORNE

Developmental Editor: Maria Tureaud (authormariatureaud.com)
Copyeditor: Cassandra Friday (copyeditsbycass@gmail.com)
Cover designer: Fay Lane (faylane.com)
Formatter: Books and Moods

PLAYLIST

"A Little Wicked" by Valerie Broussard

"Take Me Back to Eden" by Sleep Token

"Dead Lovers Lane" by HIM

"You Know Me Too Well" by Nothing But Thieves

"Words as Weapons" by Seether

"Cut Deep" by Matt Maeson

"Call Me" by Shinedown

"Le Disko" by Shiny Toy Guns

"Closer" by Kings of Leon

"Nazareth" by Sleep Token

"Big Bad Wolf" by In This Moment

"Watch the World Burn" by Falling In Reverse

"The Hourglass" by Ben Crosland

"Ode to a Conversation Stuck in Your Throat" by Del Water Gap

"Lost In You" by Three Days Grace

"Rain" by Sleep Token

WARNING

Death Shall Bow contains content that may be triggering or disturbing to some. This book is a work of fiction, and I in no way condone or encourage such behaviors in real life. If you wish to go in blind, know you have been warned. Your mental health matters.

Trigger warnings include, but are not limited to:
Strong language, sexually explicit content, brief suicidal ideation, gore/blood, on page death and murder, blood play, sexual assault (not the love interest), self-harm (blood pacts), and genital mutilation.

If you have any questions regarding the content of this book, please feel free to reach out: Gemma_Ashborne@att.net

Enter at your own risk.

And welcome to Anathema.

For anyone who has ever been told they're "too much" or to "calm down," this one is for you.
Give 'em hell, babe.

CHAPTER 1

WE WHO SEEK THE DARKNESS

"To control one's darkness is a gift. One bestowed upon those who seek not the dawn, but rather, those who would wield the shadows burst forth in Fate's light. Those who fear not the company of Death, but hunger to become him." – Chapter 11, Page 1, *The Book of Shade*

Death's metallic tang slithered between my teeth, sparked across my skull, and settled in my clenched jaw. Not the taste of *my* imminent doom though. No, the flavor was that of a Susan Bell: thirty-eight, lawyer, no notable family to mention. A drifter set to bypass Cottage Grove on her way to a convention in Spokane, or so Susan thought anyway. What she got instead? I-5's center divide, up close and personal. And me, well, I'd known about it for days. The same way I foresaw every other death in my podunk town. I pressed against my screaming temples. Head trauma. Poor thing.

Another day. Another death.

But this time, I wouldn't be there. This time the call would fall on another reaper to ferry the dying woman to the afterlife, because tonight I had a date with Death himself. Whether the fucker liked it or not. Years I'd been waiting for this moment, and while part of me felt an inkling of guilt in ignoring a lost soul's cry, I brushed it away. There were far bigger things at stake.

I headed for my bedroom window—combat boots clunking against the hardwood floor—and the moon's thick red glow shone down on me: a blood moon. Rare, and precisely the thing I'd need to enact my revenge. Or at least the first step anyway. The best part? Death would be expecting me, banking on me to summon him so I might take my rightful place. That's what made my plan foolproof: hiding in plain sight. I unclenched my fists, shaking the nerves out at my sides.

Patience, Kim, patience.

The familiar call of a raven tickled my ears, and I pulled my black velvet curtains aside, dragging the window open with a squeal to allow him in.

"Poe, there you are." I tickled the playful raven's head, placing a few sunflower seeds down for him to pick at. I'm not sure when my feathered friend first showed up, years ago I'd guess, but after that first snack there was no shaking him. Not that I wanted to. He was one of the only beings in this damned world I actually trusted. Plus, he was a great listener. Never judged. I slid a finger under his wing, scratching the place he loved most. A smile crept across my face as he purred into my palm. "Tonight's the night, buddy. Can you believe it? I'm finally going home."

Head cocked to the side, he squinted up at me as I slid my handy dagger into the holster around my thigh. If I didn't know any better, I would have sworn Poe actually understood English. I mean, the dude basically carried conversation with me, just with his beady eyes and croaky caws instead of words. With a rub against my hand, he disappeared out into the night, a low fog enveloping him. I soaked in what could very well be the last glimpse I ever got of him and released a heavy sigh. "Bye, bud."

The front door crashed open. Cooper's maniacal laugh echoed down the hall, redirecting the crossed wires in my subconscious, and brought me back to attention. Game on.

His tall stature leaned against the door frame, eyes wide and restless. "You ready for this?"

"You bet your ass I am."

"Got everything we need?" he asked, motioning to my leather backpack.

I raised an eyebrow. While my supernatural genes raged in the night and the chaos, Coop was human. And while he'd accepted me for who I was without question, I knew the risk in bringing a mortal along on this mission. No way I'd chance screwing it up. Though I'd checked it about twelve times, I unzipped the bag to show him the fruits of our labor. Three vials of blood—soon to be four—vampire, reaper, and shapeshifter. The latter was damn near impossible to find. Three nights in the Nevada desert and about a thousand bug bites later, we had barely managed to steal a few drops before the shifter took off. I mean, I get it. I'd run too if I were being held at knifepoint by two randos, one with flaming eyes like something straight out of a horror movie. Not going to lie, his fear was thrilling. Delicious. Reaper genes: got to love them. Always an internal tug of war between dark and light, though mine always skewed towards the shadows.

Next, I pulled out the herbs: wolfsbane, vervain, palo santo, and frankincense. Mixing these with the holy water we'd hunted down in a small church just outside Portland—turns out holy water doesn't hold its potency when the pastor who blessed it has a sick fondness

11

for little boys—was the only way to break the skin of our next target while in the mortal world: a demon. Once we had the demon's blood, all it would take was a centuries' old spell read aloud under the blood moon and a drop of royal blood (mine), and Death would show. He had to. And then I'd take what was mine.

"What, no booze?" Coop asked with a wink.

Rolling my eyes, I rummaged through my backpack and came back with a half-empty bottle of vodka. "Right, like I'd forget the most important part."

Mirroring each other's mischievous smiles as my heavy, Victorian front door clicked shut behind us, we trotted down the stairs and stepped out into the night. The stars flickered bright in the unpolluted sky. More than temptation, nightfall was a catalyst to the ever-present thirst within us both. We lived for the solace the night brought, me especially. Cloaked in dusk, prophesying deaths became almost bearable. The discomfort lessened; the pain proved more tolerable. At night I was just…me.

My mom waved from her cozy rocking chair on the porch, tapping her watch. "Don't be too late," she mimed. A joke, seeing as I was far too old for my mommy to be giving me any real orders. But she was still my landlord, and after Coop's and my drunken escapades having woken her up on more than one occasion, I couldn't blame her. Especially considering she had no idea I wasn't planning on coming back. Not anytime soon, anyway. Seeing her upset…I couldn't do it. But I wasn't a complete asshole; I left a note. One she'd find the following morning when I was far away, and she had no chances of following me. She'd be safe, like she deserved after all she'd been through.

"Sweet of mommy dearest giving you a curfew like that," Cooper called as we swept beneath the ivy arbor separating the main house from my private studio, the full moon reflecting off the evergreen yard's central fountain.

"Yes, Sir Sarcasm. Believe it or not, she does care about me. She cares about you too."

"I know, I know." He huffed and flipped his wrist. "I've just never understood why she gets so worked up about what time you're home. I mean, nothing happens in this town…like, ever. What, is she afraid old Mrs. Cringle is going to lose her mind and sic her rat-dog on us?"

True, Cottage Grove certainly held no place among Oregon's elite destination spots. Unless you considered countless bike trails and small-time museums "the good stuff," then sure, five stars. For the souls born and raised in its historic streets though? Not so much. But none of that mattered now. Not when my real home was so close, I could almost taste it.

Anathema: the realm of eternal night. And my birthright.

Lungs laced in piney air, I chucked the car keys to Coop and climbed into the passenger seat of my ever-faithful '82 pickup. "She worries about us being out too late, because of all the axe murderers lurking in the woods ready to hack-em-slash-em."

"Right, right. Forgot about them."

"Uh huh." I grinned as Coop turned over the ignition and aimed down the wooded driveway. "And we mustn't forget the dreaded candy store robbery of '22."

Coop clutched his chest dramatically. "Oh, dear me. Taffy strewn across the streets, kites wreaking havoc on the suburban residents, balloons polluting the atmosphere. It was a horror show, I tell you!"

"A bloodbath!" I snickered and adjusted my leather glove. "But really, I think she knows. Deep down, she has to."

My whole life she'd tried to protect me from my father. From Death, and his wicked and hateful heart. That's why she'd brought me to the mortal realm to begin with, in hopes I'd never have to see him again. But she knew this day would come. She'd mentioned it once; the vengeance refracted in my eyes. I'd never seen her look so sad and proud all in one moment.

As Coop swerved about the pothole ridden lane, my heartbeat quickened. What we were about to do would be the hardest thing we'd ever attempted; the chill in my bones assured me. But I needed it: that all-encompassing fear. Of all the sensations my fatal predictions forced upon me throughout the years, fear was never one. Pain, sadness, frustration, confusion...hell, even relief washed over me on occasion, but not a single twinge of terror. But attacking a demon on a full, blood moon? When their guardians stalked the woods while they hunted? I'd need that fear now. It'd keep me sharp. Alert.

Alive, hopefully.

Coop tapped the wheel before looking my way. "Did you tell June yet?"

"Not yet." I took a swig of vodka, its harsh warmth stabbing my tongue. "I didn't want to worry her."

"Seriously? You know she's going to freak. I mean, come on, Kim." He laughed. "You're about to go after a demon, not to mention summoning Death himself. That's the sort of thing your girlfriend *should* worry about."

Oh, my sweet, kind, safe June. When my dark gifts first began to crop up around my eighteenth birthday, I had no idea how to control my astral projection. I'd found myself in hell on more than one occasion—for the record, brimstone smells like literal shit—before I crashed through Juniper's realm, Elysium, the realm of eternal light, before inevitably colliding with her in neutral territory. A sarcastic little vixen with a brat complex, she became my first thought every morning and the one I dreamt about every night. Over the years, she'd helped me hone my skills. Now, I didn't need to sleep to reach her. All I had to do was picture that beautiful face of hers, and I'd be there.

"Fine, I'll reach out to her," I said, shifting in my seat. "You know where we're going, yeah?"

"Of course. We only studied the evidence, what, thirty times?"

About a week ago, we'd gotten wind of demonic activity in the next town over. Random bodies found with their livers ripped out, singe marks on the soles of their feet, and silver coins placed over their eyes: aka a demon calling card. Usually, the mark would be something simpler, like a sigil drawn in the dirt next to the body, or a colored piece of fabric tucked into the corpse's pocket. Demons were prideful fuckers, always wanting recognition for their kills. It's why so few remained in the mortal world. They got cocky, and humans got brave. But this coin thing? Concerning. That was the mark of an old demon, one who'd hunted in the mortal world long before the realms had been closed off. It was basically a big "fuck you" to reapers, as the old human stories told of paying a toll to have their souls taken to the other side. They hated us, mostly. But hell if I'd let that stop me.

"Tell her I said hi," Coop said with a wink. "That is, if your lips aren't too occupied with…other things."

"Fuck off," I said with a laugh, and closed my eyes.

The world around me stilled, a gentle buzz settling in my ears. I built June's image in my mind's eye. Her intoxicating, mahogany eyes. The soft, tight ringlets that framed her face. The way the light danced on her rich brown cheeks. Next, I focused on feel. How soft her velvet lips felt against mine. My hands wrapped around her hips, pulling her close. The magnetic draw we'd had from day one. We joked that we had a rope tying us together, a knot anchored in both of our chests.

And just like that, I was there.

"Kim." Her voice tangled in my ears, like sweet music. "I wasn't expecting you."

I stepped towards her, the scene around us filling in. The Shroud: where we always met. Better known as purgatory to the human realm. Given our conflicting gifts—hers born in the light of a realm opposite my own—it was neutral ground. You see, reapers and ascended spirits weren't exactly supposed to fraternize. Not like we did. But somehow, whatever divine being had connected us in the first place had also gifted us a place to meet, and I was grateful. Though I wasn't a huge fan of how many times our visits had been cut short thanks to the realm's rogue monsters wanting to eat our faces off. Nightmares: hungry little shits.

I wrapped my arms around her, placing a quick kiss on her lips. "So promise not to be mad?"

Her brow creased. "Well, aren't we off to a lovely start this evening? What did you do?"

"It's not what I did," I said, pinching her butt playfully. "It's what I'm about to do."

She must have known, because fear crept into her eyes. "The blood moon…it's finally here, isn't it?"

I nodded and tucked a curl behind her ear. "We have everything we need to do the ritual. It's now or never."

Her face fell, and I lifted it gently.

"You have to understand," I pled more than stated. "I have to do this, June. This is my birthright. My people need me."

"I know; I just wish you didn't have to be the one to summon him."

Death. I offered a gentle smile. "I've got this, love. I'm not afraid of him."

"Yeah, well, maybe you should be. Attempting this alone, it's risky."

My hold on her tightened as I coaxed her head to my chest, and she rested it there with a sigh. "I'm not alone; I have Cooper. Anybody else would just get in my way. I don't need to be worried about anybody else's life hanging in the balance. But you know Coop, stubborn as shit. Wouldn't take 'no' for an answer."

Her face bobbed against me, a cynical laugh rattling through her. "One of these days, you're going to have to learn to let people in, Kim. Or you'll end up finding yourself in a scrape with nobody left to turn to."

"What, that your way of saying you're breaking up with me?" I teased.

She slapped my chest before grabbing my face and pulling me within an inch from her lips. "Just promise me you'll use that brain of yours, yeah? No rash decisions. And if push comes to shove, you—"

"I know, I know, I run."

"Like your life depends on it, woman. Because it does."

Her lips met mine, and my toes curled. This woman... I lost myself in her, her inner light dancing against the tendrils of dark magic at my fingertips. There was no way to describe it, the magnetic draw. Loving her: it'd never been a choice. Preordained by fate or magic, I'm not sure, but I couldn't get enough. Juniper was my air, my life force. And this insatiable need to be near her—especially in times such as these—consumed me. Here I was about to hunt down Death, and all I could think about was all the ways I wanted to please her. My hands, of their own volition, began to wander about her. She repaid my efforts with a satisfied moan, and I smiled against her kiss.

"You're trying to get me to stay," I whispered.

"Mm-hmm," she said, her lips moving to my neck. "Is it working?"

My heartbeat kicked up, everything in me aching to pin her to the ground and ravage her. "I'll come back. And when I do, you better be ready."

She met my gaze, a strained look on her face. "You better come back. I swear, if you go and get yourself killed, you better not land in Elysium. Cause I'll kill you again for making me worry."

Her laugh carried me back to the mortal world, the sensation of her kisses on my neck still tickling the need deep inside me. I turned to Coop, a devilish smirk on his face.

"What?" I asked.

"Sounds like somebody was having a good time." He mimicked my moan.

I slapped his arm. "Oh, whatever, you're just jealous."

"And if I was?" he asked, voice low and gravelly.

My body still aching for touch, I watched as he slid a hand up my skirt, pausing just below the good stuff. The skull tattoo covering his hand pulsed as he squeezed my thigh. Twenty-one and he was already sleeved up both arms thanks to his buddy at Royal Empire Tattoo. Dark, sinister pieces intermingled with realistic sketches of poisonous hemlock and oleander.

I wanted to tell him to do it, to guide his hand and put those long fingers to good use. Take the edge off. My mind slipped back to the drunken night we'd let slide, seeing who would blow the whistle first. But then, we just…didn't. To say he blew my back out would be the understatement of the century. Dick for days and an acute attention to detail, I couldn't even guess how many times he had sent me over the edge that night. But he was also the light of my life and my best friend, and I'd decided the following morning that risking our friendship wasn't something I was about to mess with. And then came June.

As much as I hated it, I pulled his hand from its hold on my thigh and wove my fingers through them instead. "Have I told you lately how much I fucking love you?"

"Not nearly enough, tease." He winked.

He veered the old truck past St. Augustine Cathedral—its stained-glass windows lightless—and edged onto the interstate. A cool wind raked through the window and swept across my cheek as we picked up speed. At least I could always count on two simple comforts: the night and Coop. I let that wash over me, ground me.

He shuffled about in my peripheral, his ripped jeans squeaking against the pleather seat. "So think this will work?"

"It has to. I'm ending that piece of shit, no matter what it takes."

He chuckled, squeezing my hand. "That's my girl. Give 'em hell."

The old truck wheezed past the last house on the main drag and onto a single lane, dirt road. A musty aroma crept on the breeze, carried from the eerie, mildew-riddled shed at the creek line ahead. Reduced to little more than peeled paint and rotten boards, a hand painted sign on the shack marked the safest area to wade through the creek to the other side. Coop eased the truck down the bank, and water slushed at the wheel wells.

Goosebumps walked across my limbs as the images of those murdered hikers came back to me. Three victims in two weeks, all with the same coins placed over their lifeless eyes. All brutally stripped from the world. Their poor families. While I'd let the other blood donors we'd hunted before go, I'd decided that this one—this demon—would die for what he had done. But I couldn't let Coop know that, or he'd never stick to the plan. Stubborn ass.

"Care for a little liquid courage?" I extended the bottle to him. Not too much, but just enough to take the heightened nerves down a notch. We each took a swig, and I glanced over. "You ready for this?"

"What, hoping I'd puss out?" he asked, a wicked smirk on his face. "Not a chance. We do this together, like always."

Shutting the truck off and doing away with the headlights, we allowed the darkness to envelope us. Silence wisped across my neck, and a tantalizing chill crept up my spine to meet it. This. This is what I lived for: the fear. The sensations that lurked in the shadowed unknown.

As quiet as possible, we slipped into the open air. Moonlight danced along the forest floor as we made our way into the denser areas. We'd hear it, no doubt. Demons weren't exactly stealth hunters. They liked to instill dread in their victims, chase them until their lungs give out before attacking. At least the ones who still ate human liver, that is. Most were sophisticated members of Anathema's society these days—their hunger for human flesh long since passed—at least based off my studies. But some still hungered for the old ways. And I had no doubt the fucker we were after was one of them. Coming up to an outcropping of large boulders, I motioned for Coop to sit. He came to rest at my side, and I pulled the herbs from my pack. One after the other, I emptied them into the holy water and shook. Once mixed, I dipped my blade into the concoction, and a slight sizzle radiated from my blade. Ready.

Then we waited. And waited. Twenty minutes passed without a single sound. No movement. No sightings. Nothing.

Coop tapped my arm. "What if—"

"Shh," I urged.

We sat motionless in the black, breaths so shallow they lost all audibility. Thirty minutes. Forty. Come the hour mark, I'd begun to worry we'd failed before even trying.

"I have an idea," Coop finally said. "I'll bait him."

I shook my head. "Hell no, that's way too risky."

"If we don't nail this guy, you'll never get your chance, Kim.

Please let me do this."

Considering his words, my gut tightened. He wasn't wrong. Fuck.

"Fine," I sighed. "But the second that asshole comes into view, you run, you hear me? I mean it. Get the hell out, and I'll find you when the job is done."

"You'll need me to hold him down."

I raised a hand, placing it into a ray of moonlight. The shadows inside me came trickling out, and Coop's eyes widened. "You forget," I whispered, "he isn't the only one more powerful on a blood moon."

Readying my blade, I watched Coop trek out into the open. The breeze wafted my hair about, piercing the silence with its gentle whoosh. And then, with a wink, he started yelling.

"Help! Anybody out there? I lost the path. Help, please!"

Then, we heard it. The shrill, demonic screech.

My heart seized, and shock trickled its icy touch along my forearms, every hair raised in its wake. The call, it was almost...almost human. But the undertone: feral. Again it cried out, this time leaps and bounds closer than before. Coop's sights fell on me as he stomped about to keep the incoming threat on his trail. I placed one finger to my lips, and he froze. Tilting my head to the side, I listened.

Quiet blanketed the scene once again. When the air grew thick and the unshakable sense of being watched had heightened to a near-palpable state, that's when the crunching started. At first it was low, more a throb than a harsh crunch. But once the sound's direction solidified, it'd fade away and reappear seconds later in the completely opposite direction. Behind, the noise was always behind. My palms began to sweat and tingle in intoxicated bliss. Fingers trembled. I was afraid. I was feeling. I was *alive*.

A sudden thwack against wood resounded not ten feet behind Cooper.

"What. The. Fuck." Coop's breath heaved in the stillness.

The snap of a branch resounded, this time closer still.

Next came the clinking: first one flick, then two, then three. The metallic clink of a coin being flicked in the air. Over and over. Its glimmer refracted in a moonbeam peeking through the treetops just beyond Cooper. Hand clenched around my blade, I smiled.

Got you, asshole.

The demon's shadow emerged, though his face hid behind an ornate Victorian mask. Clever. But it wouldn't save him. Not this time. I circled about, sticking to the darkest parts untouched by moonlight, studying the monster in human form.

"Lost, are we?" he asked Coop, and started a slow pace towards him.

Careful to direct his attention away from my location, Cooper slid off to the left. "I...yes. Please, can you help me find my way back?"

"I'm afraid you've come to the wrong person if you wish for help. You see," the demon said, flipping his coin once more, "I'm not here to decide if you should live or die, let alone be worthy of my help. No. That I'll leave up to Fate."

As I closed in, barely three feet from striking distance, the demon tilted his head at Coop. "Call it," he demanded.

A confused look on his face, Coop asked, "Call what?"

"Call it," the demon ordered again, a feral growl in his tone. "Heads or tails. Heads, you live, and I'll decide if that includes my help. Tails, well..."

Coop swallowed hard as I settled into position. "Tails, and you kill me, right?"

The demon laughed. "Oh, no, no. Tails, and I hunt you. I know, I'm far too gracious, giving you two chances at potential salvation. So, mortal. Call it. Heads or—"

"Tails, fucker!" I screamed, and lunged out. He dodged my blade before it could pierce his heart, but I felt it nick skin. Not a deep blow, but confirmation that the herbs had worked. I struck again, this time spinning about to cut off his access towards the woods. But he was... gone. Like disappeared-into-thin-air gone. But how? I flipped my blade about. "You can't hide from me!"

"Uh, Kim," Coop whispered, voice shaky.

I whipped around. "You were supposed to run! Why are you still—"

Following the sight line of his pointed finger, my blood chilled. There, hunched in the darkness, a set of piercing gold eyes stared back from six feet off the forest floor. The creature's hot breath clouded the worst of its undoubtedly abhorrent features, but I knew. Oh, I knew.

A hellhound. And from the looks of it, he was fucking ravenous.

CHAPTER 2

DEATH

"C oop!" I called out in the darkness, but didn't dare take my eyes off the hound. "Don't. Move."

"Wasn't planning on it," he muttered, frozen.

Okay, okay, think Kim.

Referencing what I had readily available to me as the creature began a slow stalk out from the tree line, it became apparent how royally screwed we were. A dagger. That's all I had against this monstrosity whose shoulders cleared my own, and he was on all fours.

Fuck, fuck, fuck.

This was not part of the plan. We were supposed to kick this demon's ass and be out of the area before his steroid-riddled guard dog could find us. But no. Now I had to go toe to toe with Cujo 2.0 and dodge his demon companion who—by the tingle in my gut—was still nearby, watching our every move. And my dumbass brought a human with me.

I centered myself, studying and taking in what I could about the beast. It moved slow, shoulders forward in an "I'm about to pounce" stance, and a long string of saliva dripped from its mouth. It stalked about us, a low growl rattling its teeth together.

"Listen closely," I said, and took a step closer to Coop. "When I say the word, you run. I'll catch up."

He dared a reach, rubbing his thumb against my wrist. "I can't leave you."

"You can, and you will. I'm not asking."

A firm grasp on my blade, I met the creature's glowing eyes. Feral. Hungry. Murderous. But what the hellhound and its demon boss hadn't considered? You don't mess with the people I love. And if it was the last thing I did, I'd get Coop out of these woods alive. A breeze tracing an invisible touch along my cheek, I squared my stance. Now or never.

"Go!" I screamed, and took off.

Coop's steps thrashed in the tall grass as he broke for the moonlit forest behind. Surprised he listened to me—he never did...shocker— relief gave way to immediate panic. In a rush, three hundred pounds of muscle, fur, and teeth took me to the ground. My back hit the hard earth, breath betraying me as it left my lungs. But there'd be no time to regain it as massive teeth gnashed mere inches from my face. I pulled my knife to its throat, but it became crystal clear a second too late that this beast? It was conscious. Calculating. Clever. Thrusting its head forward, it knocked the blade from my hand, leaving me with nothing but my damn hands to defend myself. This was it. My end. My headstone would read "Died as Puppy Chow"—how ridiculous.

"Over here, asshole!"

Cooper. Silly of me to assume he wouldn't loop back around and risk his life for me. The sweet idiot. The hound's head shot up, and it took off like a bullet. Shit!

I hopped to my knees, snatched the dagger, and tore into the woods. "Here, you big brute! Take me!"

Coop dodged between trees, the monster matching his every move. Heartbeat in my throat, I broke right, coming around to slide between them. But once again, the hound was one step ahead, knocking me on my ass. Before I could right myself, it was already too late. Contrary to popular belief, the most traumatic moments don't slow, they speed up. All I could do was watch as those massive jaws latched around the only person I'd ever die for. I'd ever live for.

Coop screamed in agony as the hellhound took a chunk from his shoulder. An iron perfume danced in the wind, and my heart shattered under the weight. And then it happened. The unmissable call of death.

Cooper Rollins: age twenty-one, best friend, excessive blood loss.

Panic settling in my clenched jaw, I released a piercing cry into the woods as I raced towards the threat. Pushing off the ground with all my force, I launched myself onto the beast's back, cementing my hold in its fur.

"Die, fucker," I growled, burying my dagger to the hilt right between the beast's shoulder blades.

A shrill howl released from its open mouth before it bucked me off. I hit the ground for the third time, and my elbow cracked against a rock, splitting flesh. Fresh, warm blood trickled down my arm, but I couldn't give two shits about my own well-being in that moment. I drug myself through the dead leaves, coming to rest at Coop's side.

"No, don't you dare," I snarled. "Don't you dare leave me!"

I frantically pawed at his shoulder. A thick, meaty chunk lay at his side, but that wasn't the worst of it. The hound's canine had grazed his neck…deep enough to rip into the jugular. No. No! Tearing my shirt, I blotted up the wound. In seconds, the material was soaked, my hands stained through my gloves. A cough rattled through him as he took my hand in his.

"It's okay," he whispered, another cough shaking him. Crimson seeped at the corners of his mouth. "Let me go."

"Like hell I will!"

COOPER ROLLINS: AGE TWENTY-ONE, BEST FRIEND, EXCESSIVE BLOOD LOSS!

"Screw you, Death!" I screamed. And then it clicked.

Death. He could fix this.

I ripped my shirt off completely, balling it up against Coop's neck, and placed his hand on it. "Apply pressure, I'll be right back!"

Stumbling through the darkness, I kept a watchful eye for the demon and his pet. The woods stood eerily still aside from the clomp of my steps. Gone, they had to be. But I made a vow to myself, right then and there. If it wasn't already dead by now, I'd find that hound and skin it alive. And I'd make its master watch.

Nobody hurts those I love and lives. Nobody.

I crashed back into the clearing, red-tinted moonlight shining down on the object of my desire: my backpack. Shit...I didn't get the demon blood! Hands shaky, I cast my sights to the night sky, a rageful shriek tearing from my throat. My face fell, and as if Fate herself had ordained that very moment, I saw it. There, just an inch from where I stood: small red splatters. I *had* nicked him earlier! Falling on all fours, I dipped my fingers in the now cold puddle and licked them clean. Digging through my bag, I pulled out the other three vials, downing the sickening metallic liquid within each. It'd take a moment to activate and meld with my own magic, as all spells of that caliber do, no doubt. I sprinted back into the shadows. This wasn't how it ended, damn it.

Once back at Coop's side, I heaved for breath, my sights coming to rest on his still frame. He wasn't moving, chest barely rising and falling.

"Fuck, no, no, no! Don't do this! Stay with me! Don't even think about walking into that damned light!"

I rummaged about for my knife, sticking its tip in the dirt to form a circle. At the top, I scribbled a cross, connecting it to the circle. To the right, a seven-pointed star. To the left, a spiral. And at the foot, a triangle. The four courts of Anathema. The shadows inside me began to twist and turn as my stomach soured, alerting me that the spell was forming. Wasting no time, I ripped my gloves off and slid the blade down my palm, squeezing every drop I could muster in the circle's center. Sights cast to the moon, I recited the rite.

"By way of balance, blood, change, and force, I seek a stop upon Death's course." I repeated it twice more and licked my hand clean. Blood of each court, devoured by a member of the Reigning Reaper's royal line. The final step. The one that would alert Death that I was near. And I demanded his presence.

Blue flames burst to life on the earth sketch, the flames motionless despite the wind now whipping about the trees above. It had worked. I'd bound him to his duty with that spell. Ignoring it would lead to his own demise.

He'd come. He had to.

The inferno died in an instant as if it never was, and I slid back to my best friend's side in a smoky haze. His breaths were shallow, cheeks pale. Scouring the woods for any signs of movement, I awaited Death's appearance. And waited. And waited.

Goosebumps rose up on my arms as I imagined standing face to face with Death himself, but I brushed it away. Based on the summoning spell's ingredients alone, I now had a clear idea of what dangers Anathema and its beings possessed, and the potential risks therein. And neither would stop me. I'd do whatever, *become* whatever in order to save Cooper. No matter the atrocities that awaited me, I'd kick anyone's ass who stood in my way.

I'd acquired a taste for the adrenaline rush that fear brings years ago and pursued it with the kind of enthusiasm one might expect from a die-hard groupie or a sports junkie. I knew how to function within it now, how to turn on a dime and alter my course. But this? This wasn't fear; this was terror, and I needed Death to show. Now.

Coop stirred below me, a gasp rattling through him, and his wound gushed.

"Hey, hey, hey, breathe. Lay back," I said gently, guiding his head to rest on my arm. He shivered against me, and I wrapped myself around his side for warmth.

Death, where the hell are you?

A flash across the sky peeked through the treetops. A distraction, perfect. "Look, a shooting star. Make a wish."

"I wish," he heaved through blue-edged lips, "I wish I didn't have to leave you."

A sucker punch to the gut, I fought back tears. Whatever response I may have been able to muster caught in my throat. What was I supposed to say? That he didn't have to go? That I wanted him to stay with me always? We were supposed to build a life together. We'd planned it. And for what? A slow, painful end? It wasn't fucking fair. I didn't want him to leave me; but if Death didn't show, I had no backup plan. All I could do was wait for Death to reveal himself in whatever form he chose to appear. *If* he chose to appear.

"No matter what," I choked out, "I'm with you. Always."

I snaked my hand through his and allowed the moon's calming glow to say what I couldn't. That I needed him. That I was here. That we'd always have the night. I lost myself in his shallow breaths, his chest rising and falling in perfect time with my own. And then, all at once, he stilled.

"Coop," I whispered, pushed to sit, and patted his shoulder. He didn't flinch. "Cooper…"

Again, nothing. I pressed my ear to his chest, heartbeat clapping against my ribs. He wasn't breathing.

"No, no, no." Hands frantic, I began to hyperventilate, and my vision blurred.

A frosty presence settled about the forest, the wind dying all at once. My gut snarled. The unmissable scent of putrid rot curled itself through the air. I snapped to my feet, sights honed in on a silhouetted figure at the tree line, its head cocked to one side. It studied us like a beast would its prey. Flesh gripped between forefinger and thumb, I squeezed: pain. This was no hallucination. Death, it seemed, had shown after all. A shiver ran up my spine and settled at the base of my head as the dark onlooker stalked closer.

"My, my," the figure *tsked* in a haunting tone. "It seems you've landed yourself in quite the predicament tonight, my daughter."

"Death," I said, resting Coop's head before jumping to my feet.

"Father," he insisted. "But you may call me Cadagon if you deem it more fitting."

He drifted over the fallen leaves towards me, a sinister grin splayed across an otherwise concealed face. A cloak, the same shade as fresh blood, veiled his true identity. Whatever horrors lurked beneath that hood, I could only imagine. Though something told me deep down that I didn't want to know. Alarms rattled in my skull. Get out. Run. Save yourself. But one look at Cooper silenced them all. For him, I'd walk through hell itself.

"P-please," I begged behind clenched teeth, "He's dying, and I can't stop it."

A disturbed chuckle slipped through Cadagon's grin. "That's what mortals do: they die."

No. Not Coop. Not now. My breaths grew uneven, strained. "It's not his time. We have to—"

"What is, is." He quickened his pace towards me. "Now come, walk with me. I haven't long before my visitation spell ends; we must go."

"Go? I—"

"You summoned me here to take your rightful place on the throne, did you not?"

Sure, that was the initial goal, but things had changed. There was clearly a higher priority here. I forced a brave face despite every bone in my body rattling. "I'm not going anywhere with you until you heal him. He's not breathing, and I know you can save him. Please help me!"

Cadagon ceased his quick steps, and his sick smile fell from his face. I knew my pleading could be misinterpreted for weakness, but it was my best friend we were talking about. When it came to those I loved, I knew I was weak. Hell, I'd outright admit it. But I didn't care what I'd have to do to save him: plead, barter, threaten. Anything I had to, I would. Death closed the distance between us in the blink of an eye.

"You'll do as you are told," he barked down at me.

"Not until you save him." I may not have been an expert on reapers, but I knew somehow, without a doubt, that saving Cooper would be no feat for a creature of Cadagon's stature.

The air chilled. "Death is to be decisive. A finite end, Kimberly."

Fuck it, fear be damned. I stepped towards him. "But you can stop it, can't you?"

"Yes, but—"

"Then do it," I begged, attention falling on Coop once more. Minutes without oxygen, his skin had taken on a sickly purple hue. Tears tore free. Though terror gnashed inside, I held my ground, unwilling to budge. "Please do this for me!"

Cadagon drew closer and released a guttural growl. "Fine, I'll save your *pet*. But at a price."

A heavy price, I had no doubt. My gaze landed on the blood now seeping from Coop's open mouth. I coaxed his head into my lap. "Yes, anything, just save him!"

"As you wish, Princess," Death muttered, his wicked grin returned.

I brushed a strand of hair from Coop's face and shuffled to allow the reaper access to his motionless body. Useless, aside from lending my lap as a pillow. Cadagon flipped Coop's head side to side with little care.

On impulse, I slapped his hand before I could think it through. "Be careful with him. Shit."

Cadagon's head shot up, hood falling away to reveal deep-set eyes ignited with living flame, and my very spirit quivered. What. The. Hell.

"This is the first and last warning you will receive," Death said, ashen hair adrift in the steady breeze. "Treat me with the respect I deserve. If you do not, I will simply take you by force and leave this bag of bones here to rot. Do I make myself clear?"

The overwhelming urge to reach out and slap him across the face rose from the depths inside me. The arrogant bastard. But without his help, well…I nodded.

"Good." Cadagon refocused on the task and traced his lanky finger across Cooper's forehead, then his chest. "He was bitten by a hellhound. I'll need assistance to restructure his fractured insides. But you must know I cannot restore him to his original self. Not here."

"What do you mean?"

Without pause, Cadagon snatched my right hand and buried the tip of an unforeseen blade an inch deep into the flesh. My body seized at the tear of muscle, and I ripped my hand away.

"What the hell!" I shrieked, blood spurting all over Coop's still torso.

"Do you want to save your friend or not?"

"Of course I do—"

"Then stop your ceaseless blabbering and let me work." He grabbed my hand back, dipped his fingertips into the pooled blood in my palm, and traced it around Cooper's eyes and jaw. Head bowed, he slid a single, thin line of crimson across Coop's pierced lip. "Hold his head firm."

Two fingers to the sky, he inhaled a sharp breath, and struck Cooper's rib cage with a balled fist. The harsh crunch of shattered bone echoed through the trees, but my best friend's body remained unresponsive. I searched for a pulse. One second, two, three, four; all blew past without a single pump. "No…no! You said you could save him! You said—"

Cadagon latched onto my arm. "Calm yourself. It's merely a rebirth, watch."

I stared for what felt like an eternity, searched for any signs of life, however small. "He's not coming back…"

"He will."

Minutes ticked by. "What if you—"

"I said, 'Silence!'" Cadagon snarled, his attention dead set ahead.

Then, like pent up water released from a dam, Coop's chest began to rise and fall once more. But his eyes remained shut. "Why…why isn't he waking up?"

"I told you," Death said, hoisting Cooper's limp body up over his shoulder. "He cannot stay here. His mortal soul has perished, and even I cannot change such things. Come, let us go. Anathema awaits."

"No. That's not possible…" My head began to pound as the weight crumbled down on me. Stay, and Coop would die. Leave, and who knows what fate he'd face in the realm of eternal night? I clenched my hands. "If we go with you, he lives?"

"Yes."

A sickening feeling settled in my stomach. Cadagon was hiding something; I could taste the sour lie on my tongue. "And what will happen to him then?"

"We've no time for this. Come with me now or he will return to the dirt."

I turned to face Death, self-preservation overshadowed by the burn in my chest. The growing rage.

"What good is saving his life if he awakens in a world that means to eat him alive? Humans don't belong in Anathema, do they?" I ground my teeth together. "Answer me, what will happen to him if we go with you?"

"I don't care what happens to him." Cadagon snatched my wrist and pulled me close, starting towards the dense trees in the opposite direction. "I've done my part; now it's your turn to uphold your end of our bargain."

"Please don't, you have to let me—"

Cadagon stopped, sighed, and placed one finger to my forehead. "Sleep."

With that, my world went black as night.

CHAPTER 3

THE REALM OF ETERNAL NIGHT

My eyelids peeled back to reveal an ornate, vaulted ceiling complete with crisscrossed beams. A ceiling I didn't recognize in the slightest. Where was I? A flash of burning irises and a cloaked face smacked my memory, and I jerked to sit, silk sheets pooling around my hips.

Cadagon.

I studied the dainty, candlelit room, its quaint space decorated to the nines. Behind, a grand cherrywood headboard boasted hand-painted skulls and roses. I hopped to my feet and began a slow walk about the room. The headboard's edges tapered off between identical stained-glass windows, raven silhouettes encased in their centers. In the corner, a brick fireplace crackled with orange flame, its banister stained in a deep mahogany. Absolutely stunning. The kind of beauty that, on any other occasion, would have made my heart skip a beat. Yet all I felt in that moment was rage. Not fear, not worry. Blind fucking rage.

Coop. Where the hell had Cadagon taken him?

I carried myself to the door and pulled at the handle. But it remained firm, locked. With a growl, I beat my bandaged fist against the thick wood. "Cadagon, you better explain yourself, or I'll...I'll—"

"You'll what?" His grating voice answered from the shadows behind me.

"Holy shit. How'd you do that?"

"This is my castle; I flow freely within its walls, uninhibited by physical technicalities." Cadagon started towards me, his crimson robe dragging along the floor behind him. "Now, what were you saying before? Ah, yes, something of a threat, I believe?"

I studied the man closer as he stepped into the candlelight. Salt and pepper locks settled about his shoulders. At his full height, I had to crane my neck to meet his gaze. He stared down his nose at me with a grin, his eyes still alive with flame. My breath caught. He truly was Death incarnate.

"Ah, frightened I see."

"You wish," I said.

The light caught his crown. Pieced together by bits of polished bone, teeth, and cooled quicksilver, it was nothing short of wicked. My confidence wavered. This was real. He was real. Which meant the danger I faced in his presence was also entirely real. But he also needed me. My mother had assured me of that when she had told me what he'd done. Of the way he'd slaughtered her people. *My* people. I was his route to redemption. Or so the fool thought. And I'd allow him to use me, so I could get close enough to end him at just the right moment, like he deserved.

I pushed my shoulders back. "Where is he?"

Cadagon grabbed his chest with jet black, stained fingers. "Why, I have no idea what you mean, Princess."

"Liar." My hands balled into fists.

"You've never known me," he said, head tilted, "and yet you have the audacity to claim you know my character?"

I forced a laugh. "My mother told me everything I need to know about your supposed character, murderer."

The king paced about, dragging his shadowed hands across the studded, leather chair near the window. "Isn't that quite the hypocritical take? Or were you not planning on killing that demon you stalked in the woods?"

My chest constricted. "That's different. He killed innocent people. He deserved it."

"And just who are you to decide what someone deserves? You are not Death." His eyes darkened. "I alone hold that title."

"For now," I said, eyes narrowing.

"You think so, do you? Well then, allow me to enlighten you." Death snapped his fingers, and the latch on the door released from the other side. "Come, it's time you learned of your heritage. Of *my* kingdom."

"I'm not going anywhere with you." I stood tall, chin high.

"Brave words for a woman with no leverage and everything to lose. You think I don't know where to find your mother? Or that I can't simply dispose of your little pet?" Darkness settled in his stare. "Death's power is mine alone to wield. So I suggest, if you'd like my sight to pass over those you so foolishly allow yourself to love, that you do as you are told. I am the king, and I have no desire to play the doting father to someone I've never known. Now move."

I hesitated in the doorway. My instincts—elevated by the buzz of Anathema's energy—told me he was bluffing. Or partially, anyway. If he'd meant to hurt my mother, my guess is he would have already done so. But on the off chance I was wrong—the conviction in his eyes strong—I had no choice. I didn't want to tag along and play right into his hands, but if I were going to find Coop and get him back to the mortal world safely, having a lay of the land wouldn't be such a bad idea. I stepped out into the spiraling staircase.

"And so it begins," Cadagon said, flaming eyes wide.

We wound through the slim hall lit by mounted candles and twisted ever downward. Each new floor boasted a single, heavy, wooden door and an alcove cut into the stone wall beside it. Centered in each sat the same carved gargoyle, its position changed from the last floor.

"This is the southernmost tower," Cadagon projected in front of me. "This tower is yours to command. I'll fill the rooms however you see fit, given you won't have much freedom until I find you to be more...cooperative."

My hands clenched. "You're locking me away in a tower? You do realize that's the epitome of a cliché, fairy tale beginning, right?"

"No, I am not locking you away in a tower. I'm keeping you safe, secure, under my watchful eye."

"And is that for my well-being or yours?"

He whirled around. "If you would like to continue being difficult, I can always have the guards put you in the courtyard stocks?"

The hall sat silent.

"I thought not. Follow."

When we reached ground level, we swept through a pointed archway ahead and out into a much grander, open space. Black and gold leaf speckled beams jutted towards a painted ceiling above, the mural depicting a canopy of autumn treetops. The branches appeared to move of their own volition and danced about in the light of the room's wide-mouthed hearth.

My heart fluttered at the sight. I'd never seen anything so

bewitching in my life; it stole the very air in my lungs. Tracing my hands along the nearest beam, its cool marble nipping at my fingers, I heaved a sigh. A hall fit for a queen. Guilt slapped me over the head. The hell was wrong with me? I was supposed to be finding a way to get Coop home. Not marveling at the architecture.

Focus, Kim. Shit.

My sights drifted about, taking stock of two exits at the room's edges, and logged it away for future reference.

"This is the south dining hall, decorated with my own personal touch," Cadagon said. "I assumed, given your absence from me all these years, that your tastes would have grown to reflect your mother's quite keenly. But based on the wonder reflected in your eyes, it occurs to me our tastes may not be so different after all."

"We're nothing alike." My jaw tensed, nails pressing into my palms. I'd never have ruthlessly killed and ran off an entire court like he had. I'd never have stolen a loved one away, hiding them as leverage like he did now.

"And yet you stand here, marveling at my handiwork," he said, as if reading my mind.

"That doesn't make us the same. I'm not a heartless monster like you."

"You say it with such conviction, it must be so." Cadagon stepped onto the sea of red jasper tiles spread across the dining hall and ushered me forward.

Hundreds of carved picture frames claimed the farthest brick wall in its entirety. I drew closer to study the people within the photos, each reflecting various faces and moments in time, but the same shadow-tipped fingers. "Who are they?"

"The Reigning Reapers before us: your family, your bloodline." His eyes drilled into me as if he expected some grand reaction. I readied a snappy response, but he huffed away whatever he'd felt and snatched my arm. "Enough of your dilly-dallying. There's more to see."

We swept through another arch into a broad hallway.

"The guest rooms," he drawled with little enthusiasm.

We stepped out onto the south wing landing, and I fought a gasp of delight. The staircases before us, illuminated by lofty, steel candelabras, jutted three separate directions in angles disregarding gravity itself. Each corridor boasted vaulted ceilings, flying buttresses, and staggered marble statues. Upon the central staircase, a giant oil painting of Cadagon—

complete with scythe and crown—hung in full view of anyone who should enter the castle. Narcissism at its finest.

"The bottom floor is of little interest to most," he said as we descended to a center landing and settled beneath an array of domed windows. "You can find the servants' quarters there. Though I don't see why you should ever need to. Right will lead you to the east wing, where you'll find the studies and washrooms. I'll send Suri to your room after our tour; she'll show you which washroom belongs to you."

"Suri?"

"Your royal dresser. But she can be quite helpful, should you need help adjusting to your new role here."

A swift smack of reality peeked through the castle's charms. "I don't need help adjusting to anything; I can take care of myself. What I need is to check on Cooper."

"You shall have Suri at your side; that is not up for negotiation. Even if you wish to order her away. And your mortal boy is fine."

I swallowed a frustrated growl. "I want to see for myself."

Cadagon ignored my plea and started down the first steps towards the main floor. I threw my head back for a deep breath when a peculiar, out-of-place passageway caught my attention.

"What about up there?" I pointed to the landing a good thirty feet above the main entrance doors. Its hall wound off into the shadows.

"That is the north wing, which belongs to me alone." His shoulders stiffened. "Your presence is not permitted in those halls without previous clearance by me, is that clear?"

My eyes hovered over the forbidden space, and curiosity tickled the back of my mind. Leverage. I'd find it there; my gut told me so. I added it to my mental list, should I need it in the future.

"I said, 'Is that clear?'" Cadagon snapped.

"Yes, yes. Crystal."

"Good." Cadagon floated down the stairs to ground level, his heels clicking against checkered white and black tiles. With the snap of his fingers, two armored guards swept in to hurl the enormous entry doors open.

"Your Highness," they muttered in unison, and fell to their knees before him.

As we neared, I tuned into their whispers.

"It's really her," one said.

"She looks exactly like Queen Amelia," said the other.

"But she's so…" The leftmost guard stood and looked me over, paying careful attention to my thick thighs, but not out of admiration.

Cadagon paused, and his attention fell on me. The curiosity plastered to his gray face said it all. He wanted to see how I would handle the disrespect. My temper boiled over, its red-hot touch trailing down my arms and into my clenched fists. Who was he to judge me?

"I'm so…what?" I hissed at the now sweaty guard.

"Uh, so perfect, Princess."

"You'd lie to your future queen, would you?" Cadagon snarled. The fire behind his eyes burned fiercer. "You will apologize for your mistruth and pay for your transgression in the manor I deem fit."

The guard quaked and fell to his knees once more. "Yes, my King. Your Ladyship, I beg your forgiveness. I meant no ill will, I assure you."

A strange buzz swirled in my veins. To my surprise, I was enjoying the guard's panicked groveling, and it unsettled me. This wasn't me. I was nothing like the beastly king at my side. I met the guard's gaze. "Forgiven."

The guard released his pinched brow. "Thank you, my Lady."

Cadagon stepped forward and pushed into the guard's face with a dark smile. "The princess may have given you grace, but I do not forgive so easily."

With the snap of his finger, the guard was reduced to a chunky puddle of dissolved matter. What remained of the liquefied man pooled about our feet, and the iron scent of blood and marrow lifted into the air. My stomach lurched as the king knelt down, his crimson robe blending seamlessly with the guard's remains.

"That should teach you," he said, and turned to the second guard. "You, clean up this mess immediately."

"A-aye, your majesty."

I found my voice. "Holy hell, you didn't have to—"

"I have no tolerance for imbeciles," he professed, like it was reason enough for his ruthlessness. With satisfaction written all over his face, he extended his hand towards the door. "Shall we?"

I bit my tongue and trailed after Death, a million questions reeling through my mind. How had he done it? Killed so effortlessly? And for such a stupid reason. So the guard had opinions on my body. Wasn't the first time someone had had an unsavory opinion about the way I looked. He didn't deserve to die for it...did he?

The hell, Kim! Of course, he didn't!

I banished the immoral thought and drug my bloodied shoes

across the entryway mat, eager to wipe all signs of the situation from my memory.

To my surprise and satisfaction, what waited outside the castle doors wasn't the light of day or a shadow of twilight, but rather glorious night. This night, however, was nothing like that of the mortal world I'd so long adored, but far deeper and darker. Electric-colored galaxies swirled above, their beauty rivaled only by the endless cascade of shooting stars. "Wow…"

"Breathtaking, is it not?"

I took another step, head still tilted back in wonder. "I've never seen anything like it. It's gorgeous."

"I'm glad you feel that way, as the night is a permanent state here."

"The realm of eternal night." I met his stare.

"Indeed. Seems as though you know more about your heritage than I thought."

Typical dick move: assuming he'd have to mansplain it all to me. But I'd been waiting for this moment for years. I kicked my head back and allowed the brilliant scene to overtake me. Cadagon was sinister and cruel: quick to anger and even quicker to kill. And yet as I stared up at that otherworldly night sky, I made a startling discovery. I felt… home. Not with him, but in this place.

"Come," he chastised from the base of the castle steps. "I haven't all day."

Again, I held my tongue, though the effort grew harder still. Sweeping across the courtyard and past a central stone fountain with horned imps, we stopped before a wrought iron gate.

With the clap of Death's hands, the gates growled open, and he made his way to the stone rail ahead. "Welcome to Anathema."

Before me, wrapped in a cloak of shadow, sat a sight unlike any I'd ever imagined. Countless buildings cascaded below us—stacked atop each other—disappearing into a dark void below. Their combined walls bore the weight of Death's castle grounds. More peculiar still were the four cobblestone paths suspended above the black abyss ahead. Their very existence spat in the face of physics.

"But how...?" My voice caught in my throat. "How is this possible?"

"You'll find that reality is quite different here than it is in the mortal world," he said, circling about me. "In the way of restrictions, we have very little. This realm bends to the Reigning Reaper's will. *My* will. Outside space and time."

I drifted forward to find a risen stone plaque at the start of each of the four paths. The marks carved into their surfaces struck a chord. Tracing my finger along the rough stone, I studied the symbols: the very same I'd scribbled into the dirt to summon Cadagon. "These paths, they lead to the four courts, don't they?"

He moved to stand before the first. "Impressive, Princess. Indeed, they do. The cross represents the court of balance, those most like us: the Reapers. The triangle, the court of blood and those who seek substance: the Vampires."

I sauntered to the next path, my memory evading me. "The spiral? What does it represent?"

Death floated towards the plaque and tapped a finger against it. "The court of utmost importance to you and I. The court of power and industry." His mouth stretched into a sickening grin. "The Demons."

"Demons, right." I nodded, palms growing sweaty as the previous night's memory rushed over me. Of the power that demon and his hellhound held. "And why exactly are they important?"

"You will learn in time." With that, Cadagon stalked back towards the castle.

"Wait, you didn't tell me about the star." But I already knew. I just wanted to gauge his words. To study his body language as he lied straight to my face, so I could use it against him. Learn my enemy.

"The star no longer holds sway," he called over his shoulder.

"Why?"

"Because it does not."

"Tell me," I snapped, and Death spun about, a warning in his eyes. But I didn't waver or break from his stare.

He growled, turned on his heel, and continued his trek to the castle. "That path once led to the Shapeshifter court, but none remain to fill its borders. And so it has no sway. Simple."

I stole a glance behind at the closed shifter gate. In the right time, I'd return. Study what I could. But I couldn't let Death catch on that I already knew. Not if I wanted to keep my edge in our little game. Catching up to him, I fell in line with his steps and stole a look his way. "What happened? Did they leave?"

"You could say that."

"But would it be the truth?"

The Reigning Reaper's jaw tensed. "My, my, you certainly ask a lot of questions, don't you?"

"I've been told that before." An insecure smile graced my lips despite my efforts to hold it in.

"I've had quite enough of them. Come, it's time you met someone very important. He's been *dying* to meet you."

Well, if that wasn't some ominous shit.

CHAPTER 4

THE FAMILY TREE

I followed Death's lead up the castle's front steps and through the main doors, mind racing. Whoever he considered important was certain to be the last person I wanted to meet. Still, if I had any hope of finding Coop, I'd have to play along. The more I knew, the more I saw, the more in control I would be. After all, information was power, and I aimed to wield mine in just the right time.

Still, I asked, "Who?"

"We're to meet Nasheesh in the main study," Cadagon replied. "And before you ask who he is and what he wants, you'll find that out soon enough." Hands clenched at his sides, he bit out, "So do us both a service and cease your mindless blabber."

My body tensed. Sure, I was one for questions; I'd always known it, but that much should be understandable given my situation. He'd basically kidnapped my best friend for shit's sake, the arrogant asshole. I had to admit though, getting under his skin brought me a sick sense of satisfaction. Going along with his plan quietly, well, where was the fun in that? I'd be the thorn in his shoe. The squeaky wheel that would drive him slowly to madness. I'd see to it. Not to mention, seeing that little vein pop out on his forehead when he was frustrated proved a reward all its own.

Prepare to be sick of me, Death.

Rounding the corner into a large study, we were met by an astonishing creature of bold and sinister beauty. His eyes refracted the candlelight, which drew more attention to his shadowed, catlike irises. A red flag bounced about inside me. The man's eyes…they were reminiscent of the demon that'd led to all this mess. To Cooper's demise. However, the eyes before me now reflected an emerald sheen in place of those I'd seen peering across the field at me that night. The uncanny resemblance unsettled and fascinated me all at once.

"My Liege," the man muttered upon Cadagon's approach, and clapped his fist against his chest. His sights fell on me. "And just who might this be?"

"This," Cadagon motioned, "would be my daughter."

The man stumbled back a step. "Your daughter? But…how? Where? Wh-when?"

"She came to me. Sought my assistance in saving her mortal—"

"Best friend," I interjected. "And don't forget, I came for my crown as well."

The man blinked, a harshness hidden within his gaze. "Well then. Isn't that lovely?"

With a nod, the Reigning Reaper turned. "Kimberly, this is Nasheesh Avarti, my personal advisor. He provides guidance in times of need."

"My eloquent Princess, I am honored." Nasheesh bent at the hip, took my hand, and placed a sloppy kiss on top.

Goosebumps reared up my arms, and not the good kind. I

snatched my hand away and wiped it on my pants without shame. "Kimber. My name is Kimber."

"Well, well," Nasheesh said with a raised brow, and turned back to Cadagon. "It seems your daughter has quite the untamed tongue, now, doesn't she? Not a speck of etiquette in that response."

Cadagon snickered. "What did you expect? She suffered a tasteless, mortal upbringing."

"How insufferable." Nasheesh grasped his chest.

"My 'mortal upbringing' was just fine, thanks. Better to be raised by mortals than wolves in sheep's clothing." I started a slow pace about the room, dragging my fingers through the flame of a nearby candle, and relished the burn. In the low firelight, the hilt of a letter opener on the desk to my right called out to me. It's then a plan began to form. A way to force Death's hand into taking me to Cooper.

The king and his confidant shared a glance and settled their attention back on me.

My gaze fixed on the lynx-like man, I dared a step closer. "You belong to the court of power, right?"

"You're upfront as well, I see." Nasheesh gawked, adjusting his robe. "Yes. I'm a member of the demon court. But that label no longer holds my duty or loyalty."

"Why not?" I asked, stealing another step closer to my goal.

"If you must know," he continued, "I find myself more closely resembling a reaper these days. At least, one would certainly think so after fifty years tucked away here in the palace. To put it plainly, my duty lies with the crown. I suppose you could say I live to serve myself to death."

Nasheesh chuckled at his own horrible joke, and Cadagon granted him a single pity laugh.

"He's served my father and me well," Cadagon chimed. "That

much, I can assure."

The pointed look they shared set my internal warning bells off left and right. They were hiding something.

Cadagon placed a hand on my shoulder, and a chill leached across my skin. "Kimberly, give us a moment. I need to have a word with my advisor."

I seized my chance, positioning myself in front of the desk with loose bits of parchment sprawled atop it. Hidden within the mess, the bone-handled letter opener winked up at me. Moving slow and steady so as not to arouse attention, I scooped the blade into my hand and tucked it behind my back, concealing my newfound weapon for the right moment.

Patience, Kim.

I slid my finger along the tip, and the blade nipped my skin. The warm roll of blood thereafter told me precisely what I needed to know. It would do the trick. Now to wait.

I waltzed to the corner of the study, leaned against a leather chair, and traced my sights across the cedar bookshelves. My mind flooded to my mom's library back home. Though modest in comparison to the one I stood in—no ladders or fancy footstools needed to reach the top of her bookshelves—I preferred it that way. Her study was homey, comforting; and I missed it. Missed her. Fuck, she had to be worried sick. But I didn't have time to dwell on such things.

I'd let myself get wrapped up in the odd splendor of Anathema, but I had to refocus on what was important: the ones I loved. Death and his ass-kissing advisor were surely conspiring as to how they might use my friend as leverage, how they could keep me under their thumb. The only problem? I didn't fold under such pressures. My life would *never* be theirs to control.

But it wasn't my life that hung in the balance in that moment. I studied Nasheesh. The king's little lapdog had gotten too trusting. Maybe he needed a lesson in regards to turning your back on your enemy. A lesson I was chomping at the bit to teach him. The advisor turned, giving me a direct path to him outside his line of vision. My chance had come.

I grasped the hilt of the letter opener still concealed behind my back and began to question. Death stood at his side. Whatever harm I managed to inflict, he might be able to simply will it away like he'd done with Cooper before. But whatever Cadagon was capable of, the essence granting him power, that same strength ran through my veins too. My confidence returned.

In one fell swoop, I crossed the room, pulled Nasheesh's arm up behind his back, and placed the blade against his neck. "Don't move, or I'll slit his throat."

"You foolish girl." Death's expression contorted. The flames in his eyes devoured his irises, and the distinct scent of ash carried in the air. Hellfire stared back at me in those orbs as Cadagon approached. "If you lay a hand on him, it'll be an act of treason!"

"Take me to Cooper, and I'll let him go. Easy," I said, yanking Nasheesh's pinned arm tighter.

Death looked me over, a smile breaking through. "An empty threat. Your bark is much bigger than your bite. And you, you're swimming in dark waters you know nothing about. Tread lightly if you do not wish to be dragged to the depths, Princess."

"You forget, old man, Death's power runs through my veins too. I wouldn't underestimate me if I were you." I feigned conviction, pressing the blade into the advisor's neck until a trickle of blood slipped down his collarbone. "Take me to him. Now."

Cadagon stopped his slow steps and raised his hands in submission.

"Don't do it, Sire," Nasheesh hissed, but his voice wavered as I pressed the blade harder against his throat.

Cadagon lowered his arms to his side but kept his palms visible as if to signify he wasn't about to make any rash decisions. "My daughter speaks with conviction, and I don't seek to have precious blood spilled this night. Not to mention, I've no intentions of sullying my relationship with the future queen. She will hold sway over this realm one day, and I intend to take *full* advantage of that. Might we be able to reach a compromise?"

Based on what I'd witnessed in the short time we'd spent together, I knew he lacked the ability to meet anyone halfway. "You? Compromise? Ha, I doubt it."

"It's true I'm a man who gets what he wants more often than not, but it's become clear that if I wish to continue to do so, I must ensure a small amount of…rapport with you." Disgust flashed across Death's face. "I propose an alliance. You and I, we can both get what we want here."

Ah, right. An alliance based solely on what *he* might gain. But if I could finagle the terms and get him to sign off in blood, it might be worth it. Shifting on my feet, I weighed his proposal. I'd studied up on blood pacts back in the mortal world. In Anathema, they bound one to their word completely. Even the Reigning Reaper didn't hold power enough to break such a deal. I readjusted my hold on the blade. "I'm listening."

Death cleared his throat. "You wish to see your pet, correct?"

"My *friend*. Cooper."

"Yes," he dismissed with a wave. "I am willing to take you to him, but I require a few things in return."

"Go on."

"Firstly, you must release my advisor."

"Simple enough," I said, and nodded for him to continue.

"Secondly, I need your word that you will tend to your duties and take up your rightful place as future queen."

Take up my rightful place. A loaded statement, I was sure, oozing with ulterior motives I'd reap the consequences of later. No way he would hand over his throne so easily. But it still seemed a straightforward enough request as far as screwing me over in the future. "And lastly?"

His expression darkened. "Riches, Princess. When you succeed me and take *my* throne, I expect my retirement to be comfortable beyond measure. Do we have a deal?"

Easy. Seeing as he'd never make it to retirement if I had anything to do with it. He'd be six feet under where he could no longer hurt anyone long before then.

I searched his face, and skepticism tickled my stomach. He hadn't bound me to his protection. Didn't insist on my firstborn child or undying loyalty. It seemed too easy. "That's all you want? Really?"

"Yes," he said, chin held high. "That's all I require."

"Nothing more?"

"Not a thing," he said evenly. "Should you agree, you will be free to visit your pet as often as you'd like, providing there are no royal duties to attend to of course."

I raised an eyebrow. "And he'll be safe here?"

"Consider him under my personal protection." The glint in his eye unsettled me.

Something deep down told me Cadagon was holding back. No way he would let me off this easy. Not a chance in hell. But in the end, there was no true choice to make. I had to find Coop, and without taking the deal, that wouldn't be an option. My decision had been made before I'd even considered it.

Free hand extended, I reached towards Death, letting his advisor fall to his knees with labored breathing. "You have a deal."

Cadagon extended his hand.

Perfect. The corners of my mouth turned up in a malicious display as I simultaneously buried the blade in his palm, then my own, and clasped our hands together. "Say the words."

Rage flickered in his stare. "A blood pact, hmm? Foolish girl. Don't you know better than to make bargains with wicked men?"

"Have you never heard of a woman scorned? I do not fear you, Death. Now say it," I snarled.

In a sickening display, he squeezed tight, bloody drops falling to the floor. The gash in my flesh screamed beneath his hold, but I didn't allow him the satisfaction of seeing me wince. His sights narrowed, our inner shadows lacing themselves together. "The deal with Death has been struck."

Cadagon led us out past the main castle grounds, heading for wherever he'd left Cooper. In the foggy haze, I could make out sizable rocks. Boulders, maybe? No, tombstones. Lots and lots of tombstones. My sights gradually sharpened as moonlight crept through the misty air. A wrought iron fence surrounded the graveyard, its slope reaching ever upwards to a peak laden in red-stained snow. Knot-covered oaks reached their bare branches down around us, sealing in the sounds of dry leaves as they tumbled through a cool breeze.

"This is the royal cemetery," Death explained. "Only nobility are permitted access to these grounds."

When we neared the top, my steps crunched in the red snow, and iron tangled itself in my nose. Sure as shit, when we reached the top, my suspicions were confirmed. Blood. But not the kind I'd expected. The blood of a tree. A particularly strange and wild thing, I stopped in my tracks. "What is this?"

"Our family tree. Every Reigning Reaper that has or ever will be must offer up a blood sacrifice to it or risk Fate's anger. She's a fickle thing, Fate. But as all goddesses do, she relinquishes quickly when the offer of blood is on the table." He motioned for me to outstretch my hand.

Reluctant, I traced a finger along its trunk. Where rough bark should be, instead lay something soft and warm. It almost felt alive. Like skin and flesh. A shiver ran through me. So odd. I braved another reach, this time confirming that it was not only skin I'd felt, but a heartbeat thumping inside. A crack began to form at the trunk's middle, parting to reveal several rows of razor sharp teeth. The fuck? Was it…smiling at me? I stumbled back, Cadagon catching me before I could tumble down the hill.

"Vicious, isn't it?" he asked, staring down at me with a smile. "But its bark is much worse than its bite. Mostly. Go on then, offer your sacrifice. It only takes one offering for it to remember you."

Hands shaky, I swallowed hard. For all I knew, this whole thing could be a trap. A way to lure me off the grounds and dispose of me before anyone knew I'd even stepped foot in Anathema. Coop's sweet face tickled my memory. For him, the risk would be worth it. I grazed the tree's sharp teeth as I inserted my hand into the black abyss within. A sinister giggle carried about us, and Cadagon's smile widened.

"Deep breath," he said.

And then the pain. The sensation of a thousand needles punched into me all at once. I bit back a scream. Asshole! He had told me it wouldn't hurt. Jerking my arm away on instinct, I watched as the tree's grin gave way to regular bark once again. Silence danced in the air. That is, until the ground began to shake, stones grinding together beneath our feet. "What's happening?"

"There," he said, pointing. "Keep your eyes there."

In stunned amazement, I studied the earth as it ebbed and flowed. The fuck? A large crevice formed, and from it, an ancient stone staircase emerged from the earth. Then the world stood still.

"The family crypt." Death led on. "Centuries of knowledge lies in these winding corridors, but you'll also find your pet down here. Come."

Shrouded in darkness, the deep stairwell cut off all light from the moonlit surface. Down so far—walls narrow and coarse to the touch—my lungs labored for a deep breath. Tight spaces weren't exactly my favorite. Hell, I'd go so far as to say they made it into the top three of my worst-fears list. But it didn't compare to my number one: losing the one man who mattered. The only man who'd ever stayed. And I'd be damned if I didn't show up for him in return.

Do it for Coop.

When we reached the stairs' end, Death clapped his hands once, and the room's torches burst to life. Four halls curved off the main room into the darkness ahead, bookshelves lining the spaces between. Engraved above each pointed entryway were the symbols for Anathema's four courts. That must be where the Reigning Reapers' counterparts lay, buried alongside the kings and queens of old. In the center of the room lay a single, ornate coffin atop a carved stone slab. My muscles tensed. "What is this?"

"Your mortal boy, as I promised."

"Is this your idea of a joke?" I asked, jaw tight.

"It certainly is no joke. You wanted to see him, and there he lies."

The shadows in me began to rile. "Shut the hell up and take me to him."

Cadagon stepped close and snatched me by the wrist. "Watch your tongue."

"Get your filthy hands off me!" My power surged, seeping from my fingertips in a way I'd never witnessed before. Tendrils cascaded to the floor. Here in Anathema, my gifts proved stronger. Connected to the source. In that moment, it took everything in me not to wield those gifts with force at Death's stupid fucking face.

"Go, look for yourself," he ordered, and thrust me towards the coffin.

One labored step after another, I dared a glance, finding a small glass window atop the coffin's surface. My heart seized, tears welling. There, eyes closed, arms crossed over his chest, lay Cooper.

"What the hell?" I snapped, hands clasped against the casket. Hyperventilation set in as I studied my best friend's unmoving frame. Dead? There was no way! This wasn't how it was supposed to happen. "You fucking liar! You said that you would—"

"I said that I would save his life," Death said coolly, expression far too calm. "And I did. Look closer. I've kept my word."

I did as Cadagon commanded, honing in on Cooper's chest. To my delight and horror, it rose and fell. Alive, but barely. Rage teemed in my veins. He'd cheated. Death had read between the lines of our agreement as to only provide the bare minimum. I whipped around. "What good is his life if he's trapped in a damn box, comatose?"

"His consciousness was never part of the arrangement." Cadagon met my gaze, eyes aflame. "Take a good look, Princess. This is what it means to be mortal, to be impressionable by more than death. Those not born to the eternal night do not belong in its shadows. As you do not belong to the light. You'd do well to remember that."

Death turned, leaving me and my broken heart crumpled on the cold cement floor. I fought back vomit. My precious, perfect, kind, crazy Coop. Mind wild, I fast-tracked through all the ways I'd failed him. Bringing him into those woods for starters, and on a blood moon no less. Using him as bait. I'd played into Cadagon's hand, walked right into his trap. Shit, what had I done? Death wasn't the only fucking monster that'd led to Cooper's demise. This—all of it—was *my* fault.

My fucking fault.

CHAPTER 5

GOOD GIRL

The transition to my love was neither effortless nor easy as in times past. I did as I'd always done, picturing Juniper's smile and warm embrace. But instead of finding myself by her side, I entered into cool, dark nothingness. A rush of wind. The tangy scent of decay. High-pitched ringing in my ear, I attempted to refocus, imagining her waiting for me. And *then*, I was there. Frazzled and confused—and sore thanks to what felt like a two-story fall on my ass—I took in my surroundings. Static coated the edges of my vision.

"June?" I called out into the silence.

No reply. No sound. Nothing. I walked farther into the woods surrounding me, tree branches crackling above. Again, I called out, "Juniper? Where are you?"

"Kim?" she rang out in the distance.

Wrong, all of it. I'd never had a hard time finding her, let alone landed with distance between us. What the hell? Steps quick, I started in the direction of her call. My best attempts at collecting myself shattered. Tears welled, blurring my vision as that first glimpse of Coop's motionless body replayed in my head over and over. I burst through the tree line and found June there: wrapped in moonlight, her frame lying amongst a field of wildflowers.

Brow wrinkled in confusion, she stood, dusting herself off. "What just happened?"

"I have no idea." I ran into her arms and buried my face in her shoulder.

"Woah, woah, woah," she cooed, fingers brushing through my hair. "What's going on? Talk to me, baby."

"Coop," I sobbed into her shoulder. "Death. He said that he'd save him! We made a pact!"

She guided me to sit on the nearest boulder. "So Coop is…"

"No, he's alive. But that asshole put him in a coma! He's just lying there in a fucking box." I leaned my head on her shoulder, her sweet jasmine scent washing over me. "I don't know what to do. I'm lost."

"Oh, come now." She lifted my chin, expression gentle. "That can't be true."

"Death did this. What if he's the only one who can undo it?"

"Then I guess you finally found a silver lining to being his daughter, because that same power runs in your veins." She smiled. "There's always a solution, Kim. You just have to find it."

Gah, this woman.

Her presence, her peace: it was like a balm to my rage. Water spilling over a flame. I heaved a breath as my tears began to dry. She was right. There had to be an answer. Wallowing in my guilt would do me no good. I pulled her hand into mine. Tracing my finger along her palm, I sighed. "Where would I be without you?"

"Dead, probably," she teased, bumping into my side. "But so would I."

A small laugh escaped me. I lingered in the memory of our first meeting—her rich brown cheeks wrapped in golden sun—allowing it to replace the looped image of Cooper's lifeless frame. Our new gifts were wild then, untamed, and still we managed to grab onto that magnetic draw pulling us across time and space to one another. She'd called out to me somehow, voice frayed with fear, and I'd followed her into what we now knew was the Shroud: a neutral plane where the manifestations of man are born. I'd always assumed we'd found each other there because it belonged to neither Anathema or Elysium, though I wasn't entirely sure. When I had found her, I'd offered her one of my shadows to ease her panic. Numb it.

"You found me when my light threatened to overtake me," she continued, and placed a quick kiss on my forehead. "You shared your shadows with me. Centered me. That's what makes us such a good team: your dark, my light. That must be why Fate assigned us to different realms. She knew we'd be too powerful together."

"My ray of sun," I whispered.

"My moonbeam," she sang in her angelic way. She guided me to sit up straight. "I think what you need is a little balance. Do you trust me?"

My jaw tensed. Trust: a fickle beast I hadn't yet mastered. Not after my dad had abandoned my mother and me. Not after discovering my biological dad was the murderous embodiment of Death. But June? June I trusted with my entire being. I met her gaze. "Of course."

"Close your eyes," she said, and I did. "Now place your hands flat on your knees."

Her hands enveloped mine in a soft touch. The warmth started slow, growing in strength as it burrowed beneath my skin. It trickled into my veins, chasing my shadows deeper still as it ebbed and flowed. A strange sensation. My magic grew curious, but steered clear.

When the light hit my heart, every muscle in my body relaxed. Peace overcame me.

"There," June said with a quick kiss. "It won't last forever, but that blessing should keep the worst of your grief away until you can find some answers."

"How'd you do that?"

Her smile grew. "What, you thought you were the only one with cool gifts?"

"You've been holding out on me," I teased.

"No, I've just been practicing. How do you feel?"

To my surprise, the brick in my stomach dissipated. My tattered nerves settled. I pulled her into my arms, sights falling to her lips. "Much better, thank you."

"Of course," she said, her face inching closer to mine.

"Can I make one more request?" I asked, brushing my thumb along her cheek. She nodded, a shiver running through her. "Distract me a little longer?"

Juniper's lips met mine, and I pulled her to my chest. The sensation of her breasts pressed tight against me sent butterflies rushing to my center. My hands latched around her hips as her tongue parted my lips gently, as if asking for permission to explore. Always so respectful. With that, I was undone. Our kiss grew ravenous, demanding. In one quick move, I pinned her to the ground. Her hand grabbed mine, guiding it to her chest, and I slid my knee between her legs, parting them.

"Your touch drives me mad, woman," I whispered.

A breathy laugh slipped through her. "I'll show you madness."

She settled, her hips grinding against me as my kiss trailed down her throat. My hands explored her breasts, massaging her peaks until her nipples hardened under the fabric. The way she fit so perfectly in my hands: it was as if we'd been made for each other. The perfume of jasmine and fresh linen overcame me—the same way it had upon our first kiss so long ago—as her sigh tickled my ear. I bit down, and she responded with a whimper as she began hiking her skirt up with frenzied movements.

"I want you," she moaned. "Right here, right now."

I nipped her bottom lip. "Tell me what you want, my ray of light. I need to hear you say it."

"Fuck me," she begged, the stark words in her kind mouth sending a dark rush through me.

I lifted her into my arms as I stood. Her legs snaked around my hips, tongue diving back into my mouth. That taste: like fresh, summer raspberries. With careful steps, I set her down on a tall boulder and slid to my knees. Skirt bundled under her back, I kissed up her thigh. She parted her legs, exposing the exact spot I aimed to please. Staring down at me, I held her gaze as I lifted my hand and gently dragged two fingers along her silky underwear.

"Gods, you're wet," I breathed, feeling my own body responding in accordance.

"Just for you," she whispered, a devilish smirk on her face.

I slid the lacy material to the side and slipped one finger across her bare center. Her moan rattled through me, and I buried a single digit inside her. Her hips buckled, grinding down instinctually. Fuck, I could get off just looking at her. But I knew this, right now, wasn't about me. It was about her. To show her just how crazy she drove me. I slid another finger deep.

"Kim," she sighed, my name in her mouth sending lightning through me.

I met her eyes as she beared down on my fingers.

"Pull it down," I demanded, motioning to her top. "I want to see all of you."

Her eyes hazed over as I swirled my thumb against her pretty little clit. She obeyed, pulling her top down for me to see her full, swollen breasts bouncing in time with her rapid grinding. I slid a third finger in as I studied her tits, and knew I had to taste them. Without pulling my fingers from her, I stood to rest over her, sliding one of her nipples into my mouth. I flicked my tongue in time with my thumb's motions against her most sensitive spot. In, out, around and around, and I knew she was close. I pulled my fingers out, leaving her on the brink.

"No," she begged breathlessly. "Come back, please."

"Not until I taste that sweet pussy," I whispered in her ear, and settled on my knees. Positioning her hips at the edge of the rough stone, I met her gaze. "Sit up. I want you to watch."

A muffled "fuck," and she once again minded. My lips trailed lightly against each of her thighs, one after the other, as I drew near. In one motion, I slid the now soaked material down her legs, baring her completely to me. I looked up to meet her gaze, her hands tangled in my hair.

"Gods, you are beautiful," I said, never taking my eyes off her as I slid my tongue down her hot core. The look on her face made me damn near feral, the way her eyelids grew heavy with pleasure. The sharp tang of her essence was like holy water on my taste buds. The very thing that would save my damned soul, and I couldn't get enough. I devoured her like I'd been starved for weeks, and she was my only means of survival. Her labored sighs ticked up a pitch as my tongue continued to swirl and teeth nipped, which only encouraged me. I heard her getting closer to the edge, her moans like a prayer upon my alter. Fuck, to worship this woman for eternity would never be enough.

"Come for me," I demanded, slamming three fingers into her. Her thighs squeezed my face, back arching. "That's it, baby. Be a good girl and show me how much you're going to miss me."

Her hips ground down hard and fierce as I slid my tongue into her, tasting the sweet, sweet essence of all she was. That, it seemed, was the final push. She screamed out as her warmth spilled down my chin, tipping me over the edge.

"That's my good girl," I moaned into her thigh as she collapsed back on the rock, completely undone.

I awoke to the crisscrossed beams of my bedroom. After June's and my night together, I'd managed to hobble my way back to the castle, her blessing spell around my heart helping ease my grief over Coop. I'd find a way to restore his mind; I just needed to figure out where to start looking for answers. Someone cleared their throat, and I about near jumped from my skin. Nasheesh stood over me like a prowling lion.

"Holy shit!" I grasped my chest. "What are you doing here?"

"Morning, your Highness," he said, tone ominous. "I've come to deliver your royal dresser as Death has commanded me. Might I introduce you to Suri, Princess?"

I sat, looking over the fuchsia-eyed demon. Her slender frame stood one pace behind Nasheesh, and the very palpable disdain for him written all over her face had me liking her already. As far as what I was to be getting ready for? Nasheesh couldn't be bothered to explain beyond, "One of the most important days of your life," before darting from the room. So you know, no pressure.

With Death's advisor gone, Suri turned to address me for the first time. A shallow curtsy, and she motioned for me to sit in the leather chair she'd placed before a grand, gothic mirror. "Please," she said. "Sit. I'll handle everything."

I looked her over. For a royal dresser, her clothes weren't nearly as extravagant as the dress she'd set out for me. While my outfit-to-be boasted a plunging neckline, bustled velvet pleating, and pointed three-quarter sleeves, hers was worn around the sleeves. A realization that didn't sit well with me in the slightest. How was Death treating the ones who so graciously attended to his needs? Like mere servants? Not in *my* Anathema. I watched her out of the corner of my eye as I sat where she'd asked, and she got to work on my ashen hair.

"I bet all of this is a bit of a shock," she said around the bobby pin clenched between her teeth. "How are you adjusting, your Highness?"

"As well as I can be, I guess, considering how much of a prick my sperm donor is," I responded before thinking.

"He *can* be a bit of a shithead, can't he—" She stopped in her tracks, panic on her face. "Oh no, I said the quiet part out loud, didn't I? Suri, you twit. I...I'm so sorry! Please forgive me!"

Laughter rolled through me until my eyes grew blurry with tears.

"Please don't apologize." I laughed again. "That man is a massive asshole, and you never have to be worried about saying that in front of me."

Her shoulders relaxed. "Oh, thank the damned. I was afraid you might ship my dumbass off to the dungeon for that one."

I snickered again. "Hell no! You have every right to have an opinion, and I have every intention of hearing it. Please continue."

A devious smile crossed her face, and as she filled me in on all the reasons Death sucked, she readied me for whatever "important" event I was about to attend. It didn't take me long to realize this chick was a keeper. Sassy. If I had to have someone attend to me, I was glad she'd be the one.

Hair finished—flowy waves settled around my shoulders with ruby gems winking throughout—Suri turned about with a corset and started towards me.

I threw my hands up, taking a step back. "Oh, hell no. I'd rather die than be forced to wear a metal cage all night."

She smirked. "The princess gets what the princess wants."

A wink, and she tossed the gods' awful torture tool into the closet and set on getting my dress on. One final tweak of the material gathered near my feet, and she turned me towards the mirror. The woman staring back at me looked nothing short of fierce. *I* was fierce. And that ferocity took hold. I was the future queen. Whatever and whoever awaited me better fear *me*. While I might be bound in a blood pact to fulfill my duties, there'd been no such agreement that I would do so quietly. If Cadagon wanted me to act like a queen, then I'd be a ruthless one.

"You look gorgeous," Suri said. "But…"

"But, what?" I asked, and prepared for the usual ass-backwards compliment about how pretty my face was or how the bustled waistline distracted the eye perfectly. I knew what people meant by those kinds of statements. That I looked good…for a thick girl.

Suri tapped her chin. "It's missing something. Ah, jewelry. I'm quite forgetful at times; it's embarrassing."

She hung an extravagant ruby necklace across my chest and extended a matching earring set.

"Gosh, that necklace is so lovely," she swooned.

The sparkle in her eyes caught my attention. It was as if she'd never seen anything more beautiful in her life than the stones that now hung around my neck. Wonder and longing lingered behind her striking, fuchsia eyes. Without a second thought, I removed the strand from my neck and handed it back.

Suri's face tensed. "Oh, goodness, I've offended you. I apologize; I only meant it looks so becoming on you."

"You keep it."

"What?" Her brows pinched together. "Me? I-I could never."

"You said it yourself: I'm the princess. I get what I want. And what I want is for you to keep it."

Her face grew still as death. Unspoken pain churned behind her eyes. "Even if I did accept it, it'd end up in the pockets of the head servants. They, well...they take what they want."

I yearned to ask what had caused such raw and glaring wounds in the young demon's life, but deep down? Our eyes told the same story: a young girl whose innocence was taken from her long before her time. Fuck men. I swallowed down my questions and placed a gentle hand on her shoulder. "I'll make sure nobody is foolish enough to take it from you. You have my word."

Suri's pointed, black nails tapped against one another as she pondered my words.

With a reassuring nod, I stepped behind, moved her hair aside, and clipped the luminous gems around her neck. Our eyes clashed in the mirror, and I lifted her chin to behold her own reflection. "There. See, it was made for you."

"Thank you," she mouthed back, sharp canines peeking behind a wide smile.

We wound through the castle's endless hallways, my attention stolen once more by the immaculate, carved sculptures around each bend. If given the opportunity, I could spend all day studying the art alone, but it wasn't the time. Not yet, anyway. Seven turns later, our feet fell on ground level, and we burst out into Anathema's eternal night.

"The king has requested your presence in the training grounds this evening," Suri said as we wrapped around the leftmost side of the gargoyle-riddled castle.

Right, "requested." More like demanded.

When the garden entrance came into view, a chuckle slipped through me. "Damn."

The iron gates—littered with black roses that swept onto the adjoining brick walls—towered a good fifteen feet above. My fingers danced along the velvet petals. "They're beautiful."

"Quite." Suri smiled and gestured ahead. "Keep straight through the gardens, and you'll find the training grounds no problem. I'll await your return."

I nodded, hoisted up my dress, and pushed through the gate, but turned back for one final word. "Wish me luck?"

"You don't need it," she said with a wink.

Unexpected in the best of ways, the garden was lush with life: flowers in various shades of red, deep charcoal-colored thorn bushes, and more gargoyles littered the scene. It was dark. Intoxicating. I twirled beneath eccentric archways, danced around knotted oaks, and gulped a hefty lungful of crisp, night air. As much as Cadagon sickened me, Anathema itself felt right. Coop would have fucking loved it. Guilt panged through my gut at the thought, but June's light settled around it, lulling it into submission.

A wicked laugh rang out ahead.

"My, my, you are quite the vision in that gown, Princess," Cadagon said, a sinister grin at his cheeks. "Go, give us a twirl, will you?"

He grabbed my hand and spun me about before I could object. I ripped from his grasp. "I have Suri to thank for that."

"So you are pleased with her service then?"

"Completely," I confirmed, and the wheels in my head began to turn. "In fact, I'd love it if she were nearby in case I need her."

He raised an eyebrow. "I'm sensing a request?"

"You said that I could do what I wanted with the rooms in the south tower. I want one of them reserved for her."

"A servant in the main corridors of the castle?" He scoffed. "Out of the question."

"Would you like me to go back to being a pain in the ass?" I forced a glimmer of defiance behind my eyes.

"I assure you, that hasn't changed as of yet." Cadagon sighed and flicked his wrist. "But I get the idea you could be even more so, given the right motivation, so I'll see it done. Now step lively; we are late."

I followed Death's lead through the somber garden to a wall of tight-knit oaks. With a simple wave, the trees creaked to each side, and he gestured to the human-sized passage now formed between the tree trunks. "This is the warriors' training grounds, a place you'll find yourself quite familiar with in time."

"I will? Why?"

"Please." Cadagon rubbed his forehead. "Try not to ask so many questions in the presence of our guests, will you?"

"Guests—"

"Ah, ah, ah, that sounds like a question."

"But—"

"Ah," he said.

"It's—"

"Ah, ah."

"Fine." I growled.

Cadagon led us into a lush green field, its four corners ruled by gruesome lion statues. Nasheesh sat perched under a gazebo near the sidelines ahead, a sizable group of onlookers just beyond him.

"Your Majesties," he called upon our arrival, and ran to greet us. "Welcome, welcome."

Sword and axe clashed in the open air, and my sights settled on the sparring match in center field. I stifled the urge to scoff. Grown men fighting. So damn primitive. Beasts, all of them. The axe bearer swung at his opponent's knee but missed, and the crowd hurled their displeasures. Based on the spectators' eccentric outfits, I had no doubt they were of personal importance to the kingdom.

"How's our champion looking today?" Cadagon asked, and placed himself on the nearest stone bench.

"Fabulous as always," Nasheesh confirmed.

The two droned on about things I didn't understand in the slightest. Champions, battle tactics, stance…you name it. And the more they talked, the more I tuned them out. The way they spoke to each other made me queasy: Nasheesh, complimenting the king's every word; Cadagon, priding himself further.

I wandered onto the field's edge, studying the two men still locked in heated battle. The taller of the two, the axe bearer, was quick and definite in his strikes, but the swordsman had bulk and muscle on his side. They swung and dodged with minimal effort, and took advantage of whatever lay in their proximity. Backed into a corner, the axe wielder braced against the southernmost lion statue and propelled himself straight into the swordsman's chest. Just like that, the battle was won. The crowd roared their approval.

"Go congratulate the victor," Cadagon's voice boomed, making me jump.

I grasped my chest. "Gods, you and Nasheesh have got to quit sneaking up on me like that. And hell no. I'm not a damn cheerleader."

Cadagon glared down at me. "Do you want the room for your servant or not?"

"Royal dresser," I corrected with a groan, and lifted the hem of my dress off the grass. "Fine, but I expect her room to be perfection."

"Do this, and it shall be."

I stepped out onto the field and swallowed hard. Why did he want me to greet the victor anyway? As some vote of confidence that his mortal-raised daughter wasn't some heathen? Ha, joke's on them. "Heathen" didn't even begin to cover it. Whatever the reason, I didn't like it or the crowd's whispered remarks.

"She has an air of strength about her," one said.

"Lovely," said another.

But they weren't all kind words.

"She's so much larger than I'd anticipated."

"That walk, it's atrocious."

I swatted their opinions away and focused instead on the warrior up ahead. Upon my approach, he removed his medieval helmet and rubbed a metal-clad hand through his jet black hair. It was impressive: the length; but not nearly as impressive as Coop's long locks. I cleared my throat and met the victor's piercing, red eyes. "Congratulations on the win."

"I always win." His deep voice poured between thick fangs.

So dude had a big ego. Got it. "You're welcome."

He looked me over with obvious disdain. "You're the lost princess, I take it?"

"Lost princess, wow. Sounds like something out of a cheesy fairy tale." He returned my smile with a blank stare. "Right, mortal thing, got it. Yes, I am. What gave it away?"

"The accent."

I hadn't even considered that, but now that he mentioned it, he did have a tinny tone to his speech. Like every word was cut a tad short and sharpened like a blade. I cleared my throat. "I can imagine that being strange to hear."

"Quite." He referenced the crowd, plastered a smile across his face, and started towards a weapons rack on the side of the field opposite the spectators.

Cadagon's pointed stare told me to follow. I exhaled, collected my dress, and tried to keep up. "I didn't get your name."

"I didn't give it."

"Right…" Okay, a little prickish.

"I suppose you'll need to know it." He sighed. "Given how much time we'll be spending with each other."

My throat tightened. "We will?"

He slid his axe into an available slot on the rack and spun to face me. "Is that not what I said? Your abhorrent mortal upbringing didn't interfere with your ability to listen, did it?"

"Alright, alright. I think we got off on the wrong foot somehow. Let's try this again." I extended my hand, though the desire to put this asshole in his place raged under my skin. "I'm Kimber, and you are?"

"Bored. Annoyed."

My blood boiled. "Okay, now you're trying to be an ass."

"Lyvias."

I looked him over, clueless.

"My name," he said nice and slow, as if I were an idiot. "Do try and keep up."

Keep it together, Kim. Don't go postal.

My jaw tensed as I forced out, "See? That wasn't so hard, now, was it?"

"Don't patronize me, Princess." He stepped closer, a threat held in his eyes, but a smile still glued to his face for the onlookers. "Let's get one thing clear, I never signed up for…this."

He gestured to the whole of me. To the body I loved. The body I was proud of.

"What are you—"

"You know exactly what I am talking about."

I gawked in disbelief. "Are you calling me fat?"

"Hardly. Dense, certainly. But I have little care about your body. I do, however, wish to rid myself of this nuisance of a conversation." Lyvias started back towards the gazebo, and in the passion of the moment, I couldn't stop myself from reacting. With a sure hand, I swept the pompous vampire's axe from its slot and cut off his exit.

"Take it back," I demanded, a lifetime of forgotten power pumping through me.

A condescending snicker released from his lips as he pushed the blade from his face. "Get out of my way."

"Not until you apologize, asshole."

His forehead creased. "Keep your voice down, will you?"

I projected across the field in defiance, "Why, because then all these fine onlookers might see how you're choosing to treat your future queen? With utter disrespect."

Hushed comments and shallow gasps began to sound from the bystanders, and Lyvias's face flushed red, damn near blending with his eyes.

"I will not warn you again," he said through his teeth.

"No, I won't warn *you* again." That was the moment it happened. The moment Anathema's true ruler was born. The very second the queen in me rose, her anger a thing to be reckoned with.

"It's clear by your childish attitude that you're a spoiled brat, not a champion." I stepped closer. The axe dimpled in the pale flesh of his throat where vine tattoos crept up to settle below his jawline. "But I warn you now. Whatever sense of entitlement you hold, I will see it all stripped from you. Your legacy: voided."

"I—"

"Do not interrupt me again," I bit out, pushing the axe's edge closer, and forced his foot back. "Now apologize for your insensitivity and," a dark smile slipped across my face, "bow to me."

"I will do no such thing!"

In one swift move, I slid Lyvias's feet out from under him. In quick succession, I pinned his throat beneath my black heel, laid the axe against his cheek, and pressed down. The threat that once lay behind his eyes now reflected something adjacent to fear, and I reveled in it. "Beg your future queen for forgiveness, oh powerful warrior."

A droplet of blood seeped beneath the axe, and his Adam's apple danced about with weighty breath.

"I beg the future queen's forgiveness," he growled.

"And?"

He crept out from beneath my foot and met my gaze. "If you make me do this, I swear I will—"

"What, you'll hurl another ruthless remark at me?" I snickered. "With a single word, I could ensure you never fight or touch a blade ever again. Strip you of your rank. Hell, if I wanted to, I could own you. And yet you question me?"

The words left a harsh and dominant taste on my lips.

Lyvias sat frozen before me—the axe at his throat—and the onlookers watched in stunned silence. I searched the gazebo, but Cadagon's sleek silhouette was nowhere to be found. Nasheesh, on the other hand, was there, and he was pissed. I flashed him a cocky wink. His expression grew borderline murderous, but he could kick rocks for all I cared. This was my show now.

"You will bow, or I will make you," I snarled down at Lyvias.

He reluctantly pushed himself to his knees and laid his forehead against the moist grass below my feet. A satisfied laugh seeped from my depths. I'd won. I tossed the axe to the ground and turned to address the motionless crowd.

"Let this be a warning," I called, and sauntered across the field with grace. "Your future queen does not take kindly to disrespect. Either learn to bite your tongue in my presence, or rest assured, I will cut it out. Do I make myself clear?"

The crowd erupted with comments, and I reveled in the fear I'd awoken in them. The power: fucking intoxicating.

"Yes, my Lady," one said.

"As you would have it, your Highness," chimed another.

"Let the decree be known."

Satisfied with every eye on me, I made my exit to the garden. I'd done it. I'd put that prick in his place and solidified myself as a threat. And though my hands shook and my mind raced, I felt good. Confident, like never before. As I rounded out of sight, a slow clap filled my ears. I shifted towards the sound and discovered Cadagon hidden amongst a weeping willow's branches, a grin of disbelief at his cheeks.

"Quite the show you put on there, Kimberly."

"You're angry."

"Angry? No, 'furious' is a more apt description." He circled about me, the scent of death in his wake.

Still seized by adrenaline, I raised my head high. "And here I thought you might be proud of me."

"Proud? Of your ridiculous outburst? Of your shaming of Anathema's most revered warrior?" Flames burst to life in his stare. "Never. You've brought shame upon me."

Nasheesh approached from the shadows and grasped Death's shoulder. "Your Highness, with all due respect, I think the princess's actions weren't altogether harmful."

I looked him over, intuition on red alert. He'd thrown invisible daggers at me the entire time, and now he suddenly supported me?

No. This was something much different. Manipulative. I studied him closely.

Nasheesh nodded. "You stood your ground. Made a decree upon your first public outing, and in doing so, solidified your place among your people. You couldn't have chosen a better audience to bear witness either. The elites amongst our society hold great weight and influence. They'll be sure your message is received throughout the courts."

Cadagon tapped his chin and met his confidant's eyes. "You truly believe that? Even considering the recipient of her punishment?"

"It was a bit of a shame," Nasheesh said. "But nothing we can't smooth over, I assure you."

Death shook his head. "Lyvias has never been known to release a grudge, except by the edge of his axe. She should have had self control, held her tongue."

They carried on their conversation, and every muscle in my body stiffened. It was one thing to be talked about, but to be talked about in front of your face as if you weren't even there? Bullshit. I'd had enough. "What's so gods' damn special about this guy? What aren't you telling me?"

They froze.

Cadagon stepped forward and placed one black-stained hand on my head. "Lyvias, my senseless daughter, is your betrothed."

CHAPTER 6

THE FOUR COURTS

I descended the south tower staircase—the bustles of my pleated, black gown clenched in my fist—and greeted the day with a wide yawn.

After my little humbling lesson with Lyvias, and Juniper's blessing, I'd slept soundly enough. But the nightmares that'd ensued in the wee morning hours had been a different story. Cooper haunted me. His confused face reeled through my mind in countless scenarios, each comprised of blood and death and straight-up disturbing shit. For hours, I'd analyzed each dream in an attempt to find some profound, hidden meaning, but settled on fact: it'd been a sick trick of the mind. It was time for answers. And Death could fuck off if he tried to get in my way.

"Good morning, Princess," Nasheesh greeted upon my entrance to the south dining hall, the usual much-too-wide grin plastered across his face. Wildly unsettling. "And might I say you look lovely today."

I yawned again. "Its eight o'clock in the morning, Nas. There's no such thing as 'lovely' at this hour."

The vein in his forehead bulged. "Nasheesh," he corrected, and fiddled with a stack of papers in his hand. "Let us start our briefing of today's events, shall we? Firstly—"

"Do you guys drink coffee here or what?"

"Why, of course we do. We aren't monsters," Nasheesh chuckled. He disappeared for a few moments, retrieved a cup of piping-hot coffee, and handed it to me.

"Food?" I batted my eyes.

"Yes." He grumbled, headed to the kitchen once more, and returned with a plate full of strange jelly. "Here, now can we—"

"What the hell is that?" My nose wrinkled as I poked the jiggling, red matter in the demon's hand. It wasn't translucent like jello, but thick and congealed.

"A breakfast tradition. One her Highness should try before she judges too harshly."

"But what is it?"

"Try it first," he sneered, and extended it to me.

I kept my eyes glued to Nasheesh as I lifted the strange item to my lips. The smirk on the advisor's face widened clear to the tops of his cheekbones, thanks to what appeared to be a double hinged jaw. It made him look...cruel. For a second, I considered his motives, red flags waving in my mind. "Poison," the dark part of me insisted. But something told me that if Nasheesh had it out for me, he'd be miles away when he attempted to take me out. He'd never be foolish enough to act on it within the castle walls. Much too risky. Paranoid: I was being straight-up paranoid. I bit down. The jelly, tart and salty, wasn't at all what I'd expected. My taste buds went into overdrive and battled the odd, yet pleasing aftertaste. "What's in it?"

"Fermented frankenberry and goat's blood," Nasheesh said,

anticipation in his eyes, like he wanted me to hate it.

But I wasn't in the business of satisfying men. Especially when they boasted that shit-eating grin they like to wield to make women feel lesser, intimidated. I nodded, snatched another jelly off the plate, and popped it in my mouth. I never broke eye contact as a pleasured moan passed my lips, the sound making him clear his throat with noticeable discomfort.

"You...you like it?" he muttered. "That's...surprising."

"Yup, that's me. Full of surprises." I winked, which finally got the rise out of him I was looking for, and he cast his eyes to the floor. "Now, what of today's business?"

I slurped my coffee and reveled in the burnt sensation against my tongue. The brew was good, but nowhere near as good as my mom's. The thought of her made my chest tighten, but I pushed it from my mind. We'd be together again soon. For now, I needed her away. Safe.

"Yes, Princess." He pulled the large planner from under his arms, licked his thumb, and flipped through the pages. "Ah, here we are. You have a meeting with Death in the grand study as soon as we finish here, which I've allotted an hour for. Once finished, you'll meet Suri in the courtyard."

I squinted. "Suri, what for?"

"Death, despite my objections, assured me she would be the best fit to show you about the kingdom today. I'm not sure how a lowly dresser would make a better guide than the royal advisor, but alas, here we are. Though I suppose he did so for my protection, to ensure you won't threaten my life again." He smoothed his coat, jaw clenched, before continuing. "Your tour of the realms will take nearly the entire day given the altering time zones within each, so I cleared the afternoon for you. However, your presence will be expected in the formal dining room no later than seven o'clock our time."

"And how exactly am I supposed to keep track of time?"

"Suri has already been informed of the matter and will be sure to have you returned for preparations." He referenced the next page in his precious planner. "It seems you will be amongst some weighty guests tonight. Your appearance can be nothing short of perfection."

I looked him over. "Perfection, huh? What kind of guests are we talking here?"

"We haven't the time for more questions. You're already late for your meeting with—"

"Death. Yeah, I know." I rolled my eyes, set the now empty mug on the nearest ornate table, and began the trek to the far side of the castle.

"Have a wonderful day, Nassie," I teased, and waved over my shoulder.

"It is Nasheesh!"

I took my sweet time about the halls. The paintings littered between doorways had a sinister nature about them that pleased my black heart. A red-splattered rendition of Van Gogh's *Starry Night* in particular caught my eye. Such bold brush strokes and fine attention to detail. I found myself swept up in its beauty for some time before I reluctantly started down the hall once again. Fricking Death, always ruining my fun. When I came to the east wing, I forced the rightmost of two giant doors open and stepped through.

My breath caught. Spiraled iron staircases granted access to the uppermost shelves, studded velvet chairs sat tucked beneath broad, oak tables, and a series of narrow isles led out in various directions. Above, ornate stained-glass windows cast the room in red-tinted moonlight. This was no study; this was a library. One I could spend the rest of my life exploring, given the chance.

Cadagon stood in the room's center, bent over a worn, leather-bound book.

"Good morning, Princess," he greeted without looking up from the page.

"Morning." I stepped in amongst the grand shelves, and the scent of parchment tangled in my nose. Delightful.

"Come, I've something to show you."

I drifted to his side, and he extended an open page towards me, an old sketch of a scythe-bearing reaper across it. "Who's the old man?"

"Valhalla." He chuckled. "The Reigning Reaper who held the throne before me."

I raised a brow. "So your dad then?"

"Father, yes. But I assure you, there was nothing remotely paternal about that man."

Hurt flickered behind his flame-filled eyes, and I considered his pain. Had he always been a monster, or had there been more to him once? Maybe he'd been forced into his role, doomed to a life he never wanted.

My mom had told me once that they'd met in the mortal world. I guess at the time, Cadagon was the front man for a metal band that—according to my mother—could have taken the music scene by storm. But in the end, he chose the throne. Flash forward to his true colors shining through when he chose to cast out my mother's people. Chasing the shapeshifters from their homes, running them out of Anathema. Separating children from their parents and burning an entire court to the ground. A story my mom had saved for my eighteenth birthday, when my own gifts had begun to appear. Though she never understood why he'd done it. In the end, it's how I'd ended up raised in the mortal world.

So regardless of how Cadagon had taken the throne, he'd allowed corruption into his heart. The past was no excuse for what he'd done to Cooper, to my mother, to the shapeshifters.

Fucking monster.

Death cleared his throat. "Valhalla was quite the ruler. Fearless, merciless, and above all, balanced. Which is the bare minimum required of the crown. It is why a reaper has, and always will, hold dominion over the throne of Anathema."

"You? Balanced?" I studied the gold draped around his neck and wrists. "I'm having a hard time seeing it."

"I blame your mother for that. Had she remained by my side, fulfilled her duties, and helped me raise you to succeed me, Anathema wouldn't be in its current condition."

"Watch what you say about her," I growled. June's light settled in my chest, curbing my rage. "And what condition?"

"A question for another time, once you have gained a better understanding of your people. For now, we shall cover basics."

He floated across the room and placed himself in one of two armchairs centered beneath a multi-paned skylight. He motioned for me to sit beside him. Cadagon extended the book once again and gestured to four points on a drawn compass.

"This reflects the basis of our world," he said. "Four courts, equally balanced. The royal bloodline—the same you and I share—is the only in existence composed of each court: demon, vampire, shifter, and reaper swim in our veins, providing us the ability to protect the people of Anathema."

My brow pinched. "We're hybrids then?"

"No," he snapped, eyes ablaze. "Hybrids were created by the original Fate and Death's misgivings, steeped in dark magic that eventually devours one's morality. Such beings were cast into another realm at the dawn of Anathema's time. A realm outside our jurisdiction."

"Why?" I asked, tempting his visible irritation.

"In order to create a hybrid, it takes heavy sacrificial magic. Banned magic." His expression darkened. "*We* are something different. This is why the throne's secondary ruler rotates through the courts upon the crowning of a new heir. With Fate and Death's blessing, our kingdom can produce Reigning Reapers naturally. By birth, not hex. This is why your rule is to be paired with the court of substance."

"The vampire court…" Lyvias. The thought of him alone sickened me, and I cracked a knuckle to release the rising tension. He really thought he could try me, test me. I took to my feet. "I won't marry him. He's a prick."

Death glared up at me. "Watch your language, Princess. Such words are unbecoming of royalty. You agreed to fulfill your duties, and this is one of them. The most important, some might argue. Like it or not, Lyvias will be your second half."

And there it was: the fine print in the agreement we'd made. Shoved into a loveless marriage without question. "You can't force me. I'll…I'll change the law. Decree that I'm to wed whoever I want, whenever I want!"

He grinned, studying me. "That would work if you were already in power. But alas, you cannot take the crown until you are wed, and until so," his eyes narrowed, "I am in control. I guess you could say that I own you."

Fury seized me, and I cocked my fist back, set to impale his stupid face. But with the snap of his fingers, I found myself pulled and invisibly bound to the chair at his side. I stared down in horror at my frozen body. Trapped in my own skin. "What is this? What are you doing to me?"

"Oh, this?" he said, the pressure in my limbs growing unbearable. "One of many gifts I possess. Now listen closely. You will marry who has been chosen for you."

"And if I don't?" I forced.

"A pact in blood is binding in all senses," he snapped. "And before you go searching for a way to release yourself from your oath, that binding doesn't pertain to you alone. If you should abandon our agreement, it would lead to utter chaos. And I assume you'd like to avoid such things, if not for any other reason than your human pet who lies defenseless as we speak."

I thrashed against his hold. "Of course you'd say that. You'll do anything to get your way."

"You'd like to think so, wouldn't you?" He pinched the bridge of his nose. "The Reigning Reaper's blood is imbued with the life force of each court and, therefore, bound to each. To deny the oath you've made would cause a severe imbalance in the realm, dissolve its inherent structure. If that happens, everyone in Anathema shall perish."

Cadagon's eyes burned with stern conviction, and I swallowed against my sandpaper tongue. This had been his plan, his trap. He'd known exactly what he was doing when he'd posed our agreement. The thought of countless innocent people dying over my right to marry made my head spin. Death knew I'd never allow such a thing. The heartless bastard.

"I see I have your attention now, hmm?" he said. He snapped once, and his unseen grasp lessened.

I turned to face him. "You're a monster."

"Why, thank you. I didn't expect such an endearing compliment, my daughter." Death chuckled, unfazed. "As I was saying, the four courts balance our realm. With cycling counterparts throughout each Reigning Reaper's rule, it ensures there are no biased rulers. Our duty as regent means we are to consider the needs of all, just the same."

"Like you considered the shapeshifters' needs?"

The flames in his eyes flared. "And what do you know about that?"

"Enough to know that you killed countless in the name of your damaged pride."

He stepped towards me. "Hold your tongue before I cut it out."

I forced my chin up, fighting his hold. "Sure, threaten me, just like you did all those innocent people. Save your excuses; I know the truth," I lied, bating him. "You threw a fit like a child, all because my mother wanted nothing to do with your sorry ass. So you killed and banished her people like they were nothing to you."

"I said, 'Hold your tongue!'"

A simple look was all it took for my airway to close. I gasped for breath, pried against my throat, and Death settled into my eye line with disturbed stillness.

"You would be wise to learn to keep your mouth shut regarding issues that don't concern you, Princess." With a snap, he released me. As I gasped for air, he walked towards the library's exit and paused. "Today's lesson will be cut short. I expect our next meeting to run more smoothly, should you wish to keep your little demon friend alive and well. Suri, is it? Do I make myself clear?"

I nodded, all the while picturing Death's head on a spike.

I found Suri at the paths outside the castle gates. Cadagon's invisible grasp still lingered around my throat, but I shoved the pain to the back of my mind. I'd handle him in due time.

"Hello, Princess," Suri called warmly, legs dangling from the top of the castle gates' wall.

I looked up. "Kimber will do just fine."

"Kimber, right." She clapped her hands together before hopping down to greet me.

A grin caught my lips. "I hear you'll be my tour guide today."

"That I will. I figured we could start with the court of power, my people. That is, if you don't mind?" Suri motioned for me to take the lead, and we strolled out the courtyard gates.

A nod from me, and Suri made her way to the landing Cadagon had shown me upon my arrival. She stepped up to the spiral-marked path, removed a slight blade from her pocket, and traced its tip across her palm. Blood, the same crimson color as mine, trickled down Suri's wrist, and she placed the open wound on the path's marker. The stone rattled at her touch, and the path stretched out to meet a newly formed gate, its iron bars suspended above the black void.

"Right this way." Suri stepped onto the swaying path.

My lungs tightened, feet refusing to shift beneath the bustles of my lacy dress. A stumble would be all it took for me to be consumed by the murky abyss below. Who knew where I'd land within the emptiness, or if I even would? The darkness glared back at me. But I was no bitch. Latching onto the fear, I allowed it to fuel me. Push me. One slow step at a time, I reached the gate. Suri knocked three times, and it creaked open.

The landscape ahead was unexpected: skyscrapers, railways, and taxis. From the castle's sight lines, it'd appeared the city had been built below, houses stacked upon houses, bearing the castle grounds' weight. I'd never expected a sight so...human. "This is the demon realm?"

"It is." Suri assessed my perplexed expression. "The court of power is heavily centered on expansion. Demons are calculating and always on the hunt for knowledge. So they built themselves a city unlike any other."

We stepped forward, and I scurried to keep up amongst the

onslaught of demons. Though their stature appeared human, each stranger we passed held their own unique attributes. Some boasted long horns, others were layered with iridescent scales, but each possessed those definitive, feline irises.

"Considering our time constraint," Suri chimed above a nearby train horn, "I figured we'd hit the key landmarks. Introduce you to demon culture."

Our first stop was Fereld Tower, perched atop a solitary hill amid the otherwise flat city. The magnificent, emerald building belonged to the Grevias brothers and held the record for tallest skyscraper in any realm, Suri assured, its topmost floors hidden in the clouds. Given the tower's unmissable display of ghoulish guards and animatronic gunmen, the brothers' power needed no formal introduction.

I tilted my head back and took it all in. "What's with all the muscle?"

"Privacy. They manufacture lab-grown, precious stones. Gemstones are a bit of a hot commodity around here. The only thing a demon likes more than technological advancement is luxury." She met my gaze. "Natural stones were diminished centuries ago, sold and traded in the mortal realm until there were none left here. The Grevias brothers were the first to cash in on geo-labs, creating an economical empire." Her grin widened. "Stones, especially precious ones, will get you far in the demon realm."

The adoration in Suri's eyes the night she'd held that ruby necklace swept through my memory, and the pieces clicked. That's why she'd been so enamored: it was part of her as much as the night was a part of me.

Next came Plavin Park, tucked along the city's south side. Contrary to what one might think, the park didn't feature a playground, lush fields, or plants. Instead, an expansive field of crumbled rocks swept beneath staggered benches and bonfire pits. At our approach, tight-knit groups took notice, whispering amongst themselves.

"Demons come here to quiet their minds," Suri said. "Back during the gem mining boom, demons communed with nature, sought it out. But when the turn of the last century hit, the city's Lord did away with all that. He claimed such practices were a distraction and stunted the industrial advancements we could make as a court." Suri looked over my shoulder before grabbing my hand. She nodded towards a group of demons growing nearer and began to stroll forward. "We have to move on; we're making them uncomfortable."

We made our way back towards the city's center and emerged from an alley into an expansive town square. Cast in streetlight, a vast array of sculptures unlike any I'd seen littered the marbled courtyard. Many were actively being sculpted. The collection ranged all over the artistic spectrum, from beast to human, tree to waterfall, each a self expression as unique as its creator.

"Welcome to Bellamy Courtyard." Suri strolled out into the endless sculptures with her hands up, exposing a rather large tattoo peeking out from her pants line. A snake maybe? "When a demon reaches age, they are led here to create a tangible piece reflecting the legacy they aspire towards. There is no time frame, no rules or regulations, just the ability to leave one's mark in an ever-changing world."

In the sparse niches of free space, sculptors ticked away at new projects, and I studied them in wonder. "How is that possible though? If everyone carved a statue, the city would be overrun."

"Upon the death of a sculptor, the remaining kin are required to do away with the artist's work. They can keep it, or they can dispose of it." Suri met my eyes. "Plavin Park, all the stones you saw..."

"They're crumbled statues...that's beautiful." To be able to say goodbye to someone you love in such a way. Wow.

"I've always thought so."

We wandered about, taking it all in until the bell on Fereld Tower chimed, echoing down the city streets. Suri insisted it was time to move on. We exited the way we came and traipsed to the next path in succession. Again, Suri bartered our entrance with her blood, but this time she spilled it across the carved, triangular plaque.

The view that greeted us oozed with old world charm. The full moon—seemingly the same moon I'd fallen in love with in the mortal world—cast an amber light across the rural lands before us: rolling hills, dirt roads, dainty cottages. Sleepy Hollow vibes.

Suri ambled down the lane towards an alcove of homes in the nearby valley. "The court of substance is quite unlike the demon's in that they've never sought advancement. The vampires are rather fond of the old ways in fact, mirroring their existence off the mortals they chose to live amongst for centuries. But two decades ago, the Lord of substance made a decision much like the demon court and called back his people from the land of the living. When they'd returned, the gates were sealed, and they've lived contained here ever since."

A thought struck me as my heels crunched down the lane. "What do they eat then?"

The eerie, naked oaks above creaked in the wind, and Suri's eyes grew dark and playful. "I'll show you."

We wound into the petite, silent town. No silhouettes drifted past the illuminated windows. No bodies graced the streets. Utter silence encompassed us. The hell? Goosebumps trailed up my arms. "Where is everyone?"

"In the woods, I'm sure, celebrating the living realm's fall equinox." She rounded the next corner. "Though they left the mortals behind, they will always revere and desire their presence again. And so they dance, drink, and reminisce. It's tradition."

When we reached the center of the cottages, she motioned to an archaic, dried-up fountain smack dab in the middle of town. A rusty, iron handle hung off the side, and she motioned for me to pull.

"Me?" I lifted an eyebrow.

"You're to be the Reigning Reaper and have inherent rights I do not." She motioned again. "For me, touching this fountain would be as blasphemous as a vampire carving a legacy statue. It's a respect thing."

Made sense. I shuffled forward and switched the lever once. Nothing.

"You have to pull harder."

"Alright, alright." I hung my entire weight on the slender lever this time, and the fountain rumbled to life. Liquid fought its way to the surface, sluggish as it gurgled up the pipes. I swayed in anticipation, curiosity piqued. At first, the blood trickled, but given a few more seconds, it grew forceful, and blood shot out onto the dirt. Suri snagged an empty bucket nearby and scrambled to catch as much of the blood as possible.

"Somebody really ought to clean this thing," she grumbled until the flow slowed. "Vampires are quite particular about their food. From what I understand, wasted blood is equivalent to murder. You'd think with a law like that, they'd keep the fountain maintained better."

"How is this even possible? I mean, blood pouring out of a fountain?"

Suri set the bloody bucket on the nearest doorstep and wiped her hands on her apron. "Now that I'm not a hundred percent sure of. Some say the flow comes from a sleeping giant below the vampire's court. That a tap of sorts was put into the giant's veins, and so the blood is ever flowing. Others claim the court's previous Lord made a deal with a baneful witch from the mortal world back before the gates were sealed, and the flow stems from the witch's coven."

My lips puckered. "Okay, that's pretty badass, I have to say."

Suri laughed before leading on. We returned to the castle courtyard yet again and wasted no time. The gates shrieked open, and we wafted across the threshold. My brow pinched. The sight before us reflected neither the flashy urban lights of the demon court nor the old-fashioned charm of the vampires. No, the reaper world teemed with…life. The sweet scent of tulips and evergreen trees carried on the wind. Reapers busied themselves all around, their black-stained hands submerged in various gardens around their log cabins. Despite the constant dribble of rain, they seemed content to tend to the plants beneath the cloudy night sky. Suri began to climb the well-kept stone path before us.

"This isn't what I expected," I said, matching her pace. A reaper—rich brown cheekbones high and sharp—bit into a fresh apple and smiled.

"What were you expecting? More of Cadagon's unique displays of darkness?"

"Yeah, kind of. But they're all so happy. Light on their feet."

Suri laughed. "Darkness still has its beautiful hold. But this is what the reapers do to increase stability here in Anathema."

I scanned the hillside. "Why does the responsibility rest on the reapers' shoulders?"

"I assure you, it doesn't. Each court provides their own unique skills to better the kingdom. But the reapers' priority is balance." She waved at a nearby couple who gave her a kind nod as we passed. "They provide the kingdom's food and materials for shelter. Providing for every court's needs. This balances out the demon court's attention to development and the vampires' focus on interpersonal connection.

The reapers' responsibility is physical. Hence, balance. Without it, the kingdom would break down, sending Anathema into the void."

My mind flashed back to the black nothingness beneath each path we'd taken. "Wow, that's dark."

"Such is life in Anathema."

"But wait, if that's true, then why didn't the world end when the shapeshifters were banished? Shouldn't Anathema already be in shambles if that was the case?" A nearby reaper overheard my question and dropped his rake before retreating into his home.

"I-I don't know," Suri stuttered, and her face flushed.

"Why won't anyone talk about it?" I erupted. My shadows began to creep from my fingertips, and the remainder of the reapers on the lane dove into their homes at the sight. "An entire court was uprooted, killed, and banished!"

"Kimber, please—"

"No. This was a travesty nobody cares to even admit happened." Rage swam in my chest. Without a second thought, I snatched the knife from Suri's pocket and stalked back to the castle courtyard. A fire burned within, red-hot and unsmotherable. I'd get my damn answers, even if I had to hunt them down on my own. I slit my palm, touched the plaque, and stalked towards the shifter court.

"Kimber!" Suri screamed from the far side of the path. "It is forbidden!"

"Yeah, well, fuck that." I stepped through the shambled gates and regretted doing so in under a second.

What the hell did I just get myself into?

CHAPTER 7

SHIFTERS AND BALLROOMS AND ONE
PAIN-IN-THE-ASS VAMPIRE

The coastal shifter town before me sat engulfed in flames. Helpless people tore through the streets, screaming and crying and dying. I hoisted my dress and peeled off into the chaos. Once in the thick of it, I cupped my hands around my mouth.

"Everyone, you have to calm down. I can get you to safety, follow me." I started down the lane, sure they would follow, but upon a quick look over my shoulder, my chest grew tight. The fire, the people, the chaos, all of it: gone.

Heartbeat pounding in my ears, I watched in stunned silence as the scene slipped back into fiery disarray. On and off, over and over it went. Tears welled as I wandered down the way I'd come. I reached for the fire but felt no burn. My fingertips grazed the cheek of a child, lost and terrified, but felt no flesh. It was torture in the loneliest way I had ever experienced. To yearn to help them, all of them, but have absolutely no means to do so. Fucking gut-wrenching.

Without warning, Cadagon's voice boomed behind, and I spun about to meet his gaze.

"When tragedy strikes in Anathema, there are consequences. This," he gestured, "is an energetic imprint. It is not real, but once was."

"You," I bit out between clenched teeth. "*You* did this. You set the wheels in motion for all of this!"

"You say it with such conviction, so it must be so." He turned on his heel, his arm extended. "Come. You are late for dinner, and I cannot hold off your insufferable guests a second longer."

A wry laugh tinged my lips. "Really? You expect me to just turn a blind eye to all of this and join you for some damn dinner party?"

"Please, Kimberly, do not make me get harsh with you again."

I started towards him. "Harsh? Is that what you call it to make yourself feel better in that shithead brain of yours? What you did to me in the library, that wasn't harsh. That was abuse. What you did to these people? Allowed to happen to an entire community? That was a ruthless dictator sacrificing his people for his own selfish desires." I stepped into his face to look up at him. "And yes, you may have the crown and its protection for now, but the day will come when you don't anymore, Cadagon. On that day, you will fear me."

His eyes burned hot. "Watch yourself."

"You can't do anything to me," I sneered. "You need me. Tell me what the hell happened."

"Or what? I am in control here, not you. Now accept your fate and join your guests for dinner." He snapped his fingers, and against my will, my feet obeyed.

"You can't force me," I shrieked over my shoulder, reeling what little parts of my body I still had control of. Which was jack shit aside from my fingers. With quick steps, I passed through the shifter gates.

"You'll pay for this."

"And that is the last bit of defiance I want to hear out of you tonight."

I pushed to respond, but my words never made it past my lips. He'd muted me, silenced my cries. The bastard. I was a prisoner in my own flesh once again, bound to do whatever the Reigning Reaper deemed necessary. But I wasn't a pawn to be ordered about. He'd answer for his insolence. I'd make him fucking bow just like my piece of shit betrothed. The men of Anathema would learn to fear me. For now, though, I'd bide my time. Study them, learn their weaknesses, their secrets. Break them down from the inside before forcing them to their knees. Anathema would no longer answer to the whims of a spoiled man-child with a god complex. Their queen had arrived, and she hungered for vengeance.

You'll taste my wrath, fuckers. Just wait.

When we came to the castle gates, Death released control of my body but held my voice hostage.

"I can keep you like this for the rest of the night," he said as if I were a five-year-old who'd gotten caught coloring on the walls. "Or you can behave and actually try to enjoy tonight's event. Which, I might add, is entirely in your honor."

A scoff rattled inside, trapped. Right, as if he'd ever do a damn thing for me that wasn't oozing with ulterior motives. But maybe this was my chance. The wheels started to turn. A big event was sure to have Anathema's elite in attendance. Parties made people loose-lipped, especially a few drinks in, which led to gossip and spilled secrets. I met Death's stare, forced the rage deep down, and nodded once, paying extra attention to my expression. Forced the doe eyes as if I was ready to submit to the reaper's will. He looked me over before finally releasing his hold entirely.

"Clean yourself up," he said. "Suri is already awaiting you in your suite. I expect you in the ballroom in no more than an hour. Do not make me wait." The flames in his eyes simmered, and he headed for the training grounds. "One hour," he called over his shoulder.

The second the reaper disappeared from sight, I crumpled onto the front stairs, limbs still heavy in the wake of Death's hold. It'd been years, and yet destruction still hung on the breeze in the shifter court. It'd snapped something in me, seeing what I'd seen. Feeling their pain as if it were my own. My hands tightened into fists. In the flames, I'd pictured my mom. Imagined her heartbreak watching her people flee and burn. The betrayal she must have felt.

"Bit off more than you could chew, I see," a deep voice called from the shadowed stoop above, jarring me. "I already get the sense that sort of thing is in your blood, but I could always take a quick taste, you know, to confirm it for you."

A chuckle slid between his fangs. Lyvias.

"I don't have time for you or your bullshit right now. Kindly fuck off, will you?"

He *tsked* and straightened his tie, a deep red that matched his eyes perfectly. Making his way down the stairs, he stopped too close for comfort. Tailored suit fit to his lean body, I hated how my breath hitched at the sight of him. I'll never understand why the gods or the universe—whoever the hell conceived life—had a habit of making assholes stupidly attractive. It feeds into their ego. Makes them even more dickish. Infuriating.

Lyvias attempted to tuck an escaped wave behind my ear, a wicked smile cutting across his face when I denied him. "Come now, my dear, is that any way to talk to your future mate? Don't you want to know what my keen sense of smell picks up on when I'm around you?"

'My dear'…gag me.

He leaned in close. "I smell...weakness. A useless, mortal-raised woman, playing dress-up as Lady Death. But this is no theater. I've trained my entire life to secure this crown. It is what I am owed, and you..." His gaze pierced me, a snarl on his lips. "You are a *disease*. A cancer. One I fully intend to carve out when the time is right. So go, pretend. While you still can."

Before I could will it back down, laughter erupted through me. This man was really about to fuck around and find out. Fine by me. The laughter grew until I was tearing up, bent at the waist. Once calm, I looked him over once and started back down the stairs towards the courtyard. In time, he would see what lay bottled up inside me. Talk was cheap. Vengeance lasts forever.

"You're more delusional than I'd suspected," he called after me. "What a complete and utter embarrassment to the throne."

A final laugh escaped as I turned to watch him take a large swig of blood from his champagne flute before he headed to the castle doors. "Yeah, well, fuck you too."

The courtyard grew still, and I threw my gaze to the otherworldly constellations above. He was impossible. Pompous and arrogant and—I sighed. If I couldn't stand being in the same room with him, how the hell was I supposed to marry him? Shit, what I would have given in that moment to talk to Cooper. To pick his brain and ask him how it was possible that he was the only good man I'd ever known. But of course, another wicked man in my life had assured that wasn't an option. Fuck.

I sat on the fountain's edge and stewed until I couldn't anymore. Unless I wanted to spend the rest of the evening as Death's personal mime, I had to get myself together. Stomach finally steadied, I stood, hiked the stairs, and reached for the castle door. That's when I heard it: the undeniable call of a raven. I flipped around, a gust carrying him to me on the wind. "P-Poe?"

I stuffed him in my bustled skirt, darted to my suite, and slammed the door behind me. Hunting for anything that might serve to conceal him, I studied the raven now hopping about on my floor, talons ticking against the hardwood. Little dude came all the way to the realm of eternal night for a snack. Un-fucking-believeable.

"What are you doing here?" I hissed at him, torn between joy and concern. Of course, Poe didn't respond, but instead climbed his way up the footboard and cocked his head with curiosity. I pursed my lips. "We have to hide you. The way Nasheesh and Cadagon view the mortal world...well, let's just say that I don't think they'd consider you an honorary guest, bud."

My bedroom door squealed open without warning, and my heart thrashed. Hellbent on protecting the unexpected piece of home now perched behind me, I blocked Poe from view as Suri rolled in like a storm.

"We have half an hour to prepare you for tonight's event." Annoyance rippled through her fuchsia eyes as she darted for the closet. "If that insufferable fool Nasheesh had—"

Suri's eyes fell on the raven now poking his head around my arm. She stumbled back a step. "What in hell's name is that thing?"

"This is Poe. Not sure how it's possible, but he followed me here from the mortal world." I patted his head and studied Suri's pinched brow. "You've never seen a raven before?"

"I've heard stories, seen a few pictures, but have most certainly never seen a live one. His eyes, they're so...beady."

I snickered, coaxed Poe onto my finger, and extended him towards Suri. "Trust me, he won't hurt you. He's a friend, I promise."

Suri stuck out a shaky hand and ran a quick finger across Poe's wings. He gave her a once-over but inevitably pressed into her touch, and the connection was made.

"See, not so bad," I said.

"He's alright. Has that so-ugly-it's-cute thing going for him." A smile brimmed at her cheeks before falling away suddenly. "Come, we must get you ready."

"I have to find a place to hide him first."

"I'll handle that for you, don't worry, Kimber."

I looked her over, weighing her promise, but folded quick. If I wasn't ready in time, it'd mean Death would come to me, and that was the last thing I wanted. I'd straight-up murder Cadagon on the spot if he touched another thing I loved. Especially my little buddy. "Okay, let's do this."

The dress Suri had prepared for the event blew the other gowns I'd worn out of the water. It was magnificent: billowed in varying charcoal and emerald layers, some sheets light and soft, others rich and deep. The bodice hugged me as if the gown and I were one, its threads bound together to accentuate my curves. I studied myself in the full-length mirror. "You've outdone yourself. It's stunning."

"I'm honored you think so," she said, pushing my wavy hair over my shoulders.

I took a deep breath. "Any idea what I'm walking into tonight?"

"Aside from a den of vipers?" she asked. "No. But whatever awaits, I know you can handle it."

I forced a smile, smoothed my dress, and headed for the door.

"You'll do great," she mimed as if Poe—now resting on her finger—had said it. "And remember, you were made for this. Don't let the assholes get in your head."

I laughed and stole one last glance at Poe. Heaviness settled in my gut. He'd never be safe outside my bedroom walls. "Lock the door behind you when you leave, will you?"

"Of course."

I raced down the tower stairs. Late and without a single idea which turns led to the ballroom, dread bubbled in my veins. But I wouldn't be shaken. Not by Cadagon or Lyvias. Not even by myself. What I'd witnessed in the shifter court—the flames, the lost souls, the chaos—it'd changed something in me. Awoken this fierce devotion to my kingdom, my people. I had a duty. And to become the ruler who would fix the division in Anathema, I'd have to suck it up. Be strong. Untouchable. No matter what curve balls Death threw at me.

As if summoned by my internal thoughts, Cadagon's disembodied voice rang through the hall. "West wing, fourth door to your right. And you made me wait."

I wrapped through hallways, drifting up and down stairs, until I spotted the door Death had mentioned. My hand turned to stone around the intricate doorknob, and I steadied my breath.

Suck it up, bitch. Shoulders back, chin high.

"Await my orders," Cadagon's voice boomed again.

Of course, always on a man's time. Or maybe not. This was my chance to make an impression. To show whoever stood behind these doors that I refused to be anyone's pawn. Especially my father's. With one final exhale, I collected my gown and pushed the doors open.

Time to give 'em hell.

"My most treasured guests," I began, splaying my gloved hand through the now motionless room. "I do apologize for my untimely arrival, but you know what they say: 'A princess arrives at the precise moment she means to.'"

The claps started slow but built with force and purpose the farther into the room I drifted. They'd bought it. Maybe I could do this after all. No, not maybe. I could. Would. Royalty: that's what was in my veins. I was so sure, I'd have offered that insufferable vampire a drink of my blood as proof. That is if I gave a damn what he thought in the first place. A contented grin across my face, I found my way to the gem-encrusted chair at Cadagon's side and sat.

"You are late," he snarled, though his forced smile never fell. "And furthermore, you ruined my carefully planned introduction."

"Didn't you hear me? I arrived when I meant to."

"You stubborn thing," he hissed, rising with striking grace, and tapped a pointed fingernail against his champagne flute. "Ladies and gentleman, if I could have your attention, please."

The clink resounded through the room—projected by his inherent abilities—and every eye settled on him.

"Thank you. Now that our guest of honor has arrived, I believe it is time we get on with the night's festivities, yes?" The room clapped and whistled in approval. "Wonderful. First, though, allow me to raise a toast." He turned his back to the crowd, and his flame-filled irises fell on me. "My daughter, it's been twenty long years since we've been in one another's presence. The notion seems simply absurd looking back on it. You are, as you were then, a beacon of light amongst the void, my dear. To think, in a few short months, we will celebrate not only the day of your birth," he turned to the audience again, "but your coronation and unholy union as well."

My throat constricted. Crowned? Married? *A few months?* My head began to spin. It was absolute insanity. I went to stand, to object, to punch him square in the jaw, but my voice and body were already stilled by the Reigning Reaper's unseen touch. I had no choice but to listen and watch.

Cadagon turned for a quick, smug smirk down at me. "If you would all raise your glasses with me. To the future Queen of Anathema: may her reign be long and prosperous."

"May her reign be long and prosperous," the crowd repeated and cheered amongst themselves.

"Now eat, drink, and dance to your heart's content." With the crowd's attention no longer on us, Death returned to my side. "Do not make a scene, or I'll bind you for the remainder of the evening."

One snap, and I was released.

"Cheap move," I said, and massaged my sore throat. "Dropping the time bomb on me in front of a crowd so I couldn't object. I'm guessing that's what this was about, right?"

"Your union to Lyvias and crowning ceremony are your duty, not a cheap move. *You* agreed to this when you summoned me, demanding your birthright. And yes. Announcing you as future regent and introducing you into society was my plan here tonight, Princess." He sighed, the look of it odd. Almost human. "These people have been waiting for you. Do you understand what that means?"

"I'm here now, what's the big deal—"

He grabbed my arm and ushered me to a quiet corner.

"The 'big deal' is that you are their hope. I was..." He pulled at his collar. "I couldn't fix what unfurled all those years ago. They blame me for everything that's happened here. You are the redemption they've dreamed of. *My* redemption. You are the solution they've wound up so tightly in their minds as a means to cope with their fears, their very real and consuming fears."

Disgust crawled across my face. "So you want me to come in and clean up your mess for you? Just absolve you of guilt?"

"Please," he rubbed his temples, "put that bit aside for one second and think about what I just told you."

I stole a glance at his pinched brow and considered his words. These people had been terrified for twenty years. Locked into loyalty to a ruler they neither trusted nor respected. I scanned the ballroom. They were dancing and smiling, all in celebration of me.

My sights fell back on Cadagon. "They seem happy. I would be too if I'd met the one set to remove you from the throne."

"Yes." The king smoothed his robe and stood tall again, a flicker in his eye I couldn't quite decipher. "Now will you put yourself aside and walk out there for the sake of your people?"

"Fine. But because *I* choose to." Shooting him a pointed glare, I started towards the dance floor, but he caught my arm.

"Wait, I've something for you." Like magic, he extended a velvet-wrapped package pulled from thin air. A wide, almost genuine smile crossed the king's face. "It is time you had this."

My eyes narrowed at Death as I took the package from his grip and released the folded corners. Butterflies ignited in my center at the sight: a tiara forged of polished bone dotted with onyx stones. It was vicious in the most breathtaking way.

"This is mine?" I met Cadagon's gaze, his grin widening in approval. I placed the tiara atop my head, and pride rushed over me, tangling in my veins like adrenaline. Power.

"Go. Meet your people, Princess."

Pride radiated through me with each step I took. But at the sound of Lyvias's self-satisfied laughter ringing out ahead, my pride turned to rage.

This shithead again.

My blood boiled, but June's warm light inside softened the edges. I heaved a breath. Asshole or not, he *would* learn to respect me, damn it. We didn't have to like each other, but assuming that killing him was off the table—maybe, I'd look into it—I'd have to learn to live with him. Unfortunately. Sights set, I snatched his hand in passing and twirled him onto the ballroom floor.

"You will dance with me," I demanded, but kept my smile wide for any onlookers.

Curiosity swept beneath his porcelain gaze. "Will I?"

"Yes. And you will respect me. Do I make myself clear?"

"Indeed." He grinned, and his red eyes burned brighter.

"Good." I lost myself in his devious smirk for a moment, the gesture resurfacing the memory of the night Coop had convinced me prom was somehow a rite of passage. He'd whirled me about the dance floor without a single care, a permanent grin plastered to his face. Such simple days, fueled by equally simple needs. Just being in one another's presence. I made a mental note to start searching for answers in the grand library I'd seen that morning as soon as the night's festivities were through. There had to be a way to get Coop back, and I'd bet it'd be hidden there in some ancient grimoire or spell book or whatever.

"Princess," Lyvias prodded, and tightened his grip around my waist. "You seem distracted."

"Not at all. I was simply...remembering." I forced a happy face. "Forgive me."

"That depends. What will you give me in return for my forgiveness?" he asked with a wink. And his smile, it seemed damn near sincere. Suspicious as hell.

"What's up with you tonight?"

He spun me out and back into his arms again. "I'm not sure I know what you mean."

"You verbally attacked me earlier, made me feel like absolute shit. And what, now you're suddenly playing nice?"

"Is it really so sudden though?"

A wry laugh escaped my lips. "Yes. You haven't insulted me since I arrived, and given your track record, you should have slipped at least two cruel jabs in by now."

"Haven't I though?" His hand shifted to the small of my back, and

I grew rigid in his arms.

"No, you haven't." I moved his hand up. "And quit dodging me like that."

"Like what?" He caught me at the waist and pulled me closer.

"Like that."

He raised a brow. "I beg your pardon, Highness, but you seem upset."

I pushed from his hold. "Well, maybe I am."

"About what exactly?" A chuckle seeped past his fangs. "That I haven't insulted you? You do realize how ridiculous that sounds, don't you?"

I tapped my foot, honing in on him. He seemed different. His talk, his mannerisms, his patience: they didn't fit. Not compared to our run-ins so far. He was up to something, and I'd be damned if I let him play me for a fool. "What's your angle?"

"Angle? There's no angle here. I merely wish to dance with my betrothed." He extended his hand. "Can we please put this silliness behind us and enjoy ourselves?"

I searched his face but found no noticeable signs of mistruth. Instead, I found a strange warmth beneath his gaze that I hadn't expected. But he was vile and cruel, and above all things, unworthy of my attention. A cat-eyed couple sauntered past—their eyes transfixed on the obvious disagreement between the future king and queen—and guilt panged in my chest. There was more to this than my own comfort. I sighed, swallowed the anger in my gut, and stepped closer, holding my hand just out of reach. "Fine, I'll dance. But you have to answer something first."

He flashed a devilish smirk. "Go on then."

"Why be kind now? Is it because we're surrounded by people? Or is it because I put you in your place back at the training grounds?"

"Hardly." He scoffed, though his eyes softened. "I would simply be a fool not to have the most beautiful woman in the room on my arm tonight, would I not?"

Of fucking *course*, this was about getting his dick wet. I shoved against his shoulders and freed myself from his hold, the rage returned. "And there you have it."

"Have what, exactly?"

"The insult I was waiting for. You're getting better at this," I said. "Really shaking it up on me."

"What are you talking about, Kim?"

My nickname on his tongue stopped me in my tracks, and I whirled back on him. "That's 'Princess' to you."

"Fine, Princess, I meant no harm. I—"

"Save it." I snatched his elbow and ripped him off the main floor, away from the guests' prying eyes. "I don't care what you were trying to say; your meaning was clear. I'm sure you have been able to use that little smirk of yours to get what you wanted in the past, but you can save it. The only company you'll have in bed tonight is your hand."

He sighed and grasped his temples. "That's not what I—Look, I was clearly an asshole before, but this marriage is going to happen whether we like it or not. Can't we be civil?"

"Civil? After everything you've said to me, you have the audacity to ask me to be *civil*?"

"I'm sorry, alright?" He threw his hands up. "What do you want from me?"

"To admit this is shit! That we don't love each other and that... sucks." I relaxed my pinched brow. Juniper overcame me: the vision of her dimpled cheeks, her giggle. I missed it all more than I cared to admit. "I have feelings for someone else, okay?"

"You do?" Lyvias broke through.

"Is that so hard to believe?"

"Of course not." He dodged my gaze. "I didn't expect such an honest answer is all."

"Honesty: it's my curse." I shrugged and sauntered out onto the empty veranda. A rosy tang drifted on the wind and carried over the balcony's edge from the castle gardens below. Lyvias disappeared for all of a second before returning with two glasses in hand. Vampire speed: I'd have to get used to that.

"It's not a curse you know," he cut in, and handed me a champagne flute. "Honesty, I mean. That's actually a very noble trait."

"Think so, huh?" I took a hefty swig of bubbly. "Seems to get me into trouble more often than not."

"I do. I believe it to be crucial in a ruler. Unforeseen situations are bound to come along. A straightforward stance is the route to a decisive solution." He clicked his glass against mine. "It unites."

"I see what you're getting at…"

"You do? Thank the gods." He tapped the railing with a dramatic sigh. "I was beginning to wonder if I might have had a little too much champagne tonight."

I chuckled. "Funny."

"Eh, sarcastic mostly, but thank you." A fang-filled smile graced his lips. "So would you care to try that dance again?"

I looked him over once more, rolled my eyes, and took his hand. "Fine, but no more spinning me around, alright? You're going to make a girl sick."

"As you wish."

We walked through the crowd, careful to appear fine. Happy even. Our people, they deserved that and more. To trust in their future rulers' ability to work together for their good. As we settled into a gentle rhythm on the dance floor, however, a sickness overcame me: the unrelenting feeling of being watched. Studied. Chills spider-walked up my arms, leaving pebbled goosebumps in their wake. I scanned the room, Lyvias's arms tensing around me.

"What is it?" he asked.

But I had no answer to give him, only the alarm bells ringing in my head. "Just act normal."

Taking stock, he spun me about the floor. All around, people were smiling, dancing, conversing, nothing of note. Pushing my sights to the room's edge—to the nooks and crannies where empty tables sat waiting for bodies to fill them when they needed a rest—I found it.

Or rather, him.

Wrapped in shadow, only his emerald eyes poking through the darkness. Who the hell was that? And why did he make me feel like a damn fish in a shark tank?

"Don't make it obvious," I whispered, "but that man in the corner, who is he?"

A nod, and Lyvias flipped me about so he could get a clear view. "Malachi. Lord of the demon court."

"Does he usually conceal himself in shadow like that?"

Another nod. "Few have seen his face, and those who have, well… let's just say their survival rate is fifty-fifty at best."

Spinning back around, I stole another glance. Only, where the fuck did he go?

"He's gone," I said, mostly to myself.

"I'm sure he is." Lyvias pulled me closer, pressing his lips against my ear. "Beware, Princess. If he allows his shadows to drop, if you catch a glimpse of his face, he will be your undoing. Whatever he aimed to gain by being here tonight, letting you see him even hidden amongst the darkness, it can't be for anything good."

While I didn't trust the man holding me in his arms for shit, his voice, the way his muscles tensed as he uttered the demon Lord's name: he was in fight mode. And that was enough to unsettle me to my core. My hands clenched, knuckles cracking under the pressure.

Note to self: stay the fuck away from Lord Malachi.

ℭHAPTER 8

WHERE THE WICKED PLAY

A loud thud sent me reeling from sleep. I waited, heart pounding in my ears, until the crash sounded once more. Hopping off the bed slowly, I slid my red velvet slippers on and headed for the door. With each step, my internal horror-junkie alarm screamed louder. This was how bitches got killed: chasing after strange noises in the night. The sound of a scuffle carried into the room, and I froze. So...not my imagination then. Someone was out there, and I'd be damned if I let them get the jump on me.

Grabbing the solid gold candlestick holder off the nightstand, I heaved a deep breath and darted out into the darkness. Wrapping down the spiraling staircase, I called out, "Whoever is in my hallway better come out now, or I swear—"

A brick house of muscle and force crashed into me, slamming me against the stone wall. Hard. Shock waves racing up my spine on impact, a scream tore through me. But before it could pass my lips, a hand clamped over my mouth. A gruff laugh tickled my ears as I flailed against my attacker's hold, but to no avail.

Shit, shit, shit.

The man's free hand cemented around my throat. Turning my head, I tried to catch a glimpse of his face, but this dude had planned ahead. Where his face should be laid a ridiculously creepy scarecrow mask instead. And while normally I'd be *so* down to be choked out by a masked man—kink bucket list item—I was anything but in that moment. Not as the edges of my vision began to darken, small light flashes warning me that my ass was about to pass out. In one final attempt, I pushed my shadows out, swung the candlestick holder with all my power, and relished the crack it made against his skull.

"Fucking bitch!" he cried out.

He looked at his hand, fresh blood on his fingertips, and the hold around my throat loosened ever so slightly. Enough for me to heave a breath and get some damn air to my brain. A growl rippled through him as his hand dove into his pocket, and a glimmer caught my eye. Oh, shit. Knife. He had a knife!

Think, Kim!

I still held the high ground, my body positioned two steps above his towering frame. If I could use his weight against him… Without hesitation, I hiked my knee up, driving my foot down on his toes with all my weight. Another cry echoed through the hall, and he stumbled back. There it was: my opening.

Buckle up, asshole.

Shoulder squared, I buried it in his gut, sending him careening down the stairs with a slurry of curses.

"Help!" I screamed, voice hoarse. "Guards, anybody, help!"

My masked attacker hopped to his feet, starting towards me once again, but incoming movement echoed up the hall, stealing his attention.

"Hear that?" I asked, heartbeat clapping in my ears. "You're trapped. Nowhere to go."

"Princess? Are you okay?" Suri called from one floor below. Her steps hastened.

"Looks like somebody had a death wish coming here tonight," I said with a smirk down at him. "I'd be happy to deliver on that."

He met my gaze, chest rising and falling rapidly. "This isn't over."

In a quick flash, glass shattered, and my hands wrapped over my eyes on instinct. When I grew brave enough, I opened them to find the window to my right destroyed. I ran to it, looking down the forty-foot drop, expecting to see a jumbled mess of broken bones and gore. But…no. He was gone. How in the hell?

"Oh gods," Suri called on approach, and she wrapped a gentle hand around my shoulder. "What happened?"

My lungs labored, throat screaming from scarecrow mask's firm hold. "Somebody attacked me."

"Who? Who attacked you?"

"I have no fucking clue. He was wearing a mask, and he jumped." I pointed to the shattered stained-glass window.

"He what?" Her eyes flashed with horror as she looked out to find exactly what I had. Nothing. "Where did he go?"

"No idea, he—" My vision grew blurry again, and my knees buckled.

Suri caught me, setting me gently on the stair. "Whoa, whoa. Breathe."

I took a moment to regain control. What the actual shit just happened? What did he want, aside from me dead? And why? A million questions rapid-cycled through my mind as the adrenaline settled in my veins. If he'd made his way through the castle unnoticed and managed to get all the way up to my room, then he was either one stealthy motherfucker…or he'd had inside help. Not good. Not good at all.

"I'll get the guards," Suri finally said.

"No," I snapped, grabbing her elbow. "No, I'll fill them in later. I just need a minute."

She nodded and placed herself on the stair by my side. Silence wrapped around us for a few long minutes before I turned, noticing what I hadn't before. Suri in six-inch heels, florescent pink fishnet stockings, and a bunny mask atop her head. Two masks, all within a few minutes…coincidence? I think not.

"Where were you headed off to so late?" I asked, warning bells chiming in my mind.

"Oh…um…I have a…a thing tonight."

I squinted. "What *kind* of thing?"

After a few awkward seconds, she caved.

"It's not what you think, alright." Unbuttoning her coat, she gave me full sight of the outfit hidden beneath. A lacy corset tied up with a pretty bow on the ass. "I have a performance, okay?"

I let a single shadow slide from my fingertip unnoticed, and it swept about her. I'd always been able to read vibes well in the mortal world, but here in Anathema my power had solidified. The shadow returned, settling near my ear to whisper, "No lies detected," before returning to its home in my bones. And while this wasn't a fool-proof method, my gut confirmed its truth.

Suri took stock of my wrinkled brow. "But I can stay if you need me? I just have to send word to—"

"No, no." I waved her off. "I'll be fine. Go have fun. I highly doubt that asshole will come back tonight after the concussion I just gave him."

"With all due respect, Kimber, you don't look fine. You were just assaulted." She pushed to stand, and a metallic clang caught our attention. She knelt down, returning with the blade scarecrow had tried to jam in my throat. "How in the damned did a hellhound blade get here?"

My blood ran cold. A hellhound blade, as in...my body stiffened. That night in the woods when I'd stabbed the demon's hound, the one who attacked Cooper. If he hadn't died like I thought... "Retaliation."

Suri's eyes shot up. "What?"

"Nothing, I—" I searched her face. His mask...Suri's mask. Suspicion welled. "Where did you say your performance was again?"

Her eyes thinned. "I didn't."

"It's in the demon court, right?"

She placed a hand on her hip, the blade jutting out of it. "Yes. Why? You're making me nervous over here, woman."

The wheels in my mind began to turn. Hellhounds and demons were thick as thieves. I stepped closer. "I'm going with you."

Her eyebrows peeked over her mask. "I'm sorry, what?"

"You heard me. I'm coming with."

"No, no, no," she said, satin-gloved hands waving. "I'm sorry, but this is not the sort of place you bring royalty. Especially after an attack like this. The place is *crawling* with hounds; it's their primary stomping grounds. I'd be an idiot to let you come, Princess."

Ah, so my intuition was right. If I tagged along, maybe, just maybe, I'd find some insight into who attacked me, get a face or a name. Gain the upper hand. My shadows danced below my skin, encouraging me. I had to go.

"Kimber," I corrected her. "Tonight, I'm *just* Kimber. And you're just Suri. And we're just friends, having a night out on the town. Yeah?"

She looked me over again.

"Please," I begged. "I'll keep a low profile, I promise."

She tapped her fingertips together. "Friends, huh?"

I smiled. "Yeah, friends."

After a moment, she nodded and started down the steps towards her room. "Okay, but you will need a mask. I am not about to bring the future queen of Anathema to an underground pleasure club without a disguise. Not to mention, it's in the dress code."

My heartbeat clapped in my ears, cheeks warming as I followed Suri. Underground pleasure club. Packed with demons and hounds. Now *this* was going to be one hell of a night, I could already tell. Juniper's sweet face swept over me, and my heart jumped. Damn, how I yearned for her. For a life we could actually spend together instead of only stolen moments. One where we lived in the same realm, and breathed the same air, and did wild and crazy things together, like what I was about to do. She'd be by my side hunting answers right along with me, I had no doubt. My ride or die. I swallowed against the ache in my chest as her light coiled around my heart. Silent encouragement: she was with me in spirit.

Suri popped her head out from her bedroom door. "Well, come in. We're late."

She pulled me by the wrist, my neck snapping back from the speed—sore throat screaming—and closed the door behind me. I watched as she rummaged through her armoire.

"I know you mean well," I said, "but you do realize your clothes won't fit me, right?"

"Oh, hush. You have curves. I have curves. We'll make it work."

A few pondering moments, and she came back with a pair of fishnet stockings, a black tube top, and a stud-riddled mini skirt. I tugged on the skirt's waistline, the fabric stretching easily. Smart girl.

"Don't forget this," she said, extending an ornate, porcelain mask to me, crimson swirls dancing along its onyx surface. Pointed horns jutted from the top. Beautiful.

Taking a step behind me, she pinned my hair atop my head and tied the mask's ribbon tight, securing it in place. With my outfit on, we shared a look in the mirror, and a wicked grin eclipsed Suri's face.

Head tilted, she swung a pair of stilettos towards me. "You look like sex on a stick."

"Speak for yourself." I returned her smile. I mean, she wasn't wrong. We both looked hot as hell. "Come on, let's get out of here!"

Her hand locked around my wrist once again, pulling me back out into the hall. Shoes clenched to our chests so as not to attract attention from any lingering guards, we wound through the halls, pausing here and there before jutting off to the next corner. On more than one occasion, I communed with the halls, allowing them to help us slip through unseen by reporting back which guards were located where. Perks of being Death's daughter, I suppose: the halls answered to both him and me.

Good castle.

That first breath of cool night air was otherworldly. This, this felt like *me*. Sneaking out, chasing the things that go bump in the night. Pursuing those who would threaten me. Coop would have been feral too, ready to fight anyone and everyone he suspected might be my attacker. His absence pained me again, like a dagger to the chest. Nope. Not tonight. I couldn't afford distractions. There'd be no lingering in the past or longing for those who couldn't be by my side, no matter how much I wanted them to be. Instead, I'd embrace Fate's kindness in bringing me Suri. Descending into a den of vipers alone would be far riskier. But this was *her* court. And something deep down told me she ran that shit.

A slice of the blade, a quick blood offering, and we burst into the demon court.

"Demons never rest," Suri said, her hold on me tight as we wove through crowded sidewalks and alleys. "Funny how humans believe it to be the vampires who are sleepless creatures of the night. Never could get their facts straight."

After what felt like an eternity, we came to the outskirts of Plavin Park, shattered rock crunching beneath our feet. Suri's elongated irises scanned the scene. She motioned for me to follow, leading us over a small knoll to an abandoned shed, the scent of mildew wafting from its crooked, wooden door. "Umm...what the—"

"Shh, shh, shh," Suri whispered. "Let me do the talking."

Four knocks against the crumbling shed, and a slot opened atop the door. Two gray eyes stared down at us.

"Password," a deep voice asked.

"Tell Daddy his prize has arrived," Suri responded with a wink.

"That'll work," the guard grumbled, opening the door for us to pass through.

A long, straight staircase lined in red lights descended before us. It was quite literally an underground club. Interesting. Bass thrummed through my body, electricity hitting my bloodstream. Time to buck up or shut up.

The space opened up all at once, revealing a scene that sent goosebumps trailing up my limbs. We waded through bodies, countless eyes taking us in as we passed. Catcalls rang out in Suri's wake, but she slapped away every reaching hand with her head held high. She oozed feminine power, and I would be lying if I said I wasn't basking in her shadow. The little badass. A dainty demon in a corset flagged Suri down as we waded onto the main dance floor.

"You're late," she called. "Daddy is pissed."

"Yeah, yeah, I know how to put him in a good mood," Suri

responded, turning to wink at me from behind her mask. "Edith, this is—"

"Uh, Lydia," I lied, extending my hand to her. "Nice to meet you."

"You too," she said, and shook my hand.

"Can you look out for her while I'm on stage?" Suri asked. "This is her first time at The Underground, and you know how the men can get handsy. Don't want anybody touching my girl."

I stepped in close to Suri. "Can I go with you?"

"It's okay; Edith will keep you safe," she whispered. "Trust me when I say that you do *not* want to attract Daddy's attention. I'll handle him and his pig-headed buddies while you look around, yeah?"

"Yeah." I nodded.

Noticing my unease, she leaned close to my ear and subtly pointed to the club's far corner. "If you need me, I'll be down that hall, three doors to the right. Keep close watch on *anyone* in a blood red suit. Those are Daddy's men, and they take what they want if you catch my drift."

Great. I squeezed her hand. "Okay. Thank you."

With a kiss on my cheek, Suri was gone. I watched her disappear into the crowd before turning to Edith. "Thank you for looking out for me."

"Of course. A friend of Suri's is a friend of mine, always."

"Same," I said, and was surprised to realize I meant it. "By the way, who is this 'Daddy' guy anyway—"

"Hey, you, Blondie," a brute of a man in a red suit called from the bar's far end, snapping his fingers at Edith. "Can we get some service over here?"

Expensive jewels dangled from his earlobes, diamond-studded watch on his wrist gleaming in the light. A ruby-encrusted mask covered half his face—designed to look as if he were crying blood—

and I could practically *smell* the power wafting from him. My shadows hissed in my marrow.

Him: he'd be my target tonight.

"Hold your damn horses, Odin, I'm coming," Edith responded, before leaning down to whisper in my ear. "I have to get back to work, but I'm here if you need anything. I'll have security keep you in their sights, Princess. Just say the word, and they'll be there."

Shit. She saw right through me. "But how?"

"I'm an aura reader." She winked. "Yours is a shade lighter than Death's. But don't worry, your secret is safe with me."

She crossed her heart as she waded back into the crowd, and my instincts told me she could give two shits about my royal status. Perfect, because I planned to be anything but myself tonight. I'd be Lydia: the carefree reaper who danced like a hoe, drank like a fish, and cussed like a motherfucking sailor, while secretly hunting for the prick who dared put his hands on me.

I pushed my way through the crowd, banking straight for the bar. Red suit—Odin, I think Edith called him—sipped his drink out of the corner of my eye. After a couple quick shots of whatever the hell pixie drink was—reminiscent of vodka with a salty bite at the end— Odin began to move about and mingle. I asked for the bartender's signature cocktail and waded out into the debauchery with a smile. To the right sat an open-door red room, complete with chairs and straps and paddles. A girl in leather rocking six-inch heels tracked her feet down a man's back, while another tightened the straps around her submissive's wrists before shoving a ball gag in his mouth. A whip snapped in the far corner, making me jump. Fuck, that was hot. My center began to throb at the sight alone.

Note to self: new kink unlocked.

But I wasn't here for that. Though, maybe I could watch just a second longer. I leaned on the door, the girl with the whip making eyes at me across the room. She looked me up and down with pursed lips before making a "come hither" motion, to which I shook my head. A smirk eclipsed her face as she settled onto her pet's lap, never breaking eye contact with me as she ground against his hard cock. Whimpers escaped her as she began to climb towards release. I watched intently, squeezing my legs together in an attempt to settle the throb between them. She was going to come. And I was going to watch it happen. Her hips picked up speed as she rode him harder, her mouth opening in a "shit, this is good" way, her hands now massaging her peaked nipples beneath the leather. In an unexpected move on my part, I mouthed, "Good girl." That was all it took for her to be undone, coming hard before crumpling on her sub's chest. She gave me pleading eyes once more, but I simply blew a kiss and headed towards the dance floor, cocktail in hand.

My hands and lips belonged to Juniper alone.

I turned, my target lost in the crowd now. Shit. I took my place among the bodies grinding all around, searching carefully for Odin. But as the alcohol hit my bloodstream, I settled into the beat and let my body take over. Being so close to the stage—performers, mostly half naked if not all, dancing in cages around the room—the bass rattled deep. So deep I felt myself begin to climb. My center throbbed. Gods, what I would have given to have June's delicate frame sitting on my face in that moment. To take that pretty little clit between my teeth and—

A hard dick settled against my ass, hands wrapping around to grasp my waist. "Let me help you get off," a deep voice rumbled.

I immediately pulled out of my rising climax, pain settling between my legs at the lack of release. "Get off me!"

"Hey, hey, calm down," the stranger said. "No need to be a bitch about it. Was just trying to give your fat ass something to fuck."

Rage boiled up inside me. Fist clinched, I spun around, cocked back, and buried it straight in his jaw. A loud crack reverberated through the dance floor, stopping those nearby in their tracks. Gasps arose as they registered who I'd hit, their mumbled words making it incredibly clear that I'd made an enemy of the wrong person. When he stood to look down at me, my stomach dropped into my toes. Red suit. Odin.

Shit. Cadagon would *kill* me if I died.

The brute of a man snatched me by my hair. "You're coming with me."

I thrashed in his hold. Edith came into view on the back most stage adjacent the ominous, red door my attacker was heading straight for.

"Odin, stop!" Edith screamed as she hopped down from the stage. "That's Suri's girl!"

"Good, then she can explain to Malachi why my face is fucking bloody."

My heart sank into my toes. Oh, fuck. Daddy…VIP…Suri…This was Malachi's club. Malachi was Daddy! I should have known. Idiot. The image of the demon Lord wrapped in darkness hunting me with his eyes flowed over me. I could *not* be seen by him. If I were caught here, there'd be no telling what kind of bullshit ammo this would give him. Future queen of Anathema seen climaxing on a random dude in the middle of a sex club. With how uptight the kingdom's elite were, I'd end up with a mutiny on my hands. Not to mention my attacker from earlier that night. Who knew if they were in cahoots.

I kicked and punched as we entered the hallway, the base dying behind us. Soundproof walls. Not good. Odin threw me to the floor like a rag doll.

"Now, be a good little bitch," he growled, grabbing a fistful of my hair with one hand and unbuttoning his pants with the other. "Open that fat mouth of yours and suck until you see stars."

"Fuck you," I said, spitting on his pants.

"Mm, I like them with some fight. Makes the game more fun."

He threw me towards the wall, pinning my cheeks between his knees. In a last-ditch effort for freedom, I looked up, feigning submission. Approval on his face, he lowered his tiny dick towards my lips, slapping my cheek once just to remind me I was at his mercy. A repressed memory—one I'd tried for nearly twelve years to forget—clattered through my skull. Of the man who stole my innocence. No...of the pig who touched a child! The reason I had never, and would never, give another man head in my life. Because I'd never had a choice. And as I stared up at Odin, I decided. I'd never be a man's plaything ever again.

Rage, red-hot and demanding, soared through me.

Before I could convince myself otherwise, I bit down on his shrimp dick until my jaw damn near cracked. Warm iron spilled into my mouth as he screamed in agony and kicked his knee into my jaw, sending me tumbling face down on the ground. Black crept into the edge of my vision. The pain in my neck from the night's first attack shot like needles up behind my face. Head spinning, I spit the hunk of severed meat on the ground beside me. Three other bodies came pouring into the hallway, blurred by the blinding pain. Hands, so many hands grabbed and pulled and pushed on me. Their voices layered over one another, creating this strange, almost feral sound. Like wolves on a hunt, cornering their prey. Before I could stop him, one of the men grabbed my mask, ripping it from my face.

"Fuck, Odin," he snarled, close enough for me to make out his words in the scuffle. "This is Death's kid!"

Odin riled as his severed manhood bled out, but didn't respond. He writhed, and in the haze, I watched him slip his mask off his sweaty face. That moment was crystal clear. Like the world stood still for one moment. Below that mask, a dark bruise lay above his right eye...right where I'd hit scarecrow earlier that night. While I had believed I'd been pursuing *him*, somehow he'd looped back around. Led me to him. He'd probably planted that damned knife, banking on me tagging along with Suri to find answers. I squeezed my eyes shut.

And I'd walked right into his trap.

Odin barked an order I couldn't quite make out thanks to the ringing in my ears, but I knew. I knew this was it: how I would die. In the darkness, at the hands of a wicked man's bruised ego.

Way to go, Kim. Idiot.

Then, all at once, a shadow eclipsed what little light shone through the hallway. The men's voices silenced aside from Odin's whimpers. My heartbeat in my ears was the only sound aside from slow, calculated footsteps coming up behind me. I watched as the men recoiled, fear in their eyes. Even Odin, piece-of-shit-no-dick, muffled his cries. The steps stopped. I turned to see what manner of beast stood over me, but before I could get eyes on him, a blur darted about the room. In its wake: blood. Three bodies hit the ground in the same second, hearts torn from their chests and crimson draining from their necks. A vampire.

No. Lyvias.

"Please," Odin begged. "Please don't kill me! I—"

"Shut your fucking mouth," Lyvias demanded, voice cool and thick. He snatched Odin from the floor, staring him straight in the eyes. "The only reason I haven't ripped that lying tongue from your mouth is to send a message to your false Lord. Think you can handle that, pup?" he bit out.

"Yes, of course, yes. I'll do anything, just don't kill me!"

Lyvias's eyes darkened as he leaned in to whisper in Odin's ear. "Tell Malachi that if he or any of his hounds touch what is *mine* again, I'll drown him in his own fucking blood."

He threw Odin to the ground, the bleeding man scampering off like a dog with its tail tucked between its legs. Lyvias's shadow encased me next. Not a single word passed his lips as he lifted me into his arms, carried me out through the bustling club—the scene motionless as they watched us pass—and out into the night.

The weight of it all and what would have surely happened if Lyvias hadn't shown up sent me into tears. He remained silent the entire time, never offering a word of comfort. But never pulling my face away from its tucked position on his chest either. He just let me cry. And cry. And cry.

When we reached the castle's top landing, he settled me into my bed and immediately left. No goodbye. No, "Are you okay?" Gone. Heartbeat pounding in my ears, an itch on my chin brought me back to reality. Dried blood. From Odin's shrimp dick. It was still on my face, in my mouth, under my nails. Shit. I'd have crawled out of my skin in that moment if it'd been an option. Men like that, they didn't see women as human. They saw them as walking holes to fuck. Silent sobs burst free as I slid off the bed and melted onto the hardwood floor, curling up into a ball. Dirty, I felt dirty. And so fucking stupid.

Three soft knocks at the door sounded, Lyvias peeking his head back through. "I've drawn you a bath."

I swallowed a sob. "You…what?"

"A bath," he repeated. "Can you walk, or shall I carry you?"

Hell if I was going to let him carry me again. While he might have saved my life, he was still the same person who'd called me a disease. A cancer he aimed to carve out in due time. "I can do it myself."

"If you wish to," he said, though his frame still haunted me.

I pushed to sit, head spinning. Odin's kick hadn't been soft, and I was feeling it. Legs wobbly, I stood, but only for a brief second before crashing back to the ground. Knees screaming from the impact, I let out a frustrated scream. If my hands hadn't been shaking so fiercely, I would have told Lyvias to fuck all the way off. But I couldn't get my body to settle down. My breathing hitched, limbs covered in permanent, nasty goosebumps.

"Are you done now?" Lyvias asked, leaning against the door frame. "Or would you like to continue being stubborn?"

"Fuck you," I bit out.

"If that's what you wish, all you have to do is ask, Princess." A smirk crept across his lips.

"In your dreams, asshole."

He looked me over before making his way to settle at my side. "Maybe, just for tonight, we could put aside our hatred and get you into a warm bath, hmm?"

My sights honed in on his blood red eyes. Within them, where I expected to find the hint of a cruel joke, I found what appeared to be something adjacent to kindness instead. No signs of deception or cruelty. I attempted to stand again, but this time my body vehemently opposed, refusing to move. I cleared my throat. "Just for tonight?"

"Of course. We can go back to planning each other's murders tomorrow, when you've had time to rest."

A weird sensation rattled through me, but I swallowed it down. No doubt this was all a part of his plan to break down my walls and get me to care. Never. But I did need him if I wanted to cleanse the remnants of the night from my skin. Wash it down the drain and hopefully forget it ever happened.

"Fine," I said, the word burning on my tongue.

Lifting me into his arms, he averted his gaze as if he were carrying the plague in bodily form instead of his betrothed. Which was fine. I didn't want to look in his stupid eyes to begin with, let alone be in his arms. Once inside the washroom, he turned his back but didn't leave.

"You can go now," I said.

"I'd rather not, in case you need a hand getting in and out."

"What, you trying to catch a glimpse?"

A snicker rattled through him as I rolled down my stockings, nearly hitting the ground again. "I assure you, I am not."

"Good."

I struggled to pull my top over my head, my jaw tender where Odin had marked me. My entire face felt like it'd been hit by a semi-truck, but I wasn't about to admit that. Not in front of Lyvias. I groaned, pain thrumming in my shoulder. I tried another angle, but this shirt wasn't coming off without a fight.

"May I help you change?" he asked.

"Abso-fucking-lutely not." I made another attempt, but ended in the same position as before. Stuck. Shit. "Fine, but if you so much as peek, I'll bitch slap you into next week, got it?"

"Oh, I don't doubt it," he said with a laugh.

He turned, eyes pinched tight, a wild grin across his face. I studied his porcelain skin as his hands effortlessly found their way to the hem of my shirt, pulling it tight around the collar to get it up over my head. I wasted no time diving into the warm bath, the burn soothing me. Silent moments ticked away, him never facing me or attempting to leave.

"You're brave," he finally said, cutting through the tension. "Reckless, but brave."

I scooped water into my mouth, rinsing the iron filth out with little care for the soapy residue it left behind. "Brave? How do you figure?"

"It's rare for someone to go toe to toe with a hellhound, especially a pack alpha. Malachi's men," he said, aimlessly picking at a chip in the door frame, "they're some of the most vicious creatures in the realm."

My muscles turned to stone as the dots began to align. Odin's attack before the club...it was an assassination attempt. Potentially ordered by Malachi himself. But what did they aim to achieve out of it all? It's not like they could kill me and ascend the throne. Malachi wasn't a Reigning Reaper. Anathema's throne answered to Death's power alone. The hell were they thinking?

"They say Fate and Death fell in love at the dawn of time," Lyvias continued. "Together, they bore many vicious creatures the human realm fell victim to. Hellhounds—creatures with split souls both man and beast—were the last of their creations. Hounds respond to one master their entire lives and viciously protect them. Their bite is deadly; even a simple nip can put a reaper in their grave."

Questions began to rapid-cycle through me, and a single image became crystal clear: amber eyes peeking through shadowed woods. Cooper's undoing. The night I'd lost him. "Can a hellhound enter the mortal world?"

His shoulders grew rigid, though he didn't turn. "I don't see why they would want to—"

"That's not what I asked. Can they?"

"Well, if they had access to a realm door, sure. Anything could."

The pieces began to fall together, encompassing me in an all-consuming fear. Those eyes...the hound that'd come for Coop and me. We hadn't followed a random demon's sloppy kill tracks; he'd led us to him. A trap. It had been them from the start.

Odin and Malachi.

A knock at the door sent us both reeling. Lyvias never turned, simply peeked his head out.

"The princess has a package," a guard muttered, to which Lyvias simply took the box and closed the door.

Alarm bells raged in my mind, a sickening sensation in my gut. Something was very, very wrong. Lyvias threw the package over his shoulder, and I nearly dropped it in my bloody bathwater. Wrapped with frayed black ribbon, the box was no larger than my hand. I swallowed hard, heartbeat in my ears as I flipped the attached tag. In handwriting I'd equate to that of a toddler, I read the note.

If you wanted a war, you should have just said so. – The Hounds

My bones vibrated as I pulled the ribbon loose and popped open the box. What lay inside sent me shooting out of the water, body screaming as panic seized every muscle.

CHAPTER 9

HYBRIDS AND SACRIFICES

The cool bite of Cooper's coffin nipped at my fingertips. While I'd tried to sleep the night before, after Odin's threat and the "gift" he'd sent, it'd proved impossible. My jaw ached—throat bruised purple as a plum—and I couldn't manage to get my thoughts under control. With nobody left to turn to, I had finally found myself in the one place I'd always been able to find comfort. With Cooper.

"I think I have a target on my back," I whispered, tracing a single finger along the coffin's fogged-glass window. But I didn't need to see in to know the truth beneath. Cooper lay as he had upon my first viewing: motionless, eyes closed, barely breathing. "And that's not even the sickest part. Bet you can't guess what was in that damn box."

Silence filled the dark halls, a nearby candle's hiss breaking the quiet. Tears welled.

"His dick, dude," I said with a laugh that didn't reach my soul. "How sick is that? Guess the hounds really have it out for me now. But don't worry, I'll find a way to take them out. Somehow…for you."

While rage still held my heart in a firm grasp, I had no clue where to start looking for ways to take those monsters out. With how effortlessly Odin had gained access to my private quarters, it was clear he had people within the castle walls in his back pocket. I had no way to confirm, but something told me that Death played a part. Who knew how deep this all went. The reasons behind it. Not that I trusted Cadagon to begin with. The bastard. I couldn't turn to the guards for protection; they served Death's will. Nasheesh was slimy at best. And Lyvias…his mood swings between helpful and cruel were too hard to navigate. Trusting anyone, aside from maybe Suri, simply wasn't an option. In the end, I didn't want to rope Suri into this mess any more than she'd already been. She deserved peace, and this wasn't her fight. It was mine.

I was completely and utterly alone.

A shrill cry echoed from the stairwell above. Like a bat out of hell, the sweet, little raven swooped in, landing on my shoulder.

"Hey, buddy," I said through my tears, running a hand across his smooth feathers. "How'd you know I'd be here, huh? Always looking after me, you silly thing."

He pushed into my touch before cawing like a maniac in my ear. I jumped, sending him back into flight mode. Before I could call him back to me, he took off down one of the four dark hallways at the room's far side. The shapeshifter hall. Poor thing was going to get himself lost. I jumped to my feet, plucked a candle off the wall, and started after him.

"Poe, where'd you go?" I called ahead.

Water dripped in random places, creating slick puddles I had to sidestep or risk falling on my ass. Though, the gentle drips soothed my frayed edges. When I reached the open spaces within, I fought back a gasp. Thirteen feet below the surface, no moonlight to encourage their growth, black roses lay in bloom. Their vines twisted and knotted over twelve coffins erected along the room's outer edges, as if they were carved into the stone walls themselves. Etched into their surfaces were faces and bodies I could only assume reflected the person inside each when they'd still been breathing. With alabaster inlays on granite, each statue's arms protruded out to extend a leather book. A sinister beauty. One that made me feel less alone for some strange reason.

Poe's call sent me reeling. I found him picking at the edges of a coffin sequestered from the rest at the room's back right corner. "There you are."

Extending my finger to him as a perch, he looked me over. To my shock, he reached out and nipped my finger hard enough to draw blood. I jerked back, a droplet falling on the stone hand. "The hell was that for?"

A second later, a thud resounded, and the book that'd once been sealed away in a solid grip lay at my feet. Poe fluttered down to it, foot clawing at the cover. Was he trying to show me something? "What is it?"

On contact, the pages rustled beneath my touch as if the book itself held life all its own. It extended the title page long enough for me to read the journal's owner: Ivy Bitters, counterpart to the Reigning Reaper Shadra. Who must have been my great, great, great, great, grandfather if I worked my timelines out correctly. The clever raven hooked his talons on my pant leg, crawling up me to perch on my shoulder. I lifted it from the mucky floor, extending my candlelight to it.

Page after page boasted accounts of love for her family and her attempts to harness her shifter transitions. Come her sixteenth birthday, she'd decided upon her secondary form: a fox. For reasons unknown, I had assumed full-blooded shifters could change forms to whatever they wanted, whenever they wanted. But according to Ivy's stories, it appeared only two clans amongst the shifters possessed such power: the Bloodbanes and the Talonborns. They were elites among their people, able to change into any form they desired with ease. She described the Talonborns as fiercely protective over their people, whereas the Bloodbanes proved far more wicked, lording their abilities over those they deemed lesser.

Hours slipped by. I devoured every minuscule detail I could glean on shifter culture. When the final entry came about, my lungs heaved in anticipation. The entry was titled, "The Day the Gates Closed."

She described in terrible detail how the Bloodbanes had conspired with human witches, binding their souls to dark incantations. Forbidden magic. Their thirst for power unquenchable, they craved the one thing they couldn't have: Death's power. When Shadra got wind of their plans, he delivered the mortal witches to their coven leader for punishment and closed the shifter gates, locking the Bloodbanes and Talonborns in Anathema. This was the first gate to be sealed off in an effort to keep mortal witches and supernatural beings from conspiring. To keep the peace. But what I didn't know was what they'd hoped to accomplish with their spell. The Reigning Reaper's powers were a gift from the original Death and couldn't be fabricated. It was in our blood, plain and simple.

My shadows buzzed, a thought blooming. This had something to do with Cadagon's murder streak, what he'd done to my mother's people, pushing the shapeshifters out of Anathema. I knew it. How, I wasn't sure, but I did. Death's intuition, I suppose.

Ivy claimed Shadra had hidden away the true details, wanting to shield her from the unsavory ones. Though she said that she'd been tempted to read his entries about it in *The Book of Shade*: an enchanted tome all Reigning Reapers, and only them, had access to.

I flipped to the next page with an anxious breath. Damn it, no! A blank page. Then another. Shuffling the pages back and forth in hopes I'd made a mistake, it became clear I hadn't. Not a single word more. My candle hissed, attracting my attention to its waning light. I'd been so immersed; I hadn't realized I'd burned through an entire candlestick. Hopping to my feet, I scooped Poe up from the floor and headed out the way I had come. While I didn't have all the answers, I now had a heading.

Why I hadn't thought of it before—probably due to it being forbidden—I wasn't sure, but I knew what I had to do. Coming back into the room's main entryway, I kissed my hand and placed it on Cooper's coffin before jutting out into the night.

The Book of Shade. That's where I'd find my answers.

I slunk back up the castle stairs and into the main foyer. Death would never grant me access to what I wanted. I'd need to bide my time. Pursue my next step with care. After tucking Poe back in my room—setting out snacks as a "thank you" for his services in finding my first lead into whatever hidden conspiracy I'd stumbled on—I touched base with Nasheesh and discovered that Fate had smiled on me yet again. Death had plans for a midnight opera showing in the vampire court, which proved perfect for me. And so I waited.

When midnight rolled around, I slipped from my room. I communed with the halls to make sure Death had in fact left before wandering through the otherwise quiet castle. Of course, I tried to ask the halls where the book was, but they shunned my request. Rude. But it didn't surprise me. It just meant time was of the essence. I headed for the castle's main landings, pausing to admire once again how the staircases defied gravity.

Now if I were a control freak like Death, where would I keep the book?

I tapped my chin, and my eyes glided about the corridors, falling on the hall Cadagon had explicitly forbidden me to enter. Bingo. The north wing: it'd be there.

"Where are you going?" Lyvias's voice cut through the hall, crimson gaze alight in the shadows.

"Shit," I said in a hush, and snatched his sweater sleeve to pull him closer. With the halls so silent, even a whisper could get me caught, let alone his dumbass talking at full volume. "Lower your damn voice."

"Ease up, will you?" He shuffled from my grasp. "I'm here to help."

"I already told you that I don't want your help." My body tensed. "What are you doing wandering the castle so late anyway?"

"I could ask you the same question, Princess." He crossed his arms to match my stance.

"You're doing it again."

His eyebrows raised in jest. "Why, whatever do you mean?"

"Dodging my questions."

"I've no idea what you're talking about."

"Ugh, you're obnoxious." I growled a tad louder than I'd planned, and the sound reverberated through the open expanses around us. In an instant, Lyvias had me in his grasp and swept up the stairs into the shadows, pinning me to the wall of the south wing hallway. He anchored his hands above me, his face a mere foot from mine, fangs pressed into his bottom lip. My stomach jumped. He was close. Too close.

"Get off." I shoved against his chest.

"Shh." He collected both my wrists in his hand and pointed to the main landing with the other.

A faint light drifted down the west end stairs and out into the open. I squinted as a figure paused to scan the stairwells, their silhouette in the exact spot I'd been standing moments before. Catlike eyes were the only visible feature in the candle's low light, but it was enough for me to recognize him.

"Nasheesh," I whispered, sights transfixed on the demon as he descended the main staircase, opened the castle's front door, took a quick look over his shoulder, and swept out into the night. "What's he doing out at this hour?"

"Based on his sneaky exit," Lyvias said and stepped back, "I'd say nothing good."

I eyed him. He had reservations about Death's confidant too? How…surprising. And suspicious. For a moment, my instincts bid me to follow Nasheesh, but the snarl in my gut reminded me where my attention was needed most. *The Book of Shade*. I started back up the stairs, though I had little idea where I was going. Lyvias tailed me.

"You seem wound up tighter than usual. What is going on?" he asked, steps even with mine.

"Nothing."

He chuckled. "You're a terrible liar, you do know that?"

"I could give two shits what you think about me right now." I started up the southbound stairs, candlelight dripping down the red carpet runners.

Lyvias stepped into my path. "I'm not leaving until you tell me what was in the box."

"I don't have to tell you anything, now—"

He grabbed my arm, though his hold was surprisingly gentle. "I bid to extend our truce."

"What?" I pulled from his hold again.

"Our truce, we said it lasted for one night, correct? Well, I think it would be in both of our best interests if we extended that timeline to just one more night."

I looked him over. "I don't see why—"

"Let me come with you."

"Why do you even care?" I reeled back on him, my shadows riling inside me. "You told me yourself you wanted to cut me out like a cancer, so why worry about me now?"

"Because I can see the fear in your eyes," he said, voice low. "And if the contents of that box scared the woman who pinned me to the ground with an axe upon our first meeting, it's clearly something I should know about."

I considered his words. He wasn't wrong. A proclamation of war with the hounds and potentially the entire demon court—considering Odin answered to Malachi—meant I'd have to tell Lyvias eventually. With one hands balled into a fist, I slid my other hand into my pocket and presented Odin's note. I heaved a deep breath. "Also, Odin's... severed manhood was in there."

A snicker escaped him before he righted his face, lips thin. "He threatened you."

"Technically, he threatened *us*," I corrected. "If I can't shake you, then so be it. But if you're going to help, I need you to know that what I'm about to search for cannot be shared with anyone. If I find out that you've even *hinted* to anyone what I'm doing, I will chop off your dick and add it to my collection. Do I make myself clear?"

He pondered for a long second, intense stare piercing my face. "You have my word."

While I still didn't trust him for shit, I had a feeling he wasn't above petty revenge. Just for tonight, we could play ally. Then I'd find out what he was hiding. "Help me find Death's quarters."

I swept through the hallway and began the climb up the north stairwell without a glance back.

Lyvias remained hot on my heels. "You do know what Cadagon

will do to you if he should find out about this..."

"If you keep your mouth shut," I hissed, "he won't."

We wound through half a dozen halls, sure to peek around each corner before a turn, when we came to the largest door in the north wing hidden in the back most corridor. Thick, stone carvings twisted around the door frame, its edges lavished in a silver-leafed lacquer.

"This is him," I said.

Lyvias squinted down at me. "You are sure?"

"It's the most eccentric piece in this hallway; it's him." I collected my nerve and coaxed the door open. Of course—as an old castle's bones tend to do—the ungreased hinges shrieked into the space ahead. A snarl resonated from deep within Death's quarters, and I swallowed hard.

"What was that?"

We both stiffened, our sights set on a drifting silhouette in the darkness, not a stone's throw from where we stood. It turned, blinking its white eyes toward us. Fuck. We didn't move. Didn't breathe. Didn't even blink, all in the hopes that somehow we'd remain unseen.

When the being finally came into full view—a slippery thing, made of swirling vapor—Lyvias leaned close, his hushed breath tickling my ear. "It's a sandman."

"A what?" I whispered back.

"A sandman. They are one of the few beings with the ability to travel between realms. I'm sure Cadagon has trained this one for his protection, but seeing as he isn't here..." He met my gaze, a challenge in his eyes. "If we move slowly and don't arouse suspicion, I think we'll be fine."

I considered for a moment. To my surprise, my shadows urged me forward, practically begged. In the end, I needed that damned book. I dared a step forward. Slow and steady, we wound into Death's quarters, careful to stay on the opposite side of the dark room. The sandman floated about, drifting in and out of the walls, but stuck to a circular path. A predictable one, which proved helpful. We just had to stay out of its way. Hell knows I had *zero* desire to figure out what it was capable of should we attract its attention.

Lyvias relaxed his rigid stance, but I didn't let my guard down. Cadagon was never to be taken lightly. While he was an absolute prick, he was a smart one. Un-fucking-fortunately. Who knew what other traps he had built into his lavish room. I broke off to the right, hungry eyes hunting for any signs of the book that'd lead me to answers about my kingdom, and Fate willing, a way to lift whatever was keeping Cooper asleep. My heart leapt at the thought alone.

A platform, visible only by the bright red runners along its stairs, hovered over Cadagon's bed. I motioned for Lyvias's attention and pointed, mouthing, "There." He nodded and started for the split staircase in slow silence. Sure enough, atop a marble pedestal crammed between Death's personal bookshelves sat *The Book of Shade*. I traced my fingers across the leather surface but felt...nothing. Not a magic tingle or a jitter of motion within. The hell? I pried at the cover, but it wouldn't budge. After a second, I realized: blood. Everything in Anathema seemed hellbent on it. Slipping my dagger from its holster on my thigh, I sliced a small cut down my palm and let a single droplet fall on the cover. But again, nothing. A frustrated sigh slipped past my lips.

"What's wrong?" Lyvias muttered.

"I don't know how to do this..."

His lips tightened. "Open a book?"

"No!" I snapped. "It doesn't react to my blood. It won't open!"

He tapped his chin. A thought reached his eyes as he leaned closer. "It's *The Book of Shade*, right? So use your shadows."

Genius! Hated him, but still. Genius.

I slipped a shadow from my fingertip, whispered my desires to it, and it crept between the pages as if it knew precisely where to go. The book fluttered to life, its pages softly swooshing as my magic dove through its contents, finally stopping on one specific entry with a thud. Lyvias and I reeled around to check the sandman's location, knowing full well that hadn't been quiet, but released simultaneous sighs when we realized it'd passed into the adjacent room. Safe. For now.

Eyes squinted in the low light, I skimmed the passage as my power slipped under my nails to settle back inside me. I blinked, confused.

"This doesn't make any sense," I said, mostly to myself. "This passage is about hybrids."

"Hybrids don't exist," Lyvias responded.

"Right…" And what does that have to do with the massacre or Coop?

Seems my power wasn't quite as on par as I'd thought. Bratty shadows, throwing me off my game. Turning to a new page, I lifted the heavy tome into my arms to see closer, and I swear the damn thing bit me. With a shriek, I dropped it, loud and hard on the floor. Without a second's pause, the sandman was there. Shoulders hunched, it shrieked, taking solid form all at once and knocking me to the ground. My entire body screamed. Damn, couldn't a girl get one day without being beaten to shit?

Lyvias jumped in, attempting to pry the being off me, but its hold was firm, as if its essence had rooted itself inside me. The sharp scent of jasmine tickled my nose, and the only way I can describe the sensation along with it? A hand. Tracing its way across my brain. Juniper's face flashed across my mind's eye, her voice calling to me in rapid visions. Distress. Something was wrong.

"Well, well," Cadagon's voice cut through like a razor. "Of all the infuriating things you've done since your arrival, this is the worst yet."

With a snap, Death called off his monster, the sandman returning to its mindless rotation through the room. I stood tall, pushing my shoulders back. He was the monster who put Cooper in a coma. Who hurt my kingdom, my people. Despite our pact, no less. "I won't apologize. I will find out what you're hiding, and you can't—"

"Silence! You have outdone yourself this time, my foolish daughter. Creeping into my sacred space, wandering about my private quarters, and what's worse, you brought company to share in my humiliation." His sights landed hard on Lyvias, and the sharp aroma of death filled the air.

"We had a deal!"

Juniper's voice cut through my mind: "Come to me, Kim." In flashes, my soul began to wander, slipping from consciousness into the astral. I tried to focus, to keep my attention fixed on Cadagon. My enemy. He stalked about, his face shifting into June's and then back again. I rubbed my palms against my face, attempting to clear my vision, but to no avail.

"You've been spoiled, Kimberly." Cadagon drew nearer. "Rottenly so. But I have learned my lesson. I've coddled you, and that certainly will not do. You must be reprimanded for your transgression here tonight. You've forced my hand."

Again, Juniper called. "I need you here. Come to me."

As Death descended, my sights blurred. I'd made a promise to her, one I fully intended to keep. That I would always come when she called. That I'd be there for her. In a final burst of foolish bravery, I hurled my shadows at Cadagon. He dodged, stalking towards me with murder in his burning irises.

"Don't you dare leave this plane of consciousness," Death growled, and took control of my hand. "You will stay!"

His thumb pressed hard against my forehead, and Juniper's face began to fade. My teeth clenched. He was cutting off my connection! Tears stung my eyes. "Don't do this. She needs me!"

"You made an oath to fulfill your role! You will remain here in Anathema," he snarled, pushing harder against my brow. "Even if that means I have to sever your connection to the astral. Permanently."

My brain began to boil. If he pushed too hard, I could lose June. Forever! I looked to Lyvias. "Help me."

His face constricted. "I can't just—"

"Please, Lyvias." While I wasn't prone to begging, the alarm in my mind had reached dire levels. "Please!"

"Damn it," Lyvias muttered. A wicked expression twisted the edges of his sharp lips upward, and with a fang-filled grin, he said, "You fucking owe me."

With his full weight, he rushed Death, toppling him to the ground. I seized my moment, latched onto Juniper's call, and tumbled through time and space.

ＣHAPTER 10

AN ACT OF FATE

I crashed hard, face-planting into a bed of dying daisies. Wind knocked from my lungs, hands shaky, I laid there until the world stopped spinning. Death. He'd tried to take someone from me. Again. He'd laid his filthy hands on me. *Again.* Rage bubbled in my stomach. While I had no way to prove it—yet—it wouldn't have fucking surprised me to learn he'd headed up Odin's attack. Sided with Malachi against me if only to keep his hold on the throne. Maybe that's how Odin had slipped past all the guards to my room in the first place. Who needs stealth when you've got the king in your damn pocket?

A scream ripped through me as I hopped to my feet, kicking the dirt with white-knuckled fists at my side.

"Kim," Juniper's sweet voice rang, her sliver of light inside tugging at me.

I ran to her and cradled her face. "Are you okay? I came as soon as I could."

"Are *you* okay?" she asked, panicked sights looking over me. "I felt you. Your shadow, it did something inside me. Something strange and...unsettling."

She placed a hand over her heart, and the light tendril she'd gifted me danced in my own chest. "Death, he tried to sever my bond to the astral plane. To you."

Her brow creased, a tight curl falling from her pinned hair. "Sever us? But why?"

"Because I'm not attending to my duties? I don't know. He's an asshole," I said with an exasperated sigh. "He caught me rummaging through his quarters, so he wanted to punish me. I don't see the big deal; I would have access to *The Book of Shade* soon anyway—"

"You opened *The Book of Shade*?" June asked, and her face contorted with concern. She took a step back, her hand in mine slipping slightly.

"Well, yeah." I looked her over.

"Why would you do that, Kimber? It's forbidden."

"I needed answers, and it seemed like the best place to start. I...I was attacked." The thirst for retribution trickled its cool touch down my limbs. Surrounded by monsters, it was becoming clear that if I wished to beat them, I'd need to become a monster myself. These crooked men who sought to tear me down and take what was rightfully mine? I'd have their heads. "I'll kill them! All of them," I seethed.

June grew still as she looked over the shadows billowing from my fingertips. "You've changed."

"I've changed?" I laughed bitterly. "How could I not when evil, spoiled men are after everything I care about? And I don't even know why! Not to mention, they tried to *kill* me!"

"I'm not saying you don't have a right to be angry. You do. But killing everyone who challenges you will only lead you down a path of darkness—"

"Look at me!" I burst. "I *am* darkness, Juniper! I'm the future Death. We've always known this."

"Yes, *future*, not current. What you did, opening that book, you don't even realize what you've done! The wheels you've set in motion! That's why its contents are for the Reigning Reaper's eyes only!" She let out a sigh. "You weren't ready, but I suppose now we have no choice. Our time has run out."

"What are you talking about?" I swallowed hard. Wasn't ready? My gaze fell into hers, the bigger question hitting me all at once. "How did you even know about that book to begin with?"

She stepped forward, her light rising to the surface and forcing me to shield my eyes. But this wasn't as it had been in times before. Such raw power. So much so, it riled the shadows now burrowing in my bones to evade her growing sunlit splendor. What the hell was happening? Heat on my cheeks, I peeked through my fingers.

"How I know isn't the priority here," June said, her voice layered in what could only be described as a symphony of twinkling wind chimes. But deeper, powerful. "This is about you and what *you* need to know. It's time you saw me, knew me. The powers at play demand it."

With one wave, she dimmed her light enough for me to lower my hand while simultaneously dropping a glamour over her eyes. A hazy white eclipsed her once dark irises, giving her a severe but beautiful edge. My lungs shrunk at the sight. She was absolutely stunning. "What is this?"

"Until recently, I had my questions. Who I was. What I was made for. Why you and I found each other as we did," she said, coming closer. "But I know now. And deep down, so do you."

I looked her over. "I have no idea what you're talking about."

"Yes, you do. Think! How were we able to meet? And here of all places, in neutral territory. Never in Elysium or Anathema." Her hand reached to mine, and the shadows in me receded. She whispered, "Where do you get *your* power from?"

My brow pinched. "Death, of course."

"Correct. But how? Why?"

"Nobody knows for sure, aside from old fairy tales handed down." I squeezed her hand tight. "What does that have to do with us?"

She pressed into me, her jasmine perfume tangling in my nose. "The story says Death fell in love at the beginning of time, and that love bore children so ravenous, they nearly drove humanity to extinction. As a promise to never do so again, Death and his lover bestowed a portion of their power to the mortals. Death and..."

My whole body stilled, the realization hitting me like a sucker punch. "...Fate."

A gentle yet pained expression eclipsed her face. "Yes. I am *your* Fate."

Oh, fuck me. How did I not see it before? How her light balanced my darkness. The way her voice could quiet my rage. Our instant connection and desire. We were destined to meet, just as every mortal embodiment of Death and Fate had before us. My heartbeat clapped in my ears. But if our abilities, our kingdoms, were born of the old gods' agreement, that meant... "We were never meant to be, were we?"

"My love, we were always meant to be, just never to last." She traced a hand along my cheek, and I winced at the sear her touch now held. "Star-crossed lovers rarely do."

"We could fight it!" Panic hit my bloodstream, my limbs shaking. "There has to be a way; this can't be the end."

Juniper shook her head, forehead wrinkled with the onset of tears. "There isn't, Kim. Trust me, I've searched and searched. But the old gods, they built this as a means to ensure what they did so long ago would never happen again."

I reached for her again, her light burning the ever-loving shit out of my palms. Shuddering on contact, I yanked my already blistered hands to my chest.

"I'm so sorry," she said, reaching out but stopping herself.

"No, no, it's okay." My head spun, a sickness settling in my stomach. The nausea grew, and as if on cue, the light tendril Juniper had gifted me twisted, my shadows escorting it from my body. Rejecting it. I fell to my knees and heaved until the light burst free, floating back to its original host. June. Fate. My love. Tears began to well. "I can't believe this was all for nothing."

Her own tears sizzled as they slid down her cheeks. "Don't say that. Without each other, we'd never have found our way to becoming the leaders our realms require us to be. I like to think we helped each other find our true selves."

The breeze danced around us, twisting our hair into wisps as it passed. Words evaded me. This…this couldn't be happening. We were supposed to be a safe space for one another, always just a call away. Why did destiny insist on my loneliness? First Coop, now June—I swallowed against my sandpaper tongue. "What now?"

Her heavy sigh hit home in my gut. Ominous. "It's my job to collect your sacrifice…before I go."

"Sacrifice? Go? I…what?"

"Yes, that's the part of the story the old tales leave out, unfortunately. As another way to keep history from repeating itself, the old gods require a sacrifice in order for each new Death to ascend their throne." Her chest bobbed, a sob slipping through. "I require the thing you love most. In exchange, you will receive unrivaled power."

"I don't want power," I snapped, wishing I could grab her and hold her and kiss her and—shit! "What good is power if it means I lose everyone I care about?"

She stepped back, spooked by my harsh tone. "I wish it wasn't so, but I have no choice. As your responsibilities bind you, so do my own."

I softened under her gaze. While my dark nature fueled my anger, this woman—this wonderful, formidable, kind woman—did not deserve an ounce of my malice. We'd both been tricked by prophecy. Cursed by the mistakes of old gods. I willed my shadows into submission, letting one slip to coil against Juniper's cheek and wipe her tears. While I couldn't touch her, my power could, and I needed her to know. To feel my love. I wouldn't allow my anger to be the last thing she saw. Like calling to like, the shadow I'd given June so long before came crawling up her arm, pooling at her fingertip. It slipped to the dirt below, slithering across the ground to slink up my leg. I swear I heard my heart crack at its return. Sacrifice. While I wanted two things fervently, one stood above the other in that moment.

"You," I whispered, my magic tucking a loose curl behind her ear. "Us. That is my sacrifice."

Her eyes closed tight, in visible pain. "I thought you might say that. And while it pains me...there is something you want more. Something deeper."

"Something I want more? What do I—"

No. Fuck, no! Cooper. I shook my head. "I won't give up on him. Ever."

"I'm afraid we have no choice. If you don't give up your hunt for a cure, the sacrifice will not be enough. Death's abilities would devour you, and your kingdom would collapse." Her sobs grew louder, melding with mine. "I'll leave your memories intact, but he will never be to you what he once was."

I fell to my knees, hyperventilating. Abandoning Cooper would be betraying my own self. He was a part of me, ingrained so deep he touched the marrow. Who would I be without my shoulder to cry on, my partner in crime, my confidant? The one person I could always, without question, count on. Either I betrayed him or my entire kingdom. How royally screwed was that? But based on the way my insides constricted, I already knew: I didn't have a choice. Anathema and its people relied on me.

I crumbled into the dirt and let the grief crush me. "Fine," I wept. "Take him from me."

Juniper's shadow stretched across me as she came to rest at my side. Without a word, she extended a knife to me, and I sliced my palm, her following suit to seal the blood pact. There would be no going back. No changing my mind. As her hand laced through mine—the tang of burnt flesh rising into the air as her heat cauterized my wound—my soul quivered, a piece of it withering and dying.

Cooper. I love you. Always.

I knelt there, lost to time. But when there were no tears left to shed, I stood, dusted myself off, and gazed upon my love for the last time, knowing I'd never be the same from that day forward. Already, I felt the cold rushing in and settling around my heart. Alone. I was utterly alone.

"I'm so sorry," June said in a hush, heartbreak palpable in her tone.

She drew near, her lips an inch from mine, and I didn't hesitate. My mouth devoured hers, and though her light burned like acid, I lost myself in her. Blisters already forming, my sights met hers. "Please don't leave me..."

"Never. I'll always be here." She pointed to my chest, where her light had lived for so long, before tapping her own. "I'll never forget you."

"Gods," I breathed, shoulders quivering. "And I'll never forget you."

I watched in stunned silence as the sky opened up. Elysium's glorious light wrapped itself around Fate herself as she gave me a strained smile. "Allow me to instill one last word of wisdom? Off the record?"

"Of course."

"Help him," she said, and began to ascend. "Your path to success depends on it. Don't let your fear be your downfall. Let someone else in, Kim. You deserve to be loved."

Light rushed from overhead as the world around us began to rapidly deteriorate.

"Who?" I called out.

"You know." Her voice tickled my ear despite our distance. "Let it be known: the deal with Fate has been struck!"

Her hands clashed together, and white light exploded around us.

"Use that beautiful brain of yours to unravel your enemies," she boomed, her voice seven and one all at once somehow. "Now go in peace and know that Fate has blessed you, Lady Death."

With the kindest, most gentle smile, she was gone.

My ray of sun enveloped by Fate.

I collapsed on the castle's front stairs, the connection between Fate and me severed like a chopped limb. Her tight hold on my heart remained, but her light no longer soothed me. Instead, wrath rose. Crumpling into a ball, the pressure overtook me, twisted my stomach into knots as my head pounded from the rising sobs. A scream tore through me, so raw and anguished it sent the birds in the nearest tree into flight.

My love: gone. Cooper: gone.

How the hell was I supposed to go on? Leaving Cooper in a box to rot. Never seeing my lover's sweet smile again. Why hadn't I known about the laws set in place by the original Fate and Death? There'd been no warning. Anywhere. Nothing in my studies of Anathema led me to believe I'd have to break my own damn heart and offer it to the old gods as a sacrifice. Why hadn't I known?

Cadagon.

He'd been forced into a sacrifice in his own time to ascend the throne, and yet he had left me unknowing. From the very beginning, he had known! Still, he'd brought Cooper here, sealed him away in that coffin, tried to sever my connection with Fate in an attempt to steal my last moments with her. Monster! He lacked compassion. Empathy. Nothing but a shriveled black heart lived in Death's chest, and everything in me wanted to rip it from his body, slide it onto a stake, and post it in the castle courtyard for all to see.

The motherfucker.

I rose to my feet, shadows thrashing about me, urging me forward. Feeding the fire burning inside. If he were capable of these things— treachery against his own flesh and blood—his wickedness knew no bounds. The shapeshifter massacre: him. My fists clenched at my sides. Odin and Malachi: also Cadagon. How else had Odin gained access to me that night? And the guards stationed below my stairwell were conveniently MIA at the precise moment I had needed them. Wind whipped around me in a frenzy as I stood. He would answer for his crimes. Every last one.

Gliding up the stairs and into *my* castle, I wound through the halls; a terribly delicious power settled on my tongue, sharp as whiskey. Servants dove away at the sight of me. Doors shut of their own will at my passing. A darkness encompassed me, and where I walked, it followed.

The voices started low and muddled at first, but as I stalked within those walls, they grew louder. Death's castle: it spoke to me with certainty. Before, the halls had merely whispered their reports, but now they answered my questions with sharp precision. The castle's invisible eyes prodded me.

"Death?" A voice trilled in my ear.

"No, that is not him..." said another from the opposite direction.

"Yes, it is Death. Though, she is a lady somehow?" a third called from a step behind.

Why the sudden change, I had neither an idea nor care in that moment. My mission was clear. Each corridor sounded a report, voicing the names of those you could find concealed within its walls. Lyvias was somewhere down below, the castle's calls muddled by the floorboards. Cadagon, on the other hand, could be found in the gardens. The walls ensured it so. I stalked out the way I had come and basked in the adrenaline flooding my veins.

The Queen in me was waking. And she was pissed.

Death sat below a bloomed apple tree, biting into a piece of its fruit. The look on his face was expectant, impatient, but above both was one unmissable truth. He was furious. "So you return—"

"Shut up!" I threw my hand through the air. A weak, invisible clutch held Death's mouth closed—as he'd done to me—but with a mere snicker he broke my control.

"Impressive." His expression remained flat. "I see you've awoken your inner strength then."

"I said, 'Quiet!'" Once more, I flung my wrist. This time my silent hold stuck. For how long, I couldn't be sure, but the concern in Cadagon's eyes encouraged me. "You will learn to treat me with the respect I deserve, old man! I am not your daughter or your protege. I am the future queen." I twisted my fingers about, willing his face to meet mine, and to my surprise, it worked. This new wave of strength: it was fueled by my rage. I could sense it now. Its essence shifted through me like thick smoke, and damn, did it feel good.

"You knew, didn't you?" I seethed. "About Cooper. About Fate. All of it, you fucking knew!"

One snap, and my hold on him lessened, allowing him to move and speak, though still restrained.

"Yes." He rubbed his throat and growled. "I did. What are you going to do about it now, Princess? What is done is done."

I paced about him, my inner shadows converting my pain to power in rapid time.

"You've made a mess of things. Things I care about and people I love have been hurt and killed by your inability to empathize with anyone but yourself. Tell me, Cadagon," I asked as a wicked grin spread across my face, "do you fear death? Because I'm about one second away from snapping your neck."

"I fear *nothing*. I cannot be killed, especially by an intolerable little brat who thinks herself a queen but is merely a spoiled child throwing a tantrum!" The king threw his hand to the wind, seeking control of me, but my body denied him. The concern on his face bordered on fear as he stared down at his hands. "You...you're blocking me out? But how?"

I adopted the condescending tone that so often spilled from his mouth. "A question for a later time."

But in all reality, I had no real answer to give. My dark gifts, they'd come of their own volition when I needed them most. When my heart had shattered and I had nothing left but a hunger for revenge. "Did you send him?"

His brow tensed. "I've no idea what you're talking about—"

"Yes, you do. Odin, did you send him?" I released a single shadow to waft around Cadagon's neck, and it gripped his throat like a viper. A trickle of blood slid down his porcelain neck, my power sharpening to split skin.

The Reigning Reaper looked up at me, and his breath caught.

"Your...your eyes..." He scurried through the dirt to the garden pond and inspected his reflection with frantic pats along his brows. When he was assured his eyes were still aflame, he relaxed. "Thank the damned."

"What, were you afraid you lost your eyes?" I chuckled. "If you don't answer my question, I just might pluck them out."

"No. I was afraid you'd stolen my spark, my flame," he snarled, and whipped around. "The flame owed to me by Fate herself until the day of your coronation, you spoiled thing."

That word on his lips made my head spin. Fate. June. Darkness took hold in me, and I lowered myself to his eye level. Taking his throat in my hands, I squeezed until a whimper slipped through him. "Fine, don't answer me. I already know you have a hand in this as you have every other horrible thing in my life since my arrival. But hear me now, Death, you will bow to me by the time this all plays out. Mark my words."

I threw him into the dirt, leaving him to wallow in his defeat. Fists at my side, I focused on controlling my breathing. Tears would have to wait until later, when the world had quieted, and I was left with no other choice but to break. A shiver ran up my spine. The thought alone terrified me, but I channeled my fury instead, setting my mind on the mission at hand. I stalked into the castle.

"The dungeon, your Majesty..." The voice I'd heard in the hall earlier reported back to me.

I decided right then and there, I liked her or him. Or...it? Whatever. Weaving through the candlelit corridors, I headed straight through to the dungeons and found Lyvias exactly where the halls reported he'd be. At the entrance to his cell, a demon guard stood watch, axe in hand.

"Open the door," I demanded, and he jumped to action.

"Aye, Highness."

The rusty bars squealed open, and I waved the guard away. Inside the mildew-drenched cell, I found Lyvias pressed against the wall, concealed in murky torchlight. I settled at his side. "Are you okay?"

"Do I look okay?" His ruby eyes blazed, and he receded farther into the corner but took notice of my crumpled expression. "Don't pity me. This isn't your doing. It's Death's."

"What did he do to you?"

He didn't respond, though his breaths heaved. I waited, but my patience began to wane in the stillness. Fine then. If he didn't want to talk to me, then so be it. I turned to leave when June's words came back to me, sharp and pointed. *Help him. Your path to success depends on it.* I froze.

Of *course* she'd meant Lyvias. Ugh! But seeing as she was literally Fate herself, I had no choice but to believe her words. Not to mention, he had put his ass on the line to help me get to June in the first place. And the way he'd rescued me at the club... A deep sigh on my lips, I returned to Lyvias, pressed nearer, and wrapped a gentle hand around his shoulder. His body tensed under my touch.

"Please," I pleaded, careful not to make any quick movements. "I have to know what he did to you."

I felt his gaze on me. "Why would you want to see this? So you can tell me I deserved it? His wrath?"

"No. Because I care."

"You don't even know me, Kim," he said in a hush.

My nickname on his tongue caught me off guard. The way he said it, the inflection in his tone, it brought Cooper's face crashing into my brain. I shook my head, forcing the haunting image away. "Maybe not. But I want to. After what you did for me…"

Silence enveloped the cell, save for the drip of water that echoed through the stone-walled space, but I remained patient. Finally, Lyvias stood—a groan on his lips—and stepped into the light. I stifled a gasp. His eyes were encased in bruises, his arms and neck covered in deep gashes. But the worst? The worst were his wrists. Deep puncture marks lined their entirety, blood still seeping.

"What happened?" I reached for his hand without thought, but he dodged my reach.

"They're bite marks."

My eyes widened. "He *bit* you?"

"No. This is courtesy of Cadagon's personal torture master. He—" His voice grew hoarse. "He made me drink my own blood. It's a deeply humiliating act for vampires, used only when dealing with the worst offenders. Those accused of treason, though it doesn't seem as though Death aims to charge me. Only to wound my pride. I vomited for hours, and yet I still can't get my own damn taste out of my mouth."

"That's sick." My nails dug into my palms. "I'll handle this. Put him in his—"

"No."

My entire body tensed. "No? Why?"

Lyvias raised his head and met my gaze. Ferocity teemed in his deep eyes, a dark chuckle lifting from him. "I'll handle it. Cadagon shall die by my hand."

His words shook me. "You want him dead?"

"More than I have ever wanted anything."

I paced about in thought. If I were about to go after arguably the most powerful person in the entire realm, having a vampire's speed and knowledge of Anathema on my side could ensure Cadagon got what he deserved. Without question. But I still didn't entirely trust

Lyvias, despite Fate's advice. If this was a trap, it'd be a clever one. I looked him over again, his shoulders sinking and hatred radiating from every inch of him. The bloodlust in his expression grew palpable, his desire clear.

I forced my eyes shut and tapped into the halls' status reports. Two guards were headed our direction, a minute away at most. Our privacy was almost absolved. "I'll see it done."

"No. I'm to be the future king. It should be me."

"And I am the future Reigning Reaper. His blood belongs on my hands."

We stood, locked in one another's vengeful stares. Lyvias broke away, grasping a sharp stone from the dungeon floor. He sliced his palm open and offered it to me. "Together?"

Whatever Lyvias's true intentions were, he was certainly the lesser of two evils in play. I needed him. Following suit, I reopened the fresh cut from my most recent deal with little effort and clasped his hand in mine.

"Together."

CHAPTER 11

DEATH'S LULLABY

After seeing to Lyvias's safe transfer to the south tower—his quarters swapped for one level below mine to ensure he'd be accessible at all times—I headed to my room.

The suite was as I'd left it: empty. In the stillness, reality washed over me, crushing me under the waves. While I'd never had the biggest support system to begin with, this felt…different. Like being in a dark room with a single, half-burnt candle as your sole means of warmth and light, only for someone to come along and snuff it out, leaving you shaking and lost. No, not someone. Cadagon. Odin. Malachi.

They were to blame. For everything.

Single-minded, corrupt men who took pleasure in other's pain; the same way it'd been in the mortal world. It's as if they got off on it: devouring the good. The kind. But why would they fucking care? To them, a life was disposable. A means to an end. And love? Their shrunken black hearts wouldn't know it if it stabbed them in the face.

Power, status, riches had their devotion. And damn anyone who got in the way. I screamed, smashing my fist against the side table. The glass vase atop it shattered on the floor.

Eyes already sore, I tried to fight the rising tears. How was I supposed to do this alone? Without June's light and encouragement and gentle touch? Without Cooper's patience, support, and ability to spin even the worst situations into a silver lining worth fighting for? Everything I'd worked so hard for—my kingdom, my ascension to the throne: it wasn't worth it. Not without my people by my side. What was I without them? Nothing. Hollow, broken. I shuffled towards my bed ready to hide in it forever when my foot came down hard on a glass shard. A hiss on my lips, I stepped back to find blood seeping below my foot. "Damn it."

With careful steps, I sat in the leather chair near the window. The cool night air wafted through, soothing me as I pinched the inch-long shard buried in my heel. After a deep breath, I pulled it clean out. Intuitively aware, a shadow slipped from my fingers and stitched the flesh back together.

Well, that's new…

The simple gesture stopped my racing thoughts in their tracks. This wasn't what Cooper or June would want. They'd want me to fight. To tap into my power and fix this for those who'd been wronged before me and those still at risk.

Pull yourself together, Kim!

Yeah, fuck the self-pity. I had a king to kill. Red silk robe trailing behind me, I wound through the halls and into the study wing. While I'd no idea what exactly I was looking for or where to find it, my newly heightened power assured me it was near. Row after row, I searched the shelves. As the hours ticked by, I flipped through dozens of books. And while interesting, I wasn't looking for mainstream history here. I needed answers about the shifters. About Cadagon himself.

With three-tiered candlestick in hand, my intuition guided me to the small study at the wing's end. Its red and black stained-glass window looked out over the castle garden, moonlight trickling through. Shelves lined in thick dust, it became apparent the room hadn't been touched in what seemed like years. Why here? But the jitter in my stomach whispered that this was the place. So I started my hunt.

When I came to the unlit back corner, my eyes snagged on a tome on the bottom shelf. More importantly, on the drag lines in the dust. This book—it'd been touched. Recently. Lifting it off the shelf, I settled in the padded chair near the window and cracked its spine. The crisp aroma of old parchment tangled in my nose as I glimpsed the handwritten title page: *A History in Treason.*

The first date went clear back to before Reigning Reaper Shadra had held the throne, when Anathema was new and fresh. The passage, written by the personal advisor at the time, claimed a being unfit for Anathema had slipped through the ether and found itself here. With two corrupt Lords backing the beast, it aimed to undo the realm borders Fate and Death had created to prevent chaos from erupting into the mortal realm.

Account after account, over the course of hundreds of years, cycled through. To my surprise, this wasn't an isolated situation. Power-hungry elites had sought to overthrow the royal bloodline since the realm's creation. Which didn't surprise me. But the fact that these situations mirrored one another was no coincidence. When I came upon the last entry, my veins turned to ice.

A first-hand account by Valhalla, Reigning Reaper of Anathema, 1910

They sought to end me. To take my power, gifted to me by Death himself, in an effort to undo the royal bloodline. But they failed. Simpleminded, they believed me killable. Poor, misguided beings they were. The Reining Reaper knows nothing of physical death during their time upon the throne. Untouchable by disease or sword, just the same. And so I crushed them and their little rebellion. Sealed them away in their realms, claiming such decisions were on the Lords' parts as not to bring hellfire down upon my own head. I've placed spies across Anathema, two-fold in the shifter court. They will not rise up again. For if they do, I will destroy their entire court. Wipe them like a smudge from history. I am Death.

What. The. Hell.

I read and reread. My fingers dented the page, questions swirling through my mind. Who would even believe it possible to overthrow the Reigning Reaper? And how? Anxiety gripped at every muscle, seizing me. If this was true, if Valhalla had to strike down a whole-ass rebellion built around overthrowing him, that meant someone, somewhere, had stumbled on a way to take out the royal line. Or at least, they'd gotten close enough to an answer to believe they could. Not to mention that little bit about the Reigning Reaper being unkillable during their rule—

"What are you doing, Princess?" a sharp whisper cut through, making me jump.

"Shit, Lyvias," I muttered, grasping my chest. "Give a girl some warning next time, will you?"

He snickered as he waded into the room. The open buttons on his black silk pajamas caught my attention, vine tattoos wrapping up his throat in full view. Along the edge near his collarbone, black and white rose petals peeked through, and it sent my mind reeling back to Cooper's sleeves. The poisonous flowers woven across his arms. I shook the memory away as Lyvias sat in the chair to my left, motioning for me to pass the book.

I referenced the halls before handing it over. "It's a treason log. And look."

Flipping to Valhalla's entry, I let the heavy-eyed vampire look it over. When he'd finished, he turned to me and muttered low, "So he can't be killed then…"

"That's not how I took it." I pointed to one specific line. "See, while he is in power he's untouchable. But—"

"When his heir takes the throne…" His eyes widened.

A wicked grin overcame me. "Exactly."

"Looks like our wedding day just got a whole lot more interesting, Lady Death." A playful smirk, and his gaze slipped from mine back to the book, kicking his feet up on the nearest desk. "You know, something else stood out to me. He mentioned putting extra spies in the shifter realm."

"That caught my attention too. Maybe it has something to do with what happened under Cadagon's rule. The shifter massacre." I tapped my chin. "But the book is blank after Valhalla's entry, so there's no way to know for sure."

"There just might be. You can reference the halls, discover who's in them. I've seen you do it."

"How did you know—"

"You did it in the dungeon before we struck our deal, did you not?" He pursed his lips, awaiting my reply.

"Well, yeah, but what does that have to do with anything?"

"Don't you get it? Your abilities. You can read energy, Kim."

Like a switch, the truth lit me up. "I could read the shifter realm."

"In essence? Yes." He leaned back and tucked his hands behind his head. "I think you could and should."

I jumped up and settled into a steady pace about the room, hand clamped to my chin. "But the castle was built to serve the Reigning Reaper. It makes sense that I can feel the halls here. I don't know if I'd be able to read the energy somewhere else."

"This whole *world* serves the Reigning Reaper; it literally bends to Cadagon's will. I think you can do this." An unfitting, gentle smile caught his cheeks, but at the realization of my skepticism, it fell from his face. "If it turns out you can't, so be it. At least you tried."

I searched his piercing stare. "Someone is awfully supportive tonight."

"Yes." He shifted forward, set his elbows upon his knees, and pressed his fingertips together. "What are you getting at?"

"For someone who wanted me dead upon arrival, it just seems strange that you're suddenly so...cheerleader-ish. Why?"

"Maybe that sharp tongue of yours finally won me over." With a stretch, he stood. "Or maybe, just maybe, I changed my mind about your heathen upbringing. Anyone who can go toe to toe with Cadagon and not buckle has my respect. So regardless of our rough start, I now know where my loyalties lie." He lowered himself into my sight line. "We're in this together, remember?"

His crimson eyes dropped to my lips, and my stomach jumped. Shit. Close, much too close. I cleared my throat but held his gaze. Was this all some clever rouse? Despite my hardened stare, he didn't break under my scrutiny. That unwavering confidence...maybe I had misjudged him. Why else would Fate have urged me to help him? Sure, he'd been rough around the edges at first—really fucking rough—but now we seemed to want the same things. A realm freed from Death's tyrannical rule and restored to its balanced state. Maybe Lyvias wasn't the worst after all. A stubborn pain in the ass, sure. "You'll come with me then?"

"Anywhere." He grinned. "Though, maybe four o'clock in the morning isn't the best time to go trotting about the courts, hmm? It can wait until you've gotten some rest, I'm sure." He rubbed his neck and heaved a weak laugh. "No offense, but you look a tad...haggard."

"Haggard?" I glared up at him. "I'm fine."

"Really, I think you should—"

"I can sleep when I'm dead." I grabbed his wrist and whirled out the door. In the corner of my eye, the future king's fang-filled smile gleamed, sending a heated flush across my chest despite my best efforts. Once we'd reached the castle's main landing, I caught his sleeve. "Hold on."

I took a deep breath, communed with the halls, and sighed. "Nasheesh is in the main foyer."

Lyvias shifted from the doorway. "What's he doing?"

"No idea. The halls don't talk that much."

"Right, right. Halls, always keeping the good stuff to themselves," he jested.

"Har-har, very funny. Now go distract him, will you?"

"On it." He winked, brandished a pair of sleepy eyes, and waltzed around the corner. "Nas, my good sir, how might you be this fine morning?"

I pressed my ear to the archway's edge and awaited my opportunity.

"You?" Nasheesh rasped. "What are you doing here? You should be rotting in a cell until the end of time."

"Oh, you haven't heard of the queen's pardon yet? It's quite good news, really. Allow me to fill you in on all the juicy details." His words stabbed sharp in the halls: my cue to move.

I stepped out low and slow, eyes peeled for any guards that might have shifted since my last hall assessment. The castle reported that the west wing patrol was approaching. I would need to move quickly or risk a run-in on the main landing. Sweeping through the shadowed corridors swift as death, I greeted the endless night sky in the courtyard with a contented laugh. Stealth: another skill to add to my repertoire. I could get used to this.

Lyvias broke through the door in record time—a minute behind at most—and sauntered down the steps to meet me, self-satisfaction written all over his face. "Good to go."

"Nasheesh?"

He cracked his knuckles, flexing a fist. "Handled."

"Wait, you knocked him out?" I blinked in disbelief.

"Don't worry about it. Let's go before somebody sees us."

We wound out the courtyard gates and paused before the dustiest path. The plaque still boasted the spoils from my last visit—the rough stone stained in my blood—but required its fill once more.

"Damn it," I huffed.

"What?"

"I forgot a knife." I gestured to the plaque. "The gate needs blood to open."

"Ah, if only there was some other way to open a vein…" Lyvias bared his fangs, and with a wink, sank them into his wrist. The sight of teeth, flesh, and blood sent a rush through my limbs, clear to my toes. Delicious fear. I'd be lying if I said I wasn't into it. Like picturing-my-own-flesh-being-brutalized-in-the-same-fashion kind of into it. So much so, my cheeks warmed at the sight and—what the hell was my problem? My blushes were reserved for June alone—regardless of destiny's screwed-up idea to part us—not some self-serving, egotistical vampire. Focus.

"Is this enough?" he asked, blood dripping off his chin.

"Uh, yeah. Plenty."

"Good." He hung his wrist over the rigid stone, wiped his mouth with his free hand, and allowed the blood to flow. Minutes trickled away, but the path didn't extend, and the gate never presented itself. His brow creased. "Did I do something wrong?"

"I don't know..." I breathed. "The gates reacted to Suri's offering; this should have worked."

"Suri opened the shifter gate?"

I shook my head. "No, I did. But she opened the other gates no problem."

"Active gates, sure, but Cadagon sealed this one away." His tone grew dark. "Sealed the shifters away. Maybe royal blood is required here."

It made sense. But I had no knife, no fangs to break the skin. Lyvias met my gaze, took my hand in his, and placed his smirk against my palm. My entire body quaked, a throb forming between my legs as his fangs grazed my wrist. Shit. Shit. Shit.

It doesn't mean anything, Kim. It's just your stupid body reacting. Nothing more.

"Don't worry," he whispered. "I'll be gentle."

I fought the urge to tell him that I'd rather him not, that rough was how I liked it. Instead, I averted my eyes. Averted all senses in every way possible. I didn't enjoy his touch. Didn't enjoy his warm breath on my skin or the flutter my heart made as his bite broke through. Not the unmissable tension radiating in my peripheral or the delicious fear it inspired. Nope. Fuck that. It rubbed me the wrong way. Or maybe the way his touch sent lightning through my entire being rubbed me the wrong way. Lyvias bit down harder, and a moan nearly escaped me. Heat trailed along my forearm, and I tore from his clutch.

"Did I hurt you?" he asked, dark playfulness in his stare.

"No, I'm fine. Let's just go." I rubbed my punctured wrist against the stone, swept down the newly formed path, and barreled into the energy imprint Cadagon had meant to keep me from. Anything to escape the lingering urge to offer my neck to Lyvias. After all, time was of the essence. I knew Death would sense my presence within the shifter court soon enough, but I'd handle him when the time came. Get in, find my answers, and get out: that was the goal.

Chaos, fire, and death greeted us, and my chest tightened as it had upon my first visit. At least now I would learn its secrets. Or I hoped I would anyway. Forcing my eyes shut, I aligned my thoughts with the surrounding turmoil. That's when it hit me: the raw, tragic energy of the massacre. I latched onto it and allowed my feet to take control. Lyvias followed a pace behind.

The energy spoke to me, telling me precisely where to stop, and I bent over to place my hand on the cracked asphalt. It buzzed beneath my touch. There. The massacre had started right there. With a shaky exhale, I pushed into the memory. Images whirled behind my eyelids and arched at my spine, sending me headfirst into what Lyvias perceived as distress.

"Hey, hey! Are you okay?" He patted my cheeks. "Talk to me."

I heard him, felt him, but couldn't see him. Couldn't respond. Just as I feared my connection to the shifter court had grown too erratic, it settled into a sure rhythm, and my eyes shot open. The once chaotic scene around me had grown eerily quiet. I searched for Lyvias in vain, stood, and started down the lane. This was it. What I'd been searching for.

The houses once engulfed in flame—now reduced to charred rubble—creaked and crackled in the smoke. Char tangled in my nose. There were no screaming children or sprinting shifters. The world stood still. Motionless bodies lay strewn about the streets, and I fought back vomit. I wandered farther still and combed the scene for any signs of life when a familiar sound pricked my ears: Cadagon's voice, but different. Younger. I turned the corner and found him on his knees in the street, Nasheesh standing over him.

The advisor pulled at the king's shoulder. "My Liege, we must go."

Cadagon didn't respond, didn't even look up from the tattered fabric clenched between his fingertips. He twirled it about. Nasheesh took notice and hoisted the reaper to his feet.

"If we stay here, you will be absorbed into this reality. The kingdom, it will perish without you."

"Then let it perish," Cadagon seethed, and drilled his flame-filled eyes into Nasheesh.

I drew closer and beheld the king's tears. There were no theatrics. Death was weeping.

Nasheesh drew closer. "I know you mourn their loss, but she brought it upon herself. Upon Kimberly. They had a life here. A life of splendor, and yet they chose to flee."

My name on Nasheesh's tongue sent chills up my spine. He was referring to my mother. To me. This must have been what my mom mentioned back home, about how she had saved us from his wrath. She ran. Smart woman. Though, I'd always known that much.

Cadagon's stare danced among the wreckage in a daze. "They'll return."

"They won't, Sire." Nasheesh tugged at Cadagon's robe once more. "Come, let us get to safety."

"No." With one snap, the Reigning Reaper sent the advisor

soaring through the gate and slammed it shut behind him.

Nasheesh beat against it, fury in his cheeks. "You fool, you'll die in there!"

"I'm already dead," Cadagon whispered to himself. The snap of a twig echoed from the shadows, and he grew rigid, alert. "Come out."

The bush rustled, but no one emerged.

"I said, 'Come out.'" He snapped his fingers, and a sturdy man drifted into sight.

The demon bowed. "Your Highness."

"You're still here?"

"We've word that a pureblood shifter may have slipped through our defenses, your Highness. We'll remain here until we can be certain."

"Good," the king growled. "Back to your work then."

"Aye, sir."

My hands balled into fists, squeezing so tight my knuckles cracked under the pressure. So it was true. He'd run the shifters out and ordered any who remained be terminated. I needn't guess or wonder anymore. He'd done it. Cadagon had killed them all.

Death placed his slender frame on a singed boulder and sighed. "It is done."

"Is it?" a familiar, feminine voice sounded from the darkness ahead.

Cadagon spun about. "You."

"What, surprised to see me?" Her silhouetted frame drew closer, stepping out from amongst the fire-riddled trees. "Or are you just surprised I'm still alive?"

His brow furrowed. "Of course not. I'm relieved, you should know that. I—"

"Save it, Cad," the woman said harshly, and hurled a rock at his head, which he dodged.

"You have to understand, I did this for us. For our—"

She scoffed and ambled closer still. "Don't lie to me. You did it for your damn self, so you could feel powerful and supreme."

"I would never do such a thing!"

"You wouldn't?" She stilled. "Like you promised you'd never hurt her? And yet here you are, dooming her to a world like this."

Her shadowed hands motioned about the burnt streets as she stepped into the light, and I choked. My mother—young and bright-eyed—floated by in a vision unseen by any for years. Vanilla and peppermint carried in her wake as I fell in line with her slow steps, studying her every move.

Death's expression grew deadly. "You know nothing of what I would or wouldn't do for that girl."

"You're correct there. I wouldn't know. I don't know you at all anymore." A cynical chuckle slipped past her lips.

"Please," he begged, and took a step towards her, his callous edges now softened. "Don't say that. You know me, just as I know you."

"Not anymore. What we knew, how we felt...you put an end to that. And I—" her voice caught. "I won't leave her here to clean up your mess. You made your bed, and you alone will lie in it."

He stood eerily still. "You didn't..."

"I have. And I would do it all over again, given the choice. Kimber won't know you. Won't have any memory of the cruel king she was unfortunate enough to call 'Father.'" She circled him, rage in her eyes. "Tell me, Cadagon, do you still hear their screams? I do."

"I merely did what needed to be done, Amelia, to protect you both," he growled. "Those caught in the cross fire, they...well, they knew what would happen."

"Kellyn Ashby. I found her, you know. Bent over the lake's edge, her face burnt beyond recognition. If it weren't for her charm bracelet she always wore, I'd have never known it was her. You know the one, with six trinkets to represent each of her six children?" My mother slowed her pace and met Cadagon's stare, unafraid. "She was the first person to accept me here as I was: a mortal, forced into a role that was never meant for me. And you killed her. My friend—" She choked on a sob.

"She was one of them!" Death snapped. "And you were always meant to rule at my side. The throne is yours as much as it is mine."

"No. No, it isn't. But you knew that, didn't you? You wanted me for a trophy." She chuckled and folded her arms. "A living testament to how free you once were before you drew the line in the sand."

Cadagon scoffed and stepped towards her. "I drew no such line; they—"

"They did," she mocked. "Right. Sensible, honest people did that."

"There was no innocence in them." His face was stern, but his eyes pleaded for understanding. "They conspired, sought to overthrow me, kill my people. They wanted to end my bloodline!"

"They *were* your people. All of them, every court, are *your* people."

"You don't understand, I have nothing against—"

She threw her hand up, and I swallowed hard.

"Save it. Save it for those lonely nights ahead. Let their cries be your lullaby, Death. Their memory echoing throughout your thoughts for eternity," she whispered, and stepped into his space. "And then, once you've grown used to their screams, may your reign end abruptly and painfully. No heir, no promise of a better tomorrow. Just you, all alone, floating out into the void."

The vision ended in static, and reality cut through. From my position on the ground, the massacre's flames seemed as though they aimed to burn the night sky itself, their blue tips clawing the treetops.

I pushed to sit, and Lyvias crouched over me.

"Thank the damned." He let out a breath, and his cinched brow relaxed a tad. "You scared me senseless."

I heaved a deep breath, mind trying to catch up with what I'd just witnessed. The images played back in bits and pieces, sending me reeling. I focused instead on the vampire hung over me like a chandelier.

"Careful, it almost seems like you were worried about me," I jested, and rubbed my aching temples.

He cleared his throat and stood. "I wasn't worried about you. I was worried about losing an asset I need to kill Death, that's all."

"Uh-huh, sure. Whatever helps you sleep at night." I grinned, snatched his hand, and hoisted myself off the ground. "Just don't go falling in love with me. It'd be a conflict of interest."

A flush danced on his cheeks. "Me, fall for you? Never."

Like a freight train, everything came back to me at once, but one specific memory screamed to be heard. Cadagon's words: *They conspired, sought to overthrow me, kill my people.* My lungs heaved for a steadying breath.

The concern Lyvias had brushed off seconds before returned—his brows cinched together—and the air between us grew tense. "What is it?"

"He did it. Cadagon ordered the hit on the shifters."

"We'd guessed as much, but why?"

My hands shook as I met his gaze. "Someone wants to end my bloodline. Permanently."

CHAPTER 12

NO SUCH THING AS COINCIDENCE

The weight of the previous night's events crushed me. Locked in my own body, trapped in my thoughts, I lost track of how many days I rotted in my bed. No water. No food. No visitors. Only nightmares. Cooper: screaming for help as he was buried alive in a box. June: lost in the woods, her light faded. And me: assassinated in every different way one could imagine. Someone—and my money was on Malachi and his hounds—wanted my entire bloodline wiped out. And for a second, I entertained the idea. It'd be easier: ceasing to exist. Who knew when Odin would walk through the door, knife in hand. Or Malachi. Or Cadagon. Death surrounded me, ready to take me out whether I liked it or not. It was all too fucking much.

Naturally, Cadagon was less than sympathetic towards my pain. Time and time again, he'd insisted I put aside my personal turmoil and consider the realm I was to lead. I'd be married, crowned queen, and murdering my own damn father all too soon.

I'd cried over it too many times to count. Soon, I'd be the sole protector of this realm. I'd be the end-all-be-all. And aside from the tentative agreement I shared with Lyvias and Suri's continued kindness, I'd be entirely alone. While my pain-in-the-ass betrothed had tried to pull me from the emotional pit I'd fallen into, being near him proved harder than I'd expected. Something about his presence—maybe his sarcastic tongue or the way he knew how to push every button with acute accuracy—reminded me of the best friend I'd lost. No, given up on. Abandoned. So I avoided Lyvias's helpful attempts and everyone else's for that matter. But eventually, Death's temper boiled over.

"Open this door immediately," Cadagon barked, and rapped his fist against the door.

I pulled the blankets off my head—hair snapping with static—and tossed a throw pillow at the door. "Go away."

"I will do no such thing," he said. "I have been more than patient with you. Collect yourself and meet me in the gardens. Now."

"You can't make me," I mumbled, and ripped the blankets back over my head. The lock turned over, its click resounding like a fallen gavel, and I popped up. "Hey, you can't just come in here!"

"You mean like you've so kindly done to me before? Sneaking into my private quarters and rummaging through things that don't belong to you?" Cadagon nudged Suri into the room, his attention fixed on her. "Go, work your magic. I need the princess both presentable and active-ready in an hour."

"Yes, sir." She bowed as Death descended the tower steps.

I groaned, fanned out on the bed, and met Suri's gaze. "Active-ready? What does that even mean?"

"It means," Suri said with a wide smile, and revealed a hidden gift from behind her back, "you get to wear this, bitch."

Clutched in her hands hung an outfit fit for a goddess: leather from sleeves to ankles, adorned in chain mesh and pointed studs; it was fierce in every possible sense. A sight so glorious, I sat up. "It's..."

"It's?"

"So..."

Suri's shoulders sank. "You hate it..."

"Are you kidding? It's freaking gorgeous!"

"But?" Worry glittered behind her fuchsia eyes.

"But nothing, really, I love it. I just—I'd have to get out of bed to wear it." I whined and flopped back into my pillow fortress.

"Alright, come on, time to get up." Suri tore the poofy sheets off me and sat at the foot of the bed. "Look," she sighed, "I'm sorry about, well, whatever it is that happened. From the looks of it, it was serious."

"I don't want to talk about it," I muttered into the mattress.

"You don't have to. Just...I'm here for you, okay? And while I don't have much to go off of, what I *do* know is a part of you wants to get out of this bed."

"Ha, not a chance."

"It's true. See, if you get up, you get to go to the training grounds."

I peeked over my blanket. "And why would I want to do that?"

A smile yanked at Suri's cheeks. "Because you start your reaper training today. You'll learn how to wield a weapon."

"That sounds exhausting."

"Fine then." Suri pursed her lips and hopped to her feet. "I'm sure the opportunity to swing a blade at Death's head comes around oh... every century or so? You'll show him next time, right?"

I jerked to sit. "What?"

"Death." Suri shrugged. "He'd have been your sparring partner today. But if you aren't interested in getting out of bed, well..."

I hopped up. "Game changer. Let's do this!"

Cadagon awaited me at the parted oaks to the training grounds, a cocky grin splayed across his face. "I assume Suri filled you in on your sparring partner today then?"

"You're damn right, she did." I sauntered past him and out onto the evergreen field with a pointed stare. "Get ready to hurt."

Cadagon matched my steps. "Funny, I was prepared to warn you of the same thing."

After a few stretches and a quick jog around the perimeter, we made our way to the weapons rack across the grass. The same rack where I had first met Lyvias. A laugh slipped through me, recalling the nearly rabid look in his eyes when I'd ordered him to bow. Compared to where we stood now, the memory seemed almost untrue. Though Lyvias seemed dedicated to our mutual cause, there was always the potential for him to turn on me after ensuring Death's demise. But that was a bridge for future Kim to cross. For now, I'd watch him. Closely. Even more reason to train, so I could protect myself should the tables turn.

Cadagon clapped, an eagerness about him. "Alright, the first step is choosing your weapon. Seeing as you're a woman, I would recommend you stay away from the axe and mace—"

"Why, because girls can't handle themselves like men do?" I scoffed. "Sexist much?"

"No—"

"Well, I choose the mace, so there." I pried the weapon from its slot, and it slammed to the ground next to me. Shit, that was heavy...

He raised a brow. "The mace, really?"

"Yes, the mace. Deal with it."

"Alright." Cadagon shook his head and settled into a low stance.

"Take a swing then."

"A swing…"

"Yes. Take up your mace and hit me. I will give you this strike, free of retaliation." Laughter danced behind the Reigning Reaper's eyes.

I strained, lifting the hefty metal a good foot off the ground, but seconds later it pelted back into the moist grass at my side. "Okay, I want a re-pick."

"Ah, so you admit I was right then?" He smirked.

"No. I just want a different one, that's all." I shuffled to the rack and studied what options remained: a longsword, bow, and spear. My fingers grazed each, weighing them in my hands, but none felt right. "I don't want any of these."

"I figured you might say that." He rummaged in unseen pockets at his hips and fished out two half-moon shaped blades. "Here, try these."

I took the curved daggers from Death's grasp and shifted them about in my hands. They were light, evenly matched in weight, and the sound they made slicing through the wind? Music to my ears. "These are more like it."

"For the time being, yes," Cadagon nodded, "but those are my personal weapons. I'll see that yours are completed in due time, so you can have them in your possession during the crowning ceremony."

"Why would I need them for that?" I asked, still whirling the blades through the air in a display one might expect from a toddler with a toy airplane. It just felt too damn cool.

"It's customary. The weapon a Reigning Reaper chooses is a testament to their rule. It bears witness to the reaper's coronation and so is uniquely imbued with trace amounts of magic transferred in the ceremony."

I stilled and looked at the daggers, then to Cadagon. If I chose the same weapons as him, would I end up on his path? Fall victim to the power and use it for selfish reasons? Not worth the risk. I handed the blades back, face stern. "I'll choose something else."

His gaze pinned me. "I know what you're thinking, but you have no reason to worry, Princess. The weapons a Reigning Reaper chooses in no way point down a specific path. The weapon will be forged with your own blood and so will react to your will and yours alone. You have no reason to fear that you will end up as another has. As…I have." Cadagon cleared his throat and snatched a spear from the rack. "Now, spread out. Five feet between us."

I pushed away my lingering questions, readying myself. The rest of the night-covered afternoon went about as one might expect for a noob. Sure, I knew my way around a combat knife well enough to take down a rouge shifter or vampire in the mortal world. But sparring with Death himself? Entirely different story. I would lunge; Cadagon would dodge—complete with fake yawn—and I'd end up knocked flat on my ass. He'd insist I get up; I'd do so, strike back with purpose and…again be knocked off my damn feet. Death taunted to coax out my wrath no doubt; but no matter what I did, I failed. By the hundredth time hitting the ground, I tapped out.

"Enough," I wheezed. "I'm done, I'm done."

Cadagon spun his spear around and released a catty chuckle. "Already? But I was quite enjoying myself."

He extended a hand to me, and I took it without a second thought. The gesture, small and insignificant as it might seem, didn't sit well. I hated him, meant to end his vicious reign, and yet I'd sparred with him. Trained with him. And if I were honest, I'd even had a little fun doing so. In the end, I reminded myself it'd been worth it. That I'd gotten first person insight into his fighting style: something I could bring back to Lyvias to prepare us for our attack.

To my unfortunate surprise, Cadagon didn't set off on his own when we reached the castle stairs. Instead, he followed me clear to the south dining hall. I glared up at him. "Meeting Nasheesh here?"

"No, why would you assume that?"

"Oh, I don't know." I crossed my arms. "Maybe because you never follow me to the south wing after one of our meetings?"

He shifted side to side, and a strange, almost insecure snicker escaped him. "To be fair, I don't know that we've ever had a meeting go as well as today's. Do you?"

"Well, no."

"Precisely. Which is why I thought we might spend some time together—" He stopped short, attention stolen by incoming footsteps.

Lyvias wrapped around the corner and called out, his face buried in a book. "Princess, I was..." He peered up from his page, noticed Cadagon at my side, and his words slowed. "...looking for you." He tucked the book under his arm. "Where were you?"

"That is not your business," Death said in a fatherly tone that creeped me the fuck out. No man in my life had the right to use that tone with me. Period.

"We were at the training grounds, and now we aren't. He was just leaving." I flashed Cadagon a dismissive glance. "Right?"

"Correct. I have many things that require my attention anyway." Head held high, he sauntered off.

"The training grounds? Explains the vicious attire. Although I must say, this outfit..." Lyvias's gaze devoured me. "It does something for me."

His wink sent heat radiating through my cheeks, and I told my body to behave. But those crimson eyes, the way they lingered a little too long on my breasts...no. We were business partners: assassins on the same mission. I would *not* fuck him. Though something told me it'd be a wild ride I'd never forget. A hate fuck...hmm. New kink maybe?

No! Stop it! Bad Kim.

When Cadagon drifted out of earshot, expectation crossed Lyvias's face.

"What?" I asked.

He folded his arms. "Care to explain what that was about?"

"What 'what' was about?"

"You and the king?" He batted his eyelashes.

"Nothing." I brushed him off and started towards the kitchen. Who the hell did this guy think he was, questioning my whereabouts? "He followed me back after training, that's all."

He stepped into my path, tapping his foot impatiently.

I looked him over. "What? It's true."

"You two seemed...chummy."

"Chummy?" My nose wrinkled in disgust. "You're delusional."

In point-zero seconds, he had me pinned against the nearest beam. Face an inch from mine, he whispered between bared fangs, "You backing out of our arrangement?"

I latched my hand around his throat. A moan rattled through him, reverberating in my palm, and the sound made me damn near feral. After so much emotional bullshit the past few weeks, a good old-fashioned fuck would have been a welcomed distraction. No messy feelings or complicated depth. Just him on his knees, wearing nothing but a rope around his wrists. Gods, the things I'd do to him...

I shoved his head back. "Haven't you learned not to threaten me by now, or do I need to teach you a lesson in manners?"

Darkness spilled across his face as his sights dropped to my lips. He pushed closer, my stomach jumping as his warm breath grazed my cheeks. "You can teach me a lesson any day, so long as you don't fuck me over. Fuck me, sure, but if you back out of our deal—"

"I wouldn't touch you if you begged," I snarled, and pushed him back, releasing my hold.

His pointed gaze carried down my body, settling between my legs. "That's funny, because I can hear your heartbeat, and it tells me otherwise."

"Enough! My stance hasn't changed, and you're not getting in my pants, so tell me why you were looking for me."

"If you say so, Princess," he said under his lashes. "Suri told me you'd gotten up today. I wanted to check on you if you must know."

His expression made my lungs seize. It was the exact way Cooper used to look when he'd decided to lay claim to someone. To make them his plaything. Or worse, his partner. I dropped my eyes to my feet. "I'm fine."

"Are you?"

"Yes." I swallowed hard. "Now if you'll excuse me, I have to go change out of this damn thing. Believe it or not, leather doesn't breathe well when you're slinging a blade around for hours."

"If you need help removing it, I could be of assistance—"

"Fuck off," I said, and pushed past him, waving a hand dismissively.

"Kim..."

The sound of my nickname on his tongue stopped me in my tracks.

"For what it's worth," he continued, "I'm sorry. For whatever happened. Your girl, is she..."

My hands clenched as I turned to him. "Gone? Yes. But she's where she belongs and so am I. It's stupid really, me allowing it to have so much control over me. But I've got a handle on it now; I won't let it affect our mission."

"Loving someone is never stupid," he said, sincerity in his stare, "and the duration of love does not dictate its depth."

Love. While I hadn't admitted it to myself, I'd always known that's what had been between June and me. That deep longing. It's why I'd had to fight the urge to follow her through that door to Elysium. To keep her with me always. Or had it all just been a cruel act of Fate? Whatever the reason, sharing more than what was absolutely necessary with Lyvias was dangerous. A liability. I wouldn't show my weakness. Not to him. I turned to leave.

"Wait." He stepped closer, popping open the book he'd stowed at his side, and turned to a dog-eared page. "There's something I wanted to show you. I found this in the grand study. I went to pull a book from the shelf above, and this fell out." He rubbed his neck. "I know it sounds weird, but I don't think it was a coincidence."

"What, you think a ghost hand-delivered it to you?"

"You're hilarious," he teased, monotone. "Anyway, I found something I think would interest you. It's about the shifters." He spun the book around and extended it, finger pointing halfway down the right-hand page. "The rest is pretty cryptic, but I think this might be important."

I scanned the page:

Two shifting houses, one born of talon, the other bane of blood, deceived. One to blame, the other to pay. Beware the void-talker.

"What do you think it means?" I asked.

"I'm not sure. I didn't get a chance to read further. Nasheesh has been up my ass all day for some reason. Seems he doesn't know what to do when he isn't at Death's beck and call." He handed the book to me. "You keep it, and let me know what you find? I've got some business I need to attend to."

I squinted up at him. "What kind of business?"

"Nothing to concern yourself with. See what you can dig up, and

I'll touch base with you soon."

With that, he drifted from the room, and I turned the tome in my hand over. A journal, it looked like. Interesting.

After a much-needed trip to the bath, a long and consuming nap, and a change of clothes, I snagged the journal and headed to the back most gardens. I read the halls around each turn to assure my late night excursion remained undetected. Anathema's glorious night lured me through the rose-covered gates, and I tucked myself beneath a blooming sickle tree just outside my view of the castle windows. If I couldn't see them, nobody could see me. Perfect.

The handwritten notebook belonged to one Barges Frain, a shifter fifteen years my senior. It seemed he had a fondness for conspiracy theories. His hyperfixation? The pureblood shapeshifter families. The Bloodbanes and the Talonborns. Lyvias wasn't kidding; him finding this couldn't be a coincidence; it was too pointed. I took a final glance around before diving in.

Barges went on to explain that the Bloodbanes and Talonborns were the strongest pureblood lines. They possessed unique abilities. While most shifters took the shape of one animal their entire lives, the purebloods could steal another *person's* identity, endless people's if they wanted to. They could transform into mythical beasts from ancient lore. Horrible creatures. The Bloodbanes celebrated their strength, lorded it over the shifters they deemed lesser. In one run-in with the eldest Bloodbane brother, Barges described it as "all the oxygen being sucked out of a room." I shivered and turned the page.

The Talonborns proved the exact opposite. Caring for their people, they sought an audience with Cadagon the moment shifters started going missing in the Evermoor Woods. They wanted the incident investigated, and in exchange offered a spy to infiltrate the Bloodbanes' inner circle. While Barges couldn't know for sure if Cadagon struck the deal, I did. The shadows tickling under my skin assured me so.

Death: always ready to sacrifice others to save his own skin.

For years, Barges had researched. Studied. Crossed countless theories off his list. Come the last chunk of his journal, he'd landed on his magnum opus. Before the massacre, rumors spread of the Bloodbanes forming an alliance with a cult stemming from the demon and vampire courts. He believed that the rumors were not only true, but that the Bloodbanes were sacrificing the missing shifters in the Evermoor Woods…to create a hybrid. One strong enough to change the royal bloodline. Absorb it somehow. My mouth went dry.

Hybrid. As in, the passage I'd opened to in *The Book of Shade*.

Head spinning, I closed the journal. How would something like that even be possible? The royal bloodline had been the work of the old gods. No earthly being would have the ability to change that.

A footfall on loose stone caught my attention. Lifting my sights, I watched as Nasheesh came into view. The advisor ambled onto the path before me and stole a glance over his shoulder. It was two o'clock in the morning; what was he up to? After a final scope of the garden, Nasheesh hurried off down the path. Hunched down low, I slowly followed his wide footprints and found myself before the training grounds' ancient oaks.

At first, everything appeared normal. Weapons sat neatly in their racks, lion statues still guarded the field's four corners. Then all at once, my shadows knotted in my stomach. They ushered me forward, heightening my senses. "Look closer," they seemed to murmur inside me. My heart fell into my toes.

There, hidden in the dark gazebo, someone lurked.

"Hey, you!" I yelled, feet slushing through the wet grass. From such distance, I couldn't make out the stranger's identity aside from illuminated, feline eyes. A demon. The nearer I drew, however, the more scarlet the eyes grew, taking on the appearance of both demon and vampire at once. But beneath it, hellhound. What the actual fuck? My pace slowed. I studied the figure, its shoulders hunched in an animalistic way, and again the magic in my blood eased me forward. I stole a step, and the silhouette mimed along. I stepped, it stepped. I stopped, it stopped.

And so it went: move for move until a memory so foul and repressed cemented me in place. Of that bloody, fateful night when I'd let harm come to my best friend. The hound: how he'd circled me, planned his attack. Odin.

With my full chest, I screamed out, "Guards! Intruder in the training grounds!"

He lingered there for some time, allowing the silence to tangle around us. But at the sound of approaching footsteps, he took off. In a flash quicker than anything I had ever seen, he tore off towards the trees. I bolted after him, weaving and ducking between branches. His thrashing footsteps grew faint the farther into the woods I got, until finally, they disappeared altogether. My body stilled and twisted in every direction in hopes I'd pick up the trail, but like a mist, he'd evaporated. Gone.

"Coward!" I yelled, nails cutting into my palms. "Come out and face me!"

When my breath had finally settled, I trudged back towards the castle. Not two steps forward, my foot snagged on the forest floor, and I crumbled to the ground like a sack of potatoes.

"Damn it." I cocked my head back, expecting a rock or a stick or really anything other than what I got. But no. My heartbeat quickened as I shuffled backwards through the pine needles. Face down in his own blood—eyes still wide with terror—lay a castle guard, his throat flayed wide open. I sucked in a tight breath, pushed a shaky foot out before me, and tapped the guard once. Nothing. Dead. Then the rest came into focus. Another guard's lifeless body, five feet ahead. Then another. And another. Lined up in the exact path I'd taken to pursue the trespasser.

He'd killed them all. Displayed them behind me without me noticing.

Oh, shit. I hopped to my feet. The sharp scent of iron carried on the breeze. Of all the deaths I'd predicted in my life, I'd never been witness to a scene so gruesome. I fought the urge to vomit, turned to leave, and found one last horrific sight for me alone, scribbled across a boulder ahead in fresh blood.

See you again soon, dearest.

My mouth turned to sandpaper.

CHAPTER 13

STAY

I sought out the only person I could think of in that moment. The sole person who was even remotely trustworthy all thanks to a blood pact. Finding Lyvias in his room, I shook him awake. He hopped to his feet, eyes scanning the room in panic.

"Kim?" He rubbed his eyes. "What's going on? Are you okay?"

My lip quivered, no matter how hard I fought it. "No...I don't think I am."

Without hesitation, he snatched a thick wool blanket from his reading chair and draped it around my shaking frame. Settling me at his side on the bed, he pulled me to his chest, wrapping his strong arms around me. At first I resisted, but the comfort felt so, well, comforting. His thigh pressed against mine, and I shuddered. Hot to the touch as if a fire raged within him, his body called to me like a moth to a flame. I hadn't realized until that moment how much I'd missed physical touch. To be held. Protected. The kind of closeness Coop and I'd had—that constant need to be near one another—it'd died along with my sacrifice to Fate, and I'd unknowingly craved it.

Tears welled against my will. June and I were stolen moments. Ones I felt didn't truly belong to me somehow. Altogether different from the consistent love I'd felt from my best friend. And Lyvias, as much as I didn't want to admit it, reminded me of the lost friendship I still mourned. So I relaxed into his embrace and soaked it in a moment longer as the night's memories thrashed through my head. Blood. Death. A promise most foul.

Lyvias remained patient. Didn't ask questions or press for answers. When the tears finally stopped, adrenaline rush leaving my bloodstream, I glanced up at him. "Thank you," I whispered, slipping from his hold.

"Anytime," he said with a gentle smile. "Even Lady Death needs comfort now and again."

His words rang true. Maybe I'd been going about this all wrong. Trying to keep things in, handle it all myself. Just maybe. "Yeah."

Clearing his throat, he faced me. "Now care to tell me what has you so frightened, Princess? I can't kill what I don't know about."

"You're ruthless." A shallow laugh slipped past my lips.

I filled him in on my discoveries in the journal. How it was becoming more and more clear that the sins of Anathema's past traitors had returned to haunt Lyvias's and my rule. Our future on the throne. I didn't know if it was our mutual desire for revenge or the compassion he'd shown me, but I held nothing back. The Talonborns. The Bloodbanes. The disappearances in the Evermoor Woods and how Barges believed it to be an attempt at creating a hybrid.

"You've got to be fucking kidding me," he said under his breath, pacing about. "But what would be the point? No one aside from Fate can challenge Death. It's impossible."

"That's what I thought too. There has to be something we're not seeing. Something we're missing."

We sat silent for some time until Lyvias's brow pinched. "This is all quite serious, but it doesn't explain the fear in your eyes. What aren't you telling me, Kim?"

I bit my cheek, iron spilling over my tongue.

"Nasheesh," I started, hands shaking. "I saw him, slinking about like he does. So I followed his path to the training grounds and found somebody hiding. I assume they were waiting for him."

"Go on." He crossed his arms.

"Somebody with red, feline eyes."

"Wait…as in, demon and vampire?"

Taking a deep breath, my sights fell into his. "And somehow more? Different? I don't know, but something tells me it was Odin."

He squinted. "But Odin's a hellhound."

"I know it sounds crazy, but I feel it in my bones." The vision of tattered flesh overcame me. "He killed the guards who came to my aid, used their blood to leave a message."

Lyvias stiffened, his hands balled into fists. Thick veins bulged up his forearms, and I had to keep myself from imagining what a pretty necklace they'd make.

"What kind of message?" he growled, jaw flexing.

"See you again soon…" I left out the "dearest" part, but more for myself than him. It was sick. Mocking. I was nobody's dear. Not anymore.

Lyvias took to his feet once again in the fraction of a second and spanned the room in wide, heavy strides. "'See you again soon'? Like hell he will. I swear if that monster comes within a foot of you, I'll— fuck! I should have killed Odin when I had the chance."

"Lyvias," I snatched his pant leg and tugged him to my side, "it was just a scare tactic, I'm sure."

"But if you're—"

"I'm fine," I assured him, though my skin crawled. "I just need answers. Some insight. That's all."

"With all due respect, you don't look fine." He rested a hand on my trembling shoulder.

What was this? This *thing* blooming between us? My hatred for him melted away by the second, and it made the air feel thin, walls tightening around me. I'd allowed him to see me break. Shared my weakness. What was wrong with me? With a new kind of fear racing through my veins, I shot to my feet and headed for the door.

He caught my wrist, spinning me back towards him. "Stay with me."

His words hit hard in my center. "What?"

"You heard me." His eyes burned. "Let me watch over you tonight. Keep you safe."

I considered his offer. While the thought of my empty room scared me shitless, this proved far more terrifying. Staying with him, allowing him to be closer than the night had already brought us... "I don't think that's a good idea, Lyvias."

"And sleeping alone after such a brutal experience is?" He tugged at my hand with a sigh. "Come on, it's not what you're thinking. I'm not asking you to lay with me like that. Stay, please?"

Heartbeat in my ears, I weighed his words. The guards had done nothing to protect me. Death couldn't be trusted. And now we knew Nasheesh had something to do with it all. Who knew what connections he might have hidden amongst the castle? I pursed my lips. For my safety, that's all it was. "Alright. But you sleep on the floor."

With a crooked grin, he nodded. "Whatever you wish."

Climbing into his still warm sheets, guilt tangled in my center.

How could I boot him from his own bed, especially after all his comfort and concern? Damn stubborn bloodsucker. I reached down through the darkness and grabbed his hand.

I groaned. "Fine, come up here. Just keep your hands to yourself."

"Of course," he said, voice gravelly as he weighted down the mattress with his tall frame, leaving a foot between us. His breath grew heavy with sleep. "We'll figure this out, Kim. I promise."

And for the first time, I believed him without a single doubt.

Weeks passed. I searched the studies high and low for anything relating to hybrids and how one might create one. What purpose they served. But nothing. Lyvias sought out answers in the vampire realm, hunting through old tomes in the town library. But he too came out empty-handed. It was as if somebody had scrubbed all record of the word from history. Hidden it away.

For all we knew, they might have. My enemies—our enemies—were many. And whatever they were planning, it hinged on me being left in the dark. Unknowing.

Come nightfall a week before coronation, I could evade Death no longer. I waltzed through the halls, the hem of my charcoal gown sweeping behind me as I headed straight towards what was sure to be the most awkward dinner that'd ever been. Who did Cadagon think he was anyway, demanding I join him for dinner? By now, he knew I loathed him and his company. Cadagon knew my hatred, and therefore, wanted me to suffer in his presence. Yeah, sounded like the kind of dick move he'd pull.

When the doors to the ballroom came into view, I paused and heaved a deep breath.

"Just keep him fooled," I whispered to myself. The less he knew, the better our chances at taking him out. Simple enough, you know, aside from the deduction skills Death had acquired throughout his time on the throne, skills which had snagged liars far more talented than me in the past. Nevertheless, I had to try. One exhale, and I entered the ballroom.

To my surprise, the room boasted neither eccentric decorations nor riled castle staff. Instead, the scene proved rather humble, informal, and inherently unsettling as all hell. In the room's center, a single table boasted two chairs, its cozy surface lit by wax-covered candelabras. The rest of the room was dusted in shadow. Amongst the shallow candlelight, Death waited.

"You came," he greeted, an ill-fitted smile at his cheeks.

"Like I had a choice?" I sat in the leather chair at his left, seat squeaking against my gown.

"True, but still. I'm glad you did."

I scoffed. "You? Glad?"

"Believe it or not," he shifted in his seat, "I do possess the ability to feel an array of emotions, Princess. The same as you."

"Mm, right."

I studied him as he rushed to fill my glass with wine. His unsure movements jutted up red flags, disturbing me to the core. He looked so...nervous. What was he hiding? I snatched the wine glass and considered the fact that it could very well be laced with poison, given his urgency to pour it.

"So you've had a good day, I take it?" He placed the half empty wine bottle at the table's edge.

"Now you're asking me about my day? Okay, what the hell's going on?"

"I simply thought, given our busy schedules, you and I haven't had an appropriate amount of time to..." Again, his face seized in an odd grin. "...chat. Get to know one another."

"I don't think that's necessary."

"Princess, you wound me. I give you all this," he motioned about the castle, "and you can't be bothered to spare some time on me?"

"It's nothing personal. I just try to keep my time spent with murderers to a minimum. You know, no similar interests and all." I flashed a condescending smirk and set my wine glass back on the table.

"Smart," he said, snapping for a member of the waitstaff for a taste test. "But if I wanted to poison you, Kimberly, I would never waste such a fine wine in the process."

The slim man took a sip, making sure to wipe the edge where his mouth touched before sliding the cup back to me. When I felt enough time had gone by without the poor man keeling over, I nodded to dismiss him and kicked back a heavy swig. The sharp tang stung my taste buds. Its warmth rushed down my chest, and I relaxed a twinge. I met Cadagon's gaze, tapping the glass. "Again, nothing personal. Just wouldn't put it past you to strike me down so you can hoard the throne for yourself."

His eyes narrowed. "You say it with such conviction, so it must be so."

A snarl rose in my throat. How many times had he brushed my accusations off in such a blasé fashion since I'd arrived? I swigged another mouthful of wine. "If you're as innocent as you claim, then why don't you defend yourself? You just let it happen."

"A coping mechanism, I suppose. To ward off the hurtful things which seep so easily through your lips. Tonight of all nights, I—"

"What did you expect?" I burst. "I'd show up tonight, and we would share some grand father-daughter dinner together? Reminisce about my childhood maybe? That we'd have a heartfelt conversation and carry on about our day like a normal family?"

"And if I did?"

"Ha." I chuckled, venom seeping into my words. "Then you're an even bigger fool than I thought."

Despite my expectations, he didn't snap back, didn't threaten me in an invisible choke hold or send my feet wandering down the halls. No. He simply sighed and waved over a member of the waitstaff who'd emerged from amongst the darkness.

"I believe the princess and I are ready for our meal now, if you'd be so kind." With an "Aye, Highness," the man bowed and disappeared into the shadows from which he'd come, Cadagon's attention on me once again. "Let us discuss the details of your coronation while we wait, yes?"

"If we have to."

"We do. Tell me, have you considered what you might want that day? Anything at all, and I will make it happen. Such is customary in the crowning of a new ruler." He spun a silver dinner knife about the table, the embers in his irises stiller than I'd seen.

"Not really, no. I'm not exactly jazzed about the whole situation."

"That makes me sad to hear. Your wedding day should be a joyous occasion."

My lips tightened. "It would be if I had a choice in the matter."

"You are not happy with your alliance to Lyvias?" he asked between modest sips from his ruby-encrusted goblet. "Here I thought you two were getting along quite swimmingly, moving about the castle together and what have you. You've moved into his quarters, have you not?"

Shit. I tensed but kept my composure. Had he overheard our discussions? Our plans? No. He was far too calm to know such things. This was another attempt at baiting me in hopes I'd offer information.

I willed my face into an even expression. Controlled. He wouldn't break me.

I shrugged and gulped the last of my wine. A buzz carried in my veins as the alcohol took hold. "He's fine, I guess. It's not like arranged marriages are about the people involved anyway. It's just business."

"You'll grow to love him in time."

I fought back a cynical laugh. Like he had any fucking idea what love was. Power and control and manipulation, sure. But his cold heart was incapable of love. He'd single-handedly destroyed every person who got close enough. His expectant stare on me, I heaved a relieved sigh when the waitstaff re-entered and interrupted us. They placed covered plates on the table, offered a quick bow, and darted from the room. Food. Distraction. Good.

"Ah, here we are." The king rubbed his hands together with human-like anticipation and lifted the silver domes from atop both plates. A brilliant, intoxicating sweetness wafted about us. "I had this meal prepared special; it's my absolute favorite."

"What is it?" I poked the grayish-purple hunk on my plate.

"Candied revel. A rare, meaty flower I had sought from the shifter realm."

My ears perked. "This is from the shifter realm?"

"It's the only place you can find them. Even there, they thrive in only one location. Go on, take a bite. You'll love it; I'm certain."

Hesitant, I sliced a piece from the flower slab and placed it in my mouth. It was sweet and succulent as he'd said, and yet a bad taste lingered on my tongue. Though the food wasn't to blame, but rather his frivolous explanation of where it'd hailed from. He'd banished people from the shifter realm, locked it away, and condemned anyone who went there against his will. Yet he'd allowed someone to harvest within it? And for a flower, no less. Of course he did, because it served *his* selfish desires. My wheels began to turn. This…I could use this to *my* advantage.

The fool had played right into my hands.

"Where in the shifter realm?" I asked, chewing another bite.

"The outskirts of the Evermoor Woods. Why do you ask?"

"Just curious." The Evermoor Woods: exactly where shifters had disappeared all those years ago. Yeah, way too coincidental. I put on my best smile. "Well, I love it. I think I'd like it served at the wedding."

"Wonderful news, I'll see it done—"

"Actually, I'd like to do it," I said a little too urgently.

Reel it in, Kim.

"You wish to do the work yourself?" Cadagon looked me over. "But why? The staff can see to the entire harvest in no more than an evening."

My lungs tensed as I searched for a reason he'd buy. "I was thinking it might be a good bonding opportunity for Lyvias and me. Give us some alone time before we're locked into this whole marriage thing."

Or better still, the opportunity to snoop around, get an idea of what'd happened there. If Malachi and Odin were reenacting the sacrificial cult's motives from the past, there had to be some sign present. Cadagon looked me over once more, but I kept my expression innocent.

Come on, old man Death, take the bait.

"I think it's a splendid idea." He grinned, the usual madness behind his stare. "Can you believe it? Only seven more days until your unholy union."

My stomach heaved. "Right."

Seven short days, and I'd be Mrs. Kimberly Kraven, wife to Lyvias Kraven, Queen of Anathema. Hands shaky, I set my fork down. Right. I'd had quite enough sugary flower meat and thoughts about the future for one night.

"Revels are best served fresh," he muttered between stuffed cheeks. "I'll make sure your schedule is cleared a few days before the ceremony."

"Perfect. Lyvias and I will need a map of the area you mentioned, so we—"

"Wait," he nearly choked. "You didn't honestly think I was about to let you enter the shifter realm unattended, did you?" He erupted in maniacal laughter. "Out of the question. You aren't to enter the realm without my accompaniment, or have you forgotten that?"

I ground my teeth, reminding myself to stay calm and collected. But shit, Death's company would put a serious wrench in our plans. "Really, we—"

"Oh, don't worry so much, Princess. I'll be sure to give you lovebirds space. I won't follow...too closely."

My gut fell. Death: ever the thorn in my side.

Days dwindled away, like sinister laughs passing through chapped lips. My daily routine on repeat: planning, preparing, training. Stale. Monotonous. Aside from my now sparse visits to Cooper's coffin—in which both he and Poe never objected to my bitching and moaning—I had little time to myself. If any.

A semi-silver lining, I'd learned to wield dual daggers much more efficiently thanks to good old-fashioned repetition, but it didn't keep the king from knocking me on my ass each session. Stupid: me thinking I'd be a master in such a short time. Ha, no. Not even close. I blamed movie montages for that hunk of bullshit. I did my best not to let it unsettle me, what with Death's murder window fast approaching.

Meanwhile, Lyvias searched for more answers: ransacked the old study, sought out witness statements within the reaper realm, but found nothing of consequence. Aside from our original assassination plan, we were flying blind. In regards to said plan, our strategy remained the same. On my birthday—which paled in comparison to everything else set to happen that day—we'd strike. There before the people whose lives Death had thrown off balance: that's where the new queen would make her mark.

Suri had worked her hands to the bone planning every aspect around my big day, the sweetie. She'd taken it upon herself to handle all the details I had no interest in, which proved to be, well, pretty much everything. Cadagon oversaw the big-ticket items though, his insufferable control issues taking over, and left the smaller details to Suri, such as tablecloths and cutlery. But with three short days left until the big event, Suri couldn't allow me to dodge my damn dress fitting any longer. If the gown needed any tweaks, she'd have little time to correct the imperfections.

"Ugh, do I have to?" I grumbled, and dragged my feet up the south tower stairs.

"Yes, you do, Miss Whiny." Suri chuckled. "I need to know of any adjustments you might want me to make. It's important."

"It would be if it were the real deal." The words came out before I could catch them. Gods, I hated the way I had to monitor every word that escaped my mouth, even my own damn feelings.

"Right," Suri sighed, and pushed open the door to my suite. Once inside, she flipped the lock and turned back, her eyes soft and apologetic. "I know you are unhappy about this, but I hope you also know how thankful I am for your desire to serve your kingdom, to restore balance for me and everyone else who has lived in Cadagon's shadow for so long."

That's all it took for me to remember precisely why I'd agreed to take the throne from the start: for those who deserved more than Cadagon had offered them. Those like Suri. As I looked her over, I couldn't help but be overcome with gratitude. I'd never have survived all this without her. "You know I appreciate the hell out of you?"

"You're damn right I do. Though I wouldn't argue if you say, gifted me a matching pair of earrings for that necklace you gave me. You know, as a 'thank you' for all my hard work," she teased with a wink.

"Bitch, done! You've more than earned it."

We shared a laugh before she walked to the closet and pulled out a stuffed dress bag.

"Alright, Kimber. You ready?"

I exhaled, lifted my head, and stood tall. "As ready as I'll ever fucking be."

The dress Suri laid on the bed in no way resembled the traditional, white ball gown customary in western, mortal culture. Not in the slightest. See, this gown appeared woven together by literal strands of Anathema's night sky. Its jet black tone and color-changing sequins caused my lungs to seize. A goth's wet dream. It far surpassed Suri's creations thus far. Though beautiful on the hanger, nothing could have prepared me for how it appeared on. Hair loose around a lacy, heart-shaped neckline, I choked up. It hugged my curves in all the right places, accentuated my voluptuous shape seamlessly. I sucked in a breath. This dress hadn't simply been made for me, it was me incarnate; and though I had little excitement reserved for my own big day, the power it lent made the whole thing easier to swallow.

"Do you like it?" Suri asked, and fluffed the lace-laden skirt.

Mouth gaping wide, I met her stare.

"Do I like it?" I blinked. "Are you kidding? It's fucking gorgeous!"

"Anything less simply wouldn't do." She patted my shoulder, face alight. "Is there anything you'd prefer I changed? Fixed? I was worried the glitter may have made it a little too flashy for your liking."

"Not at all, it's brilliant. How did you get the sequins to change colors? It's—"

"Magical?" She grinned. "Yes, because it is. I had it imbued with a little something extra for you."

"Extra?"

Pride resonated across her face. "A calming spell, to help soothe your nerves. Took me a bit to find, but one of my regulars at the club had an underground potion hookup."

The second she said it, it clicked: the confidence, the security. It was like I'd been wrapped in a permanent hug. I turned and yanked her to my chest. "Thank you."

Her arms tightened around me. "Of course."

A knock boomed at the door, and after a nod from me, Suri opened it.

Cadagon stood in the doorway, shoulders back, hands clenched behind him in his usual, smug persona. His jaw tensed the second he saw me in my gown.

"You look—" he choked.

"Look?" I asked.

"You look like—"

"Like what? Spit it out, Death."

"Like a true queen," he finally said, and I smiled against my better judgment.

What was wrong with me? I hated him, didn't give a shit about his opinion, and yet the compliment sank in like it held stock somehow. I needed to get my ass into therapy and get a handle on the daddy issues. But regardless of my inner child's need for validation, I knew the truth. Every word spewed from Death's mouth was nothing but fancy lies, backwards compliments, and half-truths.

I stepped towards him, arms crossed. "What do you want?"

"Well," he cleared his throat, "I thought we might skip training this morning and go out to the shifter realm. Hunt some revels for the wedding reception."

"Wait...hunt? They're flowers. Wouldn't we just pick them?"

A dark smirk graced his face. "Oh, my dear daughter, you've no idea the fun you are in for this afternoon."

CHAPTER 14

DEEP IN THE EVERMOOR WOODS

Heels clicking against the cobblestone slabs in the courtyard, I trekked towards the shifter realm, Cadagon and Lyvias in tow. The leather satchel at my hip tugged at my tapered gray trousers with each step thanks to its heavy steel contents. Per Death's insistence, we'd retrieved firepower from the castle armory before we set out: long-barreled revolvers doused in tarnished, old-west charm. An unexpected weapon, given the usual swords, bows, and axes I'd seen so often.

Cadagon briefed us as we walked. "The revels are a sneaky bunch. Given the opportunity, they'd sooner pull themselves from the soil and bite off a chunk of your flesh than allow you to approach them."

"So they're an animal? Not a flower?" Lyvias questioned, nose wrinkled.

"Both. They are Plantaeanimalia, a breed stemmed from both plant and animal origin."

"I've never heard of such a thing," Lyvias responded.

I perked up. "How is something like that possible?"

"It's a mystery to me," Cadagon admitted, and snapped his fingers to part the courtyard gates. "They appeared from thin air and seem to be the only conscious plant life amongst all the courts."

"Do you think somebody created them then?" I flashed Lyvias a pointed expression. Strangeness this rare had to have stemmed from something. And given the Evermoor Woods' dark history with cult activity, I'd bet that had something to do with it.

"You're more interested than I expected you to be, Princess. It's refreshing," Cadagon said. Almost in unison, we stepped onto the shifter path. "But again, I am not sure. It would take a sinister strain of magic to have given conscious life to an unknowing organism. Such magic would fall into the necromancy witchcrafts, the kind of craft Anathema hasn't seen in quite some time. And yet here the revels grow." The gate to the shifter realm opened to reveal the massacre still on repeat, though Death didn't bat an eye. "They showed up about fifteen years ago now, give or take. Long after the times when said magic would be used. So I am left to assume it must be the whimsy of mother nature herself."

Lyvias drew closer to me, fell in line behind Death's lead, and pinched my arm.

I gave him a "not here" glare—panning between him and Cadagon—and averted my eyes to the shifter streets engulfed in flame. The sight consumed me even still: homes, storefronts, bodies, all succumbed to little more than ash and rubble. Nails pressed into my palms, my skin split.

It wasn't until we reached the forest's edge, untouched by the blaze, that my lungs settled into a steady rhythm again. The farther into the forest we drifted, the odder the trees became; once lush and piney fresh upon our entrance, limbs began to bulge and fray, their scent overtaken by the sharp smack of decay. The trees were dying. Again Lyvias hinted, eyebrows raised. Right where sacrificial magic had been rumored to take place fifteen years before, the trees themselves were rotting from the inside out. Happenstance? I think the fuck not.

"Ah, here we are," Cadagon called, and pulled his six-shooter from his robe pocket. "Keep quiet now; I'll show you how it is done."

Lyvias and I slunk down, locked on the empty field ahead, and waited. Despite the quiet, motionless scene, Cadagon didn't flinch from his pointed gun. One minute, two, three minutes, four...on it went for how long, I couldn't be sure. Then, like an oddity suited for a damn horror movie, the revel walked—I repeat, *walked*—into the open air: a giant and terrifying thing. A beautiful yellow bloom sat atop its head, but its remainder was of the most gruesome sort. Humanoid, it stalked about the field on two legs, salivating like a diseased dog, sniffing the air. One final whiff, and it snapped its petal-ridden face straight towards us, dropped to its stomach, and disappeared in the tall grass.

Delicious fear swept through me, and I squirmed in its icy grip. Ah, how long it'd been since it'd last claimed me. It didn't help that Lyvias's knee touched mine, and I swear I could feel the tension pouring between us. That urge inside to let the fear overtake me, and him too.

Chills climbed up my spine. "Shoot it."

"Patience," Cadagon whispered.

The revel's malicious growl drew closer. I raised my voice, "Shoot it now!"

"'Patience,' I said."

It thrashed ever closer. The swishing grass blades announced its approach like a shark's fin, but stopped suddenly. For two long seconds, silence swirled about us, until finally, the disturbed creature hurled itself into the air, dead set on the kill. I squinted, latched onto Lyvias's hand, and braced for impact, but the shrill clap of Death's gun sounded once, and he hit his mark with exceptional accuracy. The lifeless beast dropped to the dirt with a thud.

"Holy shit," I heaved. My sights landed on Lyvias's and my interlocked fingers, and in a heartbeat, I dropped my hold, a blush warming my cheeks. He smiled down at me, as if to assure me it was alright to have reached out, but I avoided his stare and studied the dead monster instead. A ruthless, flesh-eating flower seemed far safer than the questions lurking in his scarlet gaze.

"Its face," I said, grabbing a bare branch off the ground. "It's gone."

Cadagon nodded and stowed his gun at his hip. "Upon death, they return to their plant state, all consciousness erased. This one was quite a catch though, wasn't he? Look at him. That bloom will feed four people easily."

"Weird," I whispered, and poked at the carcass. "Should we be killing them? What if they're like an endangered species or something?"

Cadagon grabbed my elbow and led me across the meadow. He gestured to a wide hole in the earth. "See that? It's a revel den. Put your ear to the ground and listen."

"What?" My sights snapped to his. "The hell I will. What if one of those things comes flying out at me?"

"It won't," Cadagon assured.

"How do you know?"

"Each revel has their own personal tunnel. And they're very territorial." He pointed to the hole again. "Given the proximity of my kill, I can safely assume this one belonged to him. The others will fill the passage within the next week when he doesn't return, but until then it'll be vacant. You'll be fine; trust me."

"Trust you?" I scoffed.

"Please try to keep your needless jabs to a minimum. I'm being patient; given your ceaseless questions, at least try to be patient with me."

"You can't be—"

I clipped my words after connecting the look on Lyvias's face. "Façade," he mouthed just behind Cadagon's sight line.

Play nice. Keep him distracted. Right.

"Fine," I whined, and placed my ear near the burrow. The rustle of countless leaves, mixed between rabid snarls and thrashed movements reverberated below.

"There are hundreds down there," Death assured. "By week's end, their numbers will have increased by a third. The revels are as quick to breed as they are to perish."

My forehead creased. "What do you mean?"

"Precisely what I said. Their lifespan is what one would expect from a regular flower: short. But they fight to keep the species alive, reproducing at exceptional rates before they keel over and die." He knelt and eyed the beast at his feet. "It's a good thing no one lives in these parts anymore; they'd become a feast for these creatures, no doubt."

Acid burned in my chest. Glad nobody lived here? What a heartless piece of shit. "There would be people here if you hadn't killed and banished them."

Cadagon rolled his eyes, hoisted himself off the ground, and started back towards the woods. "I'll be hunting just over there. Don't wander too far."

Lyvias stepped near, setting a hand on my shoulder, and the rage in me simmered.

"Come on," he said, and we wasted no time setting off in opposite directions to investigate.

I wove through the putrid trees, slipping to the outskirts of the reaper's view, when I noticed a subtle yet unmistakable shift in the air. A gust rolled through, loosening leaves from the treetops. I anticipated the leaves' usual flutter to the ground, but instead, they fell in straight lines and far slower than gravity would have it. Weirder still, they all but halted at eye level, jittering about as if they'd been met by resistance stemming from the forest floor. Index finger raised, I thrust my hand forward, and each leaf I touched dropped to the ground like a rock. Magic? I swept my arms through the open air and was met with a dead leaf fallout. It had to be magic. What else could cause such a strange, altered reality? The real question, though, remained. What *kind* of magic?

Peering over my shoulder to reference Cadagon's location, I found him still planted a hundred yards out, hunched, gun pointed in the opposite direction. Perfect.

With a deep breath, I shuffled my leather boots across the still forest floor. Not two feet forward, my toe snagged, and I hunched down, feeling along the ground. Buried beneath soggy leaves and thick soil, I latched onto a frayed rope no thicker than my pinky finger. Grasping one end, I heaved, but it resisted, clinging to the dirt of its own will. Again, I tried. Again, it refused me. I gave it a few more attempts before I let go and brushed the hair from my face.

A strong perfume wafted in the air, and I brought my fingers to my nose. The rope, it'd left an earthy but soured smell. More than simple rot, it was unusual. Distinct. I scratched at the rope line, this time exposing the start of what appeared to be a symbol. A circle maybe? Whatever the shape, it hadn't happened on its own. This was man-made.

Unsure it'd work, I pressed my open palms against the dirt and centered myself the same way I did to read the castle halls. The energy flowed slowly at first, trickling along my senses, little urgency in its ebb and sway, but the soil confirmed a magical presence nonetheless. I laid claim to the energy imprint, fixated on it in my mind's eye, and willed it closer. A sick, hollow grasp hardened in my gut. Bloodied flesh, plumes of smoke, and grins brimming with lunacy hurled past my vision at record speed. It turned against me then; the energy zapped across my skin like an electric shock, and the soil sunk invisible teeth into my palms. I thrashed to my feet to find smoke hissing from the place my hands had rested. An evil lived there, embedded in the soil, its name unspoken for years and yet as alive as the day it'd been birthed. The cult. It really had existed.

Spinning about, I set off to find Lyvias when—to my panic and disappointment—I found Death on a sure path towards me. In a flustered whirlwind, I tore a piece from my maroon button-up, shoved it under a rock above the symbol, and rushed to cut off Cadagon's advance.

"I haven't heard you shoot yet," Cadagon called from the outskirts of the revel field. "Having trouble, are we?"

"I didn't see any over there. Do you think there's a better spot we could try?" I asked, appealing to his self-proclaimed hunter's intuition in hopes he'd ignore the direction I'd come from.

"I do, actually. Let's find that vampire of yours and head back." His gaze narrowed. "After all, the whole point of today was to spend time with your betrothed, correct?"

He searched my face, skepticism in his flaming irises.

"Of course it is," I lied, my expression calm and collected, though my stomach threatened to toss its contents. "Let's go."

I followed and denied myself a final glance at the dark symbol. Though its unknown evils weighed heavy on my mind.

We managed to bag four more revels before the afternoon had gotten away from us. Not nearly enough to feed all those who'd attend my coronation dinner the following night, but so be it. Cadagon insisted he cart the flower carcasses back to the castle—no doubt so any passerby could marvel at how good a shot he was—even though Lyvias had downed half the beasts in all actuality.

Lyvias and I headed for the south wing to share our discoveries. I communed with the halls before we started up the stairs. Cadagon would be held up in the kitchen butchering his kills for some time while Nasheesh seemed to be busying himself in the gardens. Perfect.

Once safely inside my room, I locked the door behind us. "I found something."

"What?" Lyvias asked, and drifted closer, eyes wide.

"A rope." He pursed his lips, unimpressed, and I whopped him on the shoulder. "Not any old rope; it was...weird, magic-imbued. It didn't budge no matter how hard I pulled, and the energy reading?" I shivered. "Let's just say it was dark."

"'Dark' as in sacrificial?"

The bloody, disturbed faces I'd seen in that brief but vivid energy-vision flashed across my memory. "Yes, sacrificial magic; I have no doubt."

"Fucking great." He released a sigh and started a slow pace about the room. "Did you notice anything else?"

"Yeah, actually. The rope, it had this nasty smell. I couldn't quite place it though."

He leaned against the door frame, arms crossed. "Like an earthy sourness?"

"Yeah." I looked him over. "Exactly like that. How'd you know?"

"I'm well acquainted with the scent of sulfur. Whatever you found was a mortal witch's spell, I'm sure, but I'd have to see it for myself to know precisely what strain of magic we're talking about."

"I figured you'd want to see. I left you a marker." I fiddled with my button-up's torn inseam.

He inspected my tattered blouse, and his brow creased. "You tore your shirt? But it looks so lovely on you."

"Think so?" Why the hell had I asked that? I didn't care about his opinion or validation. But the rising heat in my chest begged to differ. Shit.

Pushing off the wall, he made his way to me, stopping to drop his gaze into mine.

"Red is quite striking against your skin, and it makes your eyes glow," he whispered, tucking a loose wave behind my ear.

His touch was electric. All-consuming. Butterflies thrashed in my center and out across my limbs; and for a brief second, I let it take hold. Lyvias reached for me, his hand cupping my chin and lifting it. Desire, overwhelming and demanding, crept in as my sight fell to his full lips. A depraved smile eclipsed his face, giving way to ruthless fangs I couldn't help but picture buried in my flesh: the tear, the fear, the pain. I shivered. The sharp aroma of wine and iron carried in the air, and I would be a liar if I said that it wasn't intoxicating. Fuck, why wasn't I pushing him away? This couldn't happen. Not now. He leaned in closer, his hitched breath on my cheek, his eyes never falling from mine.

"What are you doing?" I whispered, but didn't flinch from his hold.

He snaked an arm around my waist, pulling me to him. "What, you don't like it?"

"No," I lied. "I don't."

A dark laugh carried through him as the crimson in his eyes darkened to near-black depths. "I never took you for a liar, Lady Death. Shall I wash your mouth out with soap or something more... substantial?"

I felt it then: his hard dick against my stomach; and before I could think twice, I slid my hand across him. Long, thick, pulsing at my touch; a moan rattled through him. Gods, I was already wet, and I hadn't even seen him yet, let alone... His mouth crashed into mine, forcing my head back as he bit my bottom lip. The prick of pain and gush of blood had me throbbing.

"You taste like heaven," he said, voice gravelly. He licked my blood off his lips with hooded eyes. "Will you purge me of my sins, Kim? Or will you revel in the darkness with me?"

My name on his sharp tongue was all it took. I was in his arms, resting perfectly on his hard length. His tongue battled my own as he laid me on the bed, frantically removing my clothes. Standing to his full height, he stared down at me, all the while my breath labored.

"Look at you," he praised, trailing a finger up my leg. He lowered himself down, his weight settling atop me. One hooked finger, and he snapped my bra's metal clasp, setting my breasts bouncing free. "Fuck, you're stunning."

A whimper rattled through me as his teeth sank into the soft skin above my nipple.

"Lower," I begged.

"That's it: tell me what to do. Guide my hands to damnation in your unholy temple," he moaned into my ear. "Be my ruin, that I might be yours alone for all eternity."

Guiding his attention to the exact spot I wanted, I began to grind against him. Fuck, he was thick. The thought of riding him, that throbbing mass buried deep, had me dripping. My nipple still in his mouth, he pulled me onto his lap, hands guiding my hips. Need overcame me. Who was this devastating monster beneath me? This wicked man I had no business doing anything, let alone *this*, with. Mere touches, and already I was coming to the edge. My eyes locked on his as I grabbed his throat, pushing him down and pinning him in place. Hips frantic, I moaned, riding him.

His lips ticked up as he snarled through his teeth, "There she is. There's my queen."

Faster than my eyes could catch, he flipped me off his lap and snatched my ankles, pulling me to the edge of the bed. He lowered himself to his knees, parting mine. I watched, breathless, feeling my climax still rattling inside me, begging to be set free. With my hand buried in his hair, he bit down on my inner thigh, and I cried out.

Lifting my hips, he slid my underwear off, and wasted no time burying his tongue in me. His long fingers cupped my ass, shoving me into his mouth as if he aimed to devour me whole. A nip at my clit, and I screamed out.

"Do you like that, my Queen?" he asked in a husky, needy voice.

"Yes," I said breathlessly, shoving his head back down.

He laughed against my most sensitive space, the gesture sending euphoric waves through me. With impeccable control, he flicked the tip of his tongue up and down, thumb working circles around the bottom half of my clit.

"Holy shit," I whimpered, body going wild. I tipped over the edge. Hard. Pleasure raced through me. He leaned up, placing his mouth over mine, devouring my scream. When the wave ceased, I wasted no time. Hands on his pant buttons, I went to work. I wanted—no, needed—him inside me.

"Kim," he said, and rested a hand atop mine. "Stop."

I stilled. Stop… "What? Did I…did I do something wrong?"

He laced a hand through mine. "Absolutely not, you're incredible."

"But…" My throat tightened.

"But this isn't going to happen. Not tonight."

Icy embarrassment swept through my blood, cooling the flames burning for him only a moment before. I became acutely aware of how exposed I was. Bare. I slid from his touch and headed for my closet, desperately searching for anything to hide my naked frame. How could I be such an idiot? To trust him with myself. My body. Ugh, I was so stupid.

"Please." He squeezed my shoulder from behind. "It's not you—"

"Don't touch me," I snapped, reeling.

"I need you to hear me. It's not you, it's *me*."

A cynical laugh rattled through me. "If I had a nickel for every time someone used that line, I'd be filthy fucking rich."

"But it's the truth." He backed me against the wall—all the while my arms flailing—before pinning my hands above my head. "Before you give yourself to me, there are things you need to know. About my past. About who I am. Until then, I cannot in good conscience be with you. I should have stopped this sooner. For that, I'm sorry."

"Don't pretend like you're the hero. Like you give a shit about me and my honor, Lyvias."

"I do care about you, damn it! You have no idea the things I've done in your name. The things I would do." His hands clenched, brow hardening.

I met his gaze, rage simmering. "Then tell me."

"It's not that simple."

Stunned silence settled around me as I looked him over. Here we were, facing what could be the greatest threat Anathema had ever known, and I couldn't manage to keep my head in the game. Whatever had bloomed between us, it wasn't priority, couldn't be, no matter how much my body begged otherwise. I was the queen first and foremost, and this—whatever the fuck it was—was a distraction I couldn't afford. One that could get innocent people killed should my eyes stray too far from the looming threat ahead. This…it had to end.

"Yeah," I said, and thrashed from his hold, guilt heavy as a brick in my stomach. "Well, this is simple. You and me? We're business partners. There is no 'us' or 'we' outside of what we must do for Anathema. So keep your secrets, Lyvias. Just know that if any of them put my people at risk, I'll do what I must."

"You can't mean that. You know me—"

"No, I don't. And I no longer care to. I am your queen, and that is all I'll ever be to you." I swallowed down the lump riding in my throat. "Do I make myself clear?"

He stepped back, eyes falling to my feet. "Yes, your Majesty. Please forgive me."

My heart jumped at his hardened stare, and I almost recounted my words. Almost. But I had to stand my ground for Anathema. Too many people I loved were relying on me to fix this mess and keep them safe. So instead of reaching out to him like my body begged me to, I pushed my shoulders back, head held high.

"Return to the shifter realm. Find the marker." I retrieved a pen and paper from my desk along with a small vial. I cut a line in the pad of my thumb, guiding my blood into the bottle, and extended it to him. "Draw what you find and bring it back to me."

"Yes, your Majesty." A nod, and he headed to the door. Without turning, he called over his shoulder, "Even if today is the only taste of you I'll receive, everything I've done will have been worth it."

His shadow disappeared into the hall, leaving me reeling.

CHAPTER 15

THE LORDS

I looked myself over in the mirror, lips puckered, fluffing and re-fluffing the bustle of Suri's newest creation: a gunmetal gray, Victorian gown.

"Don't worry," Suri said from her hunched position on the floor, hands buried in tulle and lace. "It's only a few Lords and their trophy wives."

I turned to her. "Right, *only* three Lords. A handful of dukes and duchesses. Oh, and the few sole leaders I need to impress before my coronation in *two* days or lose the respect of my people. But yeah, sure, no big deal."

"Take a breath, woman. If anybody can do this, it's you. Just be your badass self, and the rest will fall in line."

I inhaled a sharp breath. "I'm sorry. I didn't mean to be an asshole. I'm just stressing the fuck out. If I lose their loyalty—"

"You won't." Suri stood and grabbed me by the shoulders, a warm smile on her full lips. "They're going to see you for exactly who you are: Anathema's queen."

I wrapped her in a tight hug, exhaling slow. "Thank you. I seriously don't know what I'd do without you."

"Good thing you'll never have to find out, huh? You're stuck with me, bitch."

A laugh rolled through me. "Thank the gods for that!"

"Now get out there and show those pompous men what real royalty looks like." She placed a swift smack on my ass as she urged me towards the door.

Chin up, I meandered down the halls—polished bone tiara atop my head—and met Lyvias at the ballroom door.

He turned, eyes wide and cheeks rosy at my approach. "You look ravishing."

"I know I do." The words rolled out, and I almost felt bad. But then I remembered how he'd rejected me, bouncing around from wanting me one minute and not the next. Keeping secrets. Lying. I deserved better than that, damn it.

"Spoken like a true queen," he said, his gaze falling to his feet. "Are you ready for this?"

"You bet your ass."

He extended an arm to me, and I reluctantly took it. Showtime. The hefty doors skidded open thanks to Cadagon's magical snap, and we graced the ballroom. Upon our entry, the chamber orchestra grew silent, instrument bows clutched to their chests in reverence. The guests' cheers and claps commanded the room. I swallowed, my throat suddenly drier than the Sahara. Cadagon caught my eye perched on his velvet chair ahead. "A few guests," he'd told me. And yet a sea of visitors more suited for my coronation itself rather than a premarital ball stared back expectantly. My chest tightened.

Lyvias leaned over and whispered in my ear, "Give them hell."

I fought the smirk on my face but ultimately gave in. He was right. *I* was in control here. Lyvias led me to my place at Cadagon's side, placed a kiss on my hand—my cheeks warming where his lips had been despite myself—and turned to his chair positioned beneath mine. It struck a chord. The wrong one. Why was he below me? If we were to be partners, that shit wouldn't fly. I might be pissed at the dude, but I wasn't a fool. Ruling a kingdom required two leaders. United, if only by a mutual desire to protect our people. The citizens of Anathema knew him, respected him. And I'd need his influence if I were to gain their respect as well and not be deemed a simpleminded mortal raised as a heathen, as Nasheesh had so kindly put it upon my arrival. I was their queen. And Lyvias would be their king, whether I liked it or not.

I turned back to the crowd now gathered before us and cleared my throat. The room grew quiet. Still. Hands clasped behind my back, nails dug into my palms for grounding, I spoke.

"Honored guests, welcome! We are so fortunate to have such prestigious and influential minds in our presence this night." I panned the room, locking eyes as I went. "It is with great joy that we celebrate the coming change of an era."

Lyvias stepped to my side and laced his fingers through mine, sending goosebumps up my spine. "A change the future queen and I are excited to build with your help. We look forward to what is to come in the days ahead. Anathema, united."

Cadagon rose last but remained on his platform, his unspoken message received loud and clear: he was higher than us. "The future regents will see to a personal meeting with each of you. While you await an audience, please enjoy the refreshments, music, and great company as we celebrate your future queen and king." He nodded to the orchestra who struck a fast-paced tempo, and the crowd returned to garish conversations, feasting, and dancing.

When the last eye turned from us, I dropped Lyvias's hand.

"I didn't think I was so detestable." He winked, though the twitch in his jaw betrayed his jest.

My gut fluttered. This guy. "After last night, I'd rather crawl into a revel nest than touch you."

"Ouch." A pained snicker slipped past his fangs as he rubbed the back of his neck. "But I deserved that."

His gentle expression sent another exhilarated flush through me. Fuck, he was making it *way* too hard to hate him. And his patience… ugh, infuriatingly hot. In fear I'd do something stupid—like forgive him and pin him to the wall in a dark corner somewhere—I turned to Cadagon. "Lyvias's throne, I want it raised."

Cadagon nodded. "I'll see it done."

"I said that I want—" I froze. "Wait, did you just agree with me?"

"Yes. This weekend is all for you, Kimberly. A gift to celebrate your last two days as a mere princess and reaper." He referenced the crowd, the band, the countless vases of pitch black roses gleaming in the candlelight. "Whatever the future queen wants, she shall have."

I tapped my chin. "And if I wanted to go back to my room and crawl in bed?"

"Whatever you want *within reason*. I should have prefaced, given who I'm speaking to." Cadagon chuckled.

"Ugh, fine." It was worth a shot. "Well, at least tell me who these people are before I go and try to sell myself as their future ruler."

"There is no 'selling' going on here tonight." Death stepped closer. "You are my daughter. That alone ensures their respect. You simply need to give them a reason to remain an ally upon my retirement from the crown."

I raised an eyebrow. "And what reason would that be?"

"Such things are for you and the future king to decide. Together you will find the purpose your specific rule requires."

"What does that even mean?"

"Figure it out." Cadagon took to his seat and drank from his diamond chalice, shooing us away with the flick of his wrist.

A growl rose up in me. "You're seriously going to—"

"Go figure it out, or I will excuse myself for the evening, and you will be forced to handle the guests alone." Flames raged in his eyes.

"A night without you? As if you'd be so kind." I grimaced, wove my arm through Lyvias's, and glided into the mass of exquisite dresses and well-tailored suits.

At first, we were clunky and nervous in our approach. Lyvias would talk, and I'd accidentally interrupt him. Or he'd be silent, and I'd completely forget what words were, let alone how to speak. But beyond any belief I had coming into this whole thing, it seemed most guests truly wished to welcome us. Take Adari Melontin, the demon Duke of Wentworth Manor, for example. When conversation grew stale, Adari would interject a well-timed joke or comment on the orchestra's song choice. His husband, Tovas Wentworth, remained silent, but his gentle demeanor showed his support. Gods, I loved them. I made a mental note to plan a visit after all the dust settled to thank them for their kindness. And maybe ask them to be my adopted guncles because, damn, they were cool!

"Connection," Adari said at one point, hand never parting from his husband's, "comes from a vibe similar to what one feels in music. Once you find the rhythm, you'll be able to play whatever tune is placed before you."

They followed us through our first few exchanges, lightening the mood with their relaxed approach, until the time came to part ways.

"You kids," Tovas finally chimed, mustache wiggling below his periwinkle eyes. "You will be the change Anathema so desperately needs. The house of Wentworth is at your service, always."

His sage words rippled through me as Lyvias slipped off to the banquet table.

Change: was that to be our rule? Our mission?

Lyvias returned, two full champagne flutes in hand. I considered the events thus far, a question rattling about.

"Lyvias," I said between sips. "The nobility here, I'm having a hard time understanding. Aren't dukes usually above lords and ladies?"

He chuckled. "You're using your mortal brain. It's not the same here. A Lord has full control over his court, while a duke is his second in command and the Lord's successor should a rightful heir not be provided."

Mortal brain. Right.

"Alright, mental note made. Lord, then duke. Weird, but okay."

"Think it's time we meet them? The Lords?" he asked, searching my face.

"I do." Though one Lord in specific haunted me. Malachi. I hadn't seen him or his hound in the blustering crowd, but I could feel him somehow. Lingering in the shadows.

I finished my champagne in one chug, and without thinking, laced my fingers through Lyvias's and swept amongst the crowd once more. For show. It was all for show. He didn't comment but flashed a devilish smirk and squeezed my hand. "Don't get cocky. I'm just trying to sell us as a united front."

"Right," he said playfully.

Head full of fizz, we made our way into the crowd once again. Halfway across the dance floor, Cadagon's disembodied voice clanged through me, coaxing me towards the night's first formal introduction.

"Look to your right, Princess. There, next to the marble fountain in a paisley suit and tie, is Lord Revert Tarrant of the Reaper court. By his side is Lady Evanna Tarrant. They are personal friends. A simple handshake, and they will know your power."

I heaved a breath and hurled Lyvias towards the fountain. "Reaper Lord, this way."

"I know. But wait, how did you—"

"Hello, Lord and Lady Tarrant," I called out. "We are so fortunate to have you here celebrating with us tonight."

Lord Tarrant placed a quick peck on my hand, and Lyvias did the same with Lady Tarrant.

"We feel quite honored to have been invited to stay here in the castle this weekend," Lord Tarrant said. "I must admit, I'd forgotten the splendor of these halls. It's truly inspired, Highness."

"It is a magical place, isn't it?" I scooped another bubble-filled glass from a nearby waiter's tray. Liquid courage. I'd finally achieved a buzz, and I wasn't about to let it fade.

Lyvias offered a hand to Lord Tarrant who gladly accepted. "Tell me, is your room to your liking then, sir?"

"Oh, quite, thank you. We will sleep in comfort tonight."

Lyvias smiled, head held high. "Wonderful."

"Indeed." Lord Tarrant nodded once. "Now if I might be so bold, your Graces, I wonder if we might speak of the future? Your future."

I pressed my shoulders together and sipped from my glass. "Lyvias and I are always willing to discuss the concerns of our court leaders."

Lady Evanna's meek voice carried through. "A magnificent quality in an heir."

"Thank you kindly." I bowed my head. "By all means, tell us your concerns."

Lord Tarrant carried on from there and expressed his concerns for the quality of life in the reaper court. "My people are experiencing adverse effects due to the shapeshifters' absence. Over the past fifteen years, they've grown tense, forsaking the balance in their blood for fights and brawls amongst themselves." He swallowed hard. "I've had to increase security in the streets to keep them from unnecessary quarrels."

"With all due respect, Lord Tarrant," I said, tone patient. "I've visited your realm rather recently, and it appeared the reapers were quite at rest."

He eyed his wife who gave him a reassuring pat. "It is strange, but it only seems to happen in the wee night hours. They walk out, a strange vacancy in their eyes, and...attack one another."

Shit, not good. I searched Lyvias's face and found the confirmation I sought. I took the Lord's hand between mine and looked him deep in the eyes. "I promise you, whatever is going on with your people, we will see to a solution."

He released a sigh, his tense stance relaxing. "Well, that is quite good news indeed. Thank you, your Majesty."

The next conference belonged to Lord and Lady Drystan of the vampire court, which proved smooth and effortless. Lyvias—who clearly had a preexisting rapport with them—dominated the conversation, allowing me to play the supportive role. A wise choice: him handling his birth court. He wooed them with talk of sustainable sustenance and more supplies for the vampire's routine rituals. A few minutes in, and Lord Drystan became near putty in his hands.

Their discussion turned to static as concern spider-walked up my back, the shadows in my bones whispering their worries. I still hadn't glimpsed Malachi in the crowd, nor Odin. But Malachi was a Lord. By law, his presence was required. I felt his eyes on me. Devouring. Yet he was nowhere. And somehow everywhere. He no doubt got off on fucking with me, biding his time while he drove me mad with brief appearances and threatening notes. At least I now had solid allies to call upon, and the night had gone smoother than I'd hoped. I grabbed another glass of champagne as a nearby waiter passed and took a hefty drink. Could I have overestimated him? Expected a monster when really, I'd been dealing with nothing more than a man's inflated ego once again? After all, the asshole's attempts to take me out had all failed. Maybe I'd allowed my worry to get away from me. He was just one man in the end.

And I was Lady Death.

Once again, Cadagon's voice rang through, "Duke Jarlin Golgotha and Duchess Nova Golgotha of the demon court are on the veranda. They will prove troublesome as they have never been in support of our lineage. They believe the throne rightfully belongs to the demons. Needless to say, they are not my biggest supporters."

Cadagon chuckled, and his voice dissipated.

"Looks like we already have something in common then," I muttered under my breath.

"What?" Lyvias questioned.

"Nothing. Our next meeting is outside."

As we started towards the open veranda doors, my head began to spin, stomach soured, hands shook. I halted, withdrew my arm from Lyvias's elbow, and braced against the nearest table, careful so as not to arouse unnecessary attention.

"Is everything okay?" he asked, forehead wrinkled.

"Yeah, I, uh, I'm just a little lightheaded. Too much champagne I guess."

"You want to take a break—"

"No, no." I shook my head. "I'm fine. Let's get this over with so we can relax."

Duke Jarlin's ashen irises had been fixed on me from the moment we cleared the door, his expression smug and impartial. The air grew colder the closer we drew to the demon couple at the back most corner, as if the Golgothas themselves carried a frigid chill in their midst, and my hand tensed around Lyvias's arm.

"Keep your head up, and we'll make this one fast," Lyvias reassured as we wound through chairs to the duke and duchess's side.

"Greetings, children," the duke said, his tone clipped. "Finally, you grace us with your presence."

"We apologize for the wait," Lyvias appeased. "But the princess and I simply meant to save the best for last."

"Flippant flattery. How like a vampire." Jarlin snuffed his nose up and turned his attention to me. "And tell me, does the princess speak through her lowly counterpart often, or does the girl speak for herself?"

Oh, hell no. Rage teemed in my champagne-buzzed veins. Vision blurring, I stepped to him. "I speak of my own accord, yes, but never with much respect for those who don't offer it. I believe you owe my fiancé an apology."

Feigned shock overtook the duke's face, his white-gloved hand pressed to his chest. "You assume I meant harm in my words? Please assure me you do not greet all your guests with such hostile accusations."

My foot edged forward. "Hostile accusations? You were—"

A tense laugh escaped Lyvias, and he anchored my hip to his, the motion sending a wave of nausea through me. "No, no, dear, it's fine," he muttered, jaw ticking. "I believe Duke Jarlin merely grew impatient awaiting an audience; let us hear him out."

He flashed a wide-eyed stare at my crushing grip on his arm, hinting towards the swirling black matter slipping from my fingertips. Funny, I hadn't remembered setting them free. I pulled my hand to my face, inspecting the frantic energy within my shadows. The hell? Lyvias's touch tightened, grounding me, and willed me to gain control. A deep breath, and my power returned to rest in my bones.

"You're right," I said, body tense. I suppressed my rage, setting my attention on the duke once again. "Well, you have our ears, so tell us what matters you wish to discuss in regards to our future alliance."

"If there *is* to be a future alliance," Jarlin specified, gangly finger pointed, "you will be required to fix the issues your father has created amongst my people. And I do mean *every* single issue."

His wife giggled in agreement, the wrinkles along her eyes creased in brazen enjoyment. *Required…* Magic tingled at my fingertips with intention now, but I forcefully denounced it. The last thing I needed was to unleash my brute power on a duke. No matter how much the prick deserved it.

"I seek to restore Anathema to balance, which includes the demon court's needs as much as every other." I cleared my throat, a knot bobbing within. "What issues might I help with?"

"The list is quite substantial. But to name a few, you will be required to—"

There was that fucking word again.

"Required?" I snapped. "I am your queen. I am never—"

Lyvias tangled his fingers through mine, and I inhaled through my nose. The duke seemed a glutton for punishment, much the same way as a certain advisor I knew. Speaking of, where the hell was Nasheesh? I relaxed my fists. One asshole at a time. I glared at Duke Jarlin and said through my teeth, "*Required* to do what?"

The duke's mouth twitched in blatant satisfaction. "Yes, 'required,' as the crown on your head binds you to."

"I assure you, *nothing* binds me."

"Well then," he scoffed, projecting his voice for anyone nearby to overhear. "Given your obvious disinterest in hearing the demon court's needs, I believe our time here is finished. Should you find yourself more apt to listen, my wife and I will be in our quarters. Come now, Nova."

The Golgothas moved to leave, and that was it. My final reason. My power surged, but I willed it to mind. To reveal itself, but only slightly. A man like him would be easy to scare. They always were. And he would fear me, damn it.

"Stop right there," I demanded in a cool, controlled tone.

"Kim, don't—"

"No, Lyvias, his attitude is appalling." I headed off the couple mid-flee before they could clear the veranda, my head spinning. Black smoke curled up my forearms. "You do not leave the future king's or my presence without our permission. You are guests in our home, Duke Jarlin, and I urge you to reconsider the manner of gratefulness you've shown here tonight. Or would you rather I see you both escorted from the premises?"

The duke's ashy stare constricted. "You're bluffing."

"Am I?" I raised a hand, snapping once, and five bulky castle guards were at my side in an instant, ready to heed my orders. "Now shall I have these lovely men see you to your room to retrieve your things, or would you care to apologize for your ridiculous behavior?"

"You're just like your father," Jarlin frothed under his breath.

"*What* did you say?" My cheeks grew hot, flames burning through my veins.

"I said that we apologize," he spat. "Now call off your dogs so we can retire for the evening. This whole exchange has tired my poor wife out."

He fanned Nova in a manner that could only be described as dramatic as fuck. I nodded towards the guards, and they disappeared amongst the ballroom bustle, onlookers whispering to one another as they followed.

Expression stern, I stepped into Jarlin's space, gripping his tie with a wicked grin. "See that your attitude is greatly improved upon our next visit, Jarlin, or I'll be forced to take much more," I cinched his tie up to his throat tight and patted his chest, "aggressive measures. Do I make myself clear?"

He released a strained wheeze, his eyes murderous. "Crystal. Though, I might urge you to pay better attention to those you aim to make an enemy," he whispered as he passed, and tapped my champagne flute once. "You never know when one might sneak up, hellbent on revenge."

All warmth drained from my body as my sights fell into my glass. There, swirling in the bottom, was a fizzing tablet. Shit! Looking up in a panic, I searched for Jarlin who had seemingly vanished into thin air. The entire space stilled. Heartbeat racing, my sights tunneled onto one specific face. My knees buckled, Lyvias catching me as my glass shattered on the floor.

There, in full waitstaff attire, a tray of champagne flutes balanced on his arm: Odin.

With a wink, he disappeared into the crowd. Poison. He'd fucking poisoned me! My muscles turned to stone, body seizing as my vision went black. I heard the chaos, the gasps, Cadagon racing to my side and demanding to know what'd happened, but I couldn't see them. I couldn't feel their prying hands.

"Give her to me," I heard Lyvias growl out.

"I will handle this," Cadagon snarled back. "Step away."

"The poison is already taking hold; if you don't give her to me now, Death, she will die!"

I tried for breath, but every attempt was like sucking air through a straw. Never deep enough.

"Fine," Death finally bit out somewhere to my right. "Just save her, Lyvias. Please."

A moment later, my head hung loose as the sensation of being lifted into the air took hold. All sound dissipated, leaving me alone in utter darkness.

CHAPTER 16

ONE MORE HINT

I awoke to the sharp tang of iron, a twist in my muscles where my shadows curled in on themselves. Hiding. Burying themselves. The sensation was unsettling; it disturbed the soul.

My bedroom ceiling peeked out above, though it swayed in my blurry vision. Rolling my head to the side, Lyvias's face slowly came into view. Blood dripped from his mouth, his shirt soaked through with fresh crimson. The sharper the image became, the more my limbs shook and heartbeat quickened. Looking ever down, I latched onto bite marks in each of my wrists still bleeding out in puddles. A whimper crawled up my throat. What the hell was happening?

"Hey, hey, hey," Lyvias said, running a hand over my forehead. "It's okay, you're safe now. You're safe, Kim."

Tears rolled down my cheeks as I pushed to sit. He slid in close, supporting my back.

"You should lie still. You've lost a lot of blood." Carefully, he lifted me into his arms, settling me in my bed. Jaw tight, he began wrapping gauze around my wrists.

"What...what happened?" I finally asked, a deep cold settling in my bones.

Lyvias covered me in a wool blanket and crawled in next to me, his radiating heat stilling my shivers almost on contact. "Odin. He slipped something into your drink."

The hound's cocky grin burst through my mind, bits and pieces coming back to me. "Poison?"

Lyvias nodded in my peripheral. "Yes. But I got it out before it could take hold."

The way he dodged eye contact, his frame growing stiff against me, I knew there was more. Something he wasn't telling me. "What kind of poison?"

His breath hitched. There it was. "By the rotten taste, I'd say it was based in baneful magic. Dark." Another flash radiated through me. My shadows had grown feral, slipping about me of their own accord. A sourness settled in my gut. "Tell me, Lyvias," I forced out, mouth dry. "Tell me the truth. I can handle it."

He rolled to his back. "From what I could make out by taste alone, there were trace amounts of several beings in that poison. Or maybe 'hex' is a better word? I'm not entirely sure, but...I felt them. Their pain."

I pressed my eyes shut, hard. Coop's and my mission, the one that'd started it all, our hunt to acquire blood hailing from each court in order to draw Cadagon to us...such magic rarely lent itself without consequence. "Did it contain all four courts?"

His face fell. "Yes. Except one."

He didn't need to say it. I knew. All but reaper. All but mine.

"There's something else you should know," he muttered, hands clenching. "It attacked your body, yes, but your spirit, your essence...I almost lost you. It was as if your very spirit was rejecting your flesh, clawing free. The poison, I think it was—"

"Sacrificial," I whispered.

"Yes." He sighed. "I believe it was. And its core...one trace of blood stood out from the rest: Malachi."

Of course. The truth came crashing in. If Malachi wanted to sacrifice me, it had to be for my power: abilities granted only to the Reigning Reaper. Everything became clear in an instant. This wasn't about simply wanting to end my bloodline; it was about *replacing* it. He meant to devour me—the heir—to steal the old god's gift and take it for his own. Thus promoting him from Lord to Death incarnate.

Sobs seized me then, uncontrollable. It had never been about taking my life; it had been about stealing it. Owning me. Using me to overturn an entire kingdom by force. What's worse? I hadn't seen him coming. Not like that: in a room full of people, every eye on me. Guards posted at each door. Lords and ladies, dukes and duchesses, even Death himself at close range, and still he'd gotten to me. But Malachi knew that. He'd banked on me letting my guard down. He wanted me to know that wherever I went, he'd be there. Watching. Waiting.

A sudden thought overtook me, and I grabbed Lyvias's face. "Are you okay? The poison, did it—"

"No, Kim. I'm fine. I was careful not to swallow. Though I'm sorry to say, I think the stains might never come out." He pointed to my floor.

I chuckled. "I'll send you the bill."

We were royally fucked. A demon Lord backed by black magic. That was some supernatural reality show shit right there.

Lyvias pressed a kiss into my hair, sending a chill along my spine. He'd saved my life. Again. Risked everything for me, again. And yet, all I could muster was, "Thank you."

Brow pinched, he laid his head on my pillow, wrapping a loose lock behind my ear. After a few wordless minutes—the weight hitting us both like a crashing wave—he broke the silence. "Want to know something?"

My heart thrashed, chest warming. "I don't know, do I?"

"How about I give you a hint, and you tell me what you think?"

I stilled. Stomach twisted in invigorated knots, I nodded. Gods, those eyes. With a devious grin, he leaned closer, a silent plea to be closer in his gaze. Matching his motion, I shimmied my tattered body closer too as he wrapped an arm around my waist. The perfume of wine and consuming desire drifted about my senses, making my lungs labor.

He leaned closer. "Another hint?"

The nervous energy in my center begged to be appeased, settled. Locked in my gaze, he placed his free hand on my cheek and brushed his thumb against my bottom lip. I pressed into his touch, and familiarity encompassed me. The way I felt in his arms: it was like home. Not Anathema, but *home* home. In a sudden need to feel more, I begged through the darkness, "One more hint?"

"Okay," he breathed, and drew his mouth nearer but hovered a meager inch from mine. "But just one more."

His eyes blazed as he closed the space between us. His kiss: slow and gentle, patient and kind. This was more than need. More than desire. Warmth rolled through me, and I lost myself in the simple act, allowing myself to take shelter in his embrace. His fingers tangled in my hair, and I laced my arms around his neck—fresh bite marks on my wrists screaming—every nerve in my body alive. Pressed together, we lost ourselves in one another for what seemed like simple seconds but proved much longer.

Somewhere between passion and reality, Lyvias broke free and rested his forehead on mine. "You've forgotten something, Princess. Something Malachi can neither steal nor replicate."

My sights danced across his face.

"In two days, you'll take the throne."

Confusion twisted my features. "Yeah…"

"You'll be unkillable."

His words sank into me like a balm on sunburnt skin. He was right. If I could dodge Malachi a little longer, make it to coronation, there'd be nothing the asshole could do. I'd strike down Death, take his strength as my own, and become borderline immortal. I stared deep into Lyvias's eyes, hand brushing through his long hair. "I'm going to make this asshole rue the day he crossed me."

A growl reverberated past his fangs. "Damn straight he will, Lady Death. And I cannot wait to watch him burn."

I awoke to a strange lightness in my chest. Body still sore and rickety from the previous night's events, yet hope abounded. In twenty-four hours, I'd be deathless. And Malachi's head would be severed at my feet.

Lyvias and I had talked for hours about anything and everything, all the while he had held me tight to his chest. The kind of conversation I hadn't had since I'd lost Cooper. Hell, since before I'd even come to Anathema. Bitterness crept across my tongue. My best friend's absence still came as a shock each time I returned to it. And I always did. Here I was glaring down the barrel of my biggest life changes in little more than a day, and yet he wouldn't be there. Not to help me celebrate my twenty-first birthday, not to see me walk down the aisle, not for my coronation. But having Lyvias made it a little easier.

Lighter. Suffice it to say, I didn't aim to kill him. Not anymore. I rolled over to find my bed empty, but I slid into the muddled sheets where Lyvias had lain. His sweet scent lingered on the pillow, and I buried my nose in it. Divine.

Cooper would have loved my sarcastic, foul-mouthed betrothed. Honestly, he'd have probably tried to swoop in on him. The thought made me giggle as I crawled off the bed. June on the other hand? She would have hated Lyvias, no doubt. Not that I'd blame her. If it hadn't been for Fate and Death's cruel play, we'd still be together. My heart sank at the thought as her words came back to me in technicolor. *Let someone else in, Kim. You deserve to be loved.* I shook off the goosebumps and pushed the past from my mind. Coop. June. What was, was. I just hoped they were happy, wherever they were. They deserved that and more. They deserved…everything.

My morning was to be filled with last minute details and teatime amongst the guests in the gardens. I arrived and anxiously awaited Lyvias, anticipating his strong support at my side. But by early afternoon without a glimpse or word from him, I began to worry and excused myself to check his favorite places about the castle. The training grounds? Empty. The old study? Vacant. The dining hall? Unoccupied, aside from a guard posted at the entrance to the south tower stairwell. With nowhere left to search, I made my way to his bedroom.

"Lyvias, you alive in there?" No response. I knocked again, still nothing. When the fourth knock went unanswered, I tried the door to find it unlocked. "I'm coming in."

His room overflowed in melted candles, woven tapestries, and various gothic mirrors. Funny, I'd always assumed vampires couldn't use mirrors. Another mortal mistruth, I suppose. I strolled to the black sheet-covered bed, an envelope at the foot, and my insides snarled. It was addressed to me.

Kimber,

I don't really know where to start, so I guess I'll just come out and say it. I thought I could do this, be the king Anathema needed...the king you needed. But I'm not. I'm sorry. Please know I will always love you.

Lyvias

Confusion and betrayal and resentment twisted inside me as I crumpled the note, acid burning my throat. I'd let him in. Let him know me. Gave him a chance after everything I'd been through, and he had dipped on me in my final hour. Shadows riling within me, I tore the letter to shreds.

Gods, I'd been so dumb! A complete idiot: played by yet another man who gave zero shits what happened to anyone but himself. He'd led me on, convinced me I wouldn't be alone in all the mess I would inherit from Cadagon, the threat still looming in Malachi's wake. He'd promised we'd handle it together. All this talk about how we were a team and I wasn't alone, and I'd believed him. Trusted him. But he'd left. Abandoned me like everyone else, and I—

Fuck. Fuck!

I threw a fist at the nearest mirror, shattering it to pieces. Satisfying pain tore through me—my knuckles freshly split—as I paced about the room. Red seeped beneath the gauze on my wrist, and I wished I could remove Lyvias's mark from my flesh. Cut it out like I should have done with him. In the end, *he* turned out to be the cancer. Not me. The drip, drip, drip of blood helped steady my breath as I considered my options. Did I *need* a king at my side? After all, I'd come into this solo. Nails buried in my palms, it became devastatingly apparent that I'd end this the same way I'd started it. Alone.

A thick, sinister *tsk* rippled from the door, and my head snapped up. "Nasheesh?"

"It's a shame," he said, leaning against the door frame. "Your vampire love getting cold feet like that."

My guts churned. "What the hell do you want?"

"I merely came to check how you were fairing the day before your wedding, Princess, out of the goodness of my heart."

Filthy liar. "Goodness? Right."

"It is the truth. See, if I didn't stop by, who would have told you about the cast change in tomorrow's event?"

I clenched my fists, blood puddling at my feet. "What are you talking about?"

"Oh, so now you want my help, huh?"

"Speak," I snapped, fury building.

"There's no reason to raise your voice. It's unladylike," he baited, and stood to his full height. "I simply meant to explain Anathema's binding law upon, well, marital abandonment."

"Spit it out already, old man."

Darkness teemed in his eyes. "Come now, is that any way to speak to your future father-in-law?"

My stomach dropped. "What?"

"In plain terms?" He smirked and sauntered into the room, arrogance wafting about him. "A ruler *must* claim the throne with a counterpart, no exceptions. You will marry tomorrow with or without Lyvias. The right will pass to the next court's representative."

"The reaper court," I tried, desperate.

"Wrong." His cocky smile widened. "That time came to pass

before your half-shifter mother's rule."

My toes curled as I fought the rising dread. While a part of me knew what was coming, accepting it was another thing entirely. I'd fought so hard. Built a life despite the many attempts on it and even managed to snag a glimmer of hope in the process. But in the end, it came down to one bitter, sobering truth. I swallowed. Reaper, shifter, vampire…that left—

"The demon court, yes," he answered, seemingly reading my mind. "You will marry Lord Malachi Avarti." His grin nearly leapt from his face. "My son."

Cold, harsh clarity slapped me across the face. Lyvias's letter stole my attention for a brief moment before I turned back towards Nasheesh. My jaw ticked. "You did this. You chased him away, didn't you?" I shrieked, and hurled a nearby candle at his head. "Tell me where he is!"

He dodged effortlessly, a satisfied laugh rolling through him. "I don't know what you're talking about. He didn't want you. I mean, look at yourself; can you blame him?"

"You monster." My power thrashed to the surface, and a violent wind ripped through the room. I would end this piece of shit. Put him in an early grave like he so deserved.

"My son is the true ruler Anathema deserves," he said, walking closer, devoid of fear. "Seeing as you've managed to slip past our attempts to end your wretched bloodline thus far, we had to take more…desperate measures. He will tame you. Teach you. Or he will end you. Your choice."

"No, he won't, Nassie," I bit out, the wind around me growing more vicious. "I will take the throne alone. *My* throne. And you both will taste my blades for high treason!"

"You think so, do you?" He paused and raised an eyebrow. "I have something I think may just convince you otherwise. You see, I've taken much more than your bloodsucker to ensure your compliance, Princess."

He walked to the nearest mirror, tracing a finger along its surface. Dark magic rippled in his wake, and an image began to form. Every muscle turned to stone as I watched in horror. No. No fucking way. I fell to my knees, throat tightening. There, bound and frantic, sat my worst fear. "Mom?"

Her gaze flicked to mine. "Honey, whatever he tells you, don't listen to him! Protect yourself; that's all that matters—"

Nasheesh smashed the mirror. "Enough of that. She talks so much, your mother, drives me positively insane. That must be where you get your foul mouth from."

I stilled, rage bubbling over. My vision blurred, the magic inside me trembling. Begging me to end this bastard. Now. I lifted a hand, ready to take his head clean off his body and mail it home to his precious Malachi.

"Ah, ah," he said. "I wouldn't do that if I were you. Did you really think I wouldn't have precautions in place for another one of your little temper tantrums, child? Should any harm come to me, my associates have their orders."

There had to be a way to save her. To get to her before Nasheesh could. Death: he'd loved my mother in his own screwed-up way. He'd never let harm come to her; my instincts assured me. Sure, he hated the world—maybe even me—but not her. I tilted my head up, stance fixed. "When the king hears about this, he'll tear you apart at the seams!"

"Oh, on the contrary. You see, this whole thing was his idea to begin with."

My chest tightened. Lungs shrunk. Cadagon was wicked, sure,

but…my mother? Filthy liars, all of them! I paced about the room, lightheaded and on the verge of truly breaking. Shattering into a million pieces that I feared would never be repairable. Who did I have left to put me back together? Nobody. They were gone; and if I broke? Well, that would be it. The end. And the crooked man who stood before me: he'd win. My shadows coiled around my heart, but their comfort proved worthless.

I'd lost.

"Now that I have your full attention," Nasheesh said, and lowered himself into my sight line, lording his false power. "You will walk down the aisle, wait at the altar like a good girl, and you. Will. Marry. Malachi. Oh, and should you utter a word to anyone, try to stop me in any way or attempt to flee, I assure you: your mother will meet the same fate as the others who have denied me." He snatched my chin, jerking it upwards. "A slow, agonizing death."

CHAPTER 17

AN UNHOLY UNION

I stood, black veil hung over swollen eyes, ready to meet the ominous future that awaited me at the altar. All night I'd wept and plotted, searched for any possible way to spare my mother's life and also avoid a horrific union to Nasheesh's piece-of-shit, treasonous son. Though, try as I might, I found no way to ensure both. The gods' awful truth? Nasheesh had me trapped, backed into a damn corner with nowhere to go.

On bended knee, Suri tended to my bustled gown, her sights on me.

"Are you okay?" She asked, voice almost a whisper.

I didn't respond. There was nothing to say. Nothing to be done. So I forced a smile that didn't reach my eyes and nodded.

"You are a shitty liar; you do know that, right?" Suri's gaze lingered, but she didn't press.

Her expression said that she knew more was afoot than just my altogether understandable disdain for an arranged marriage. Little did she know an imminent marriage to a man I'd never met, let alone loved, was now in store. As much as I yearned to spew the awful news about my mother, about Lyvias, about Nasheesh, I choked it down like a mouthful of gravel. The less Suri knew, the safer she was. Though it killed me, I knew I had to suffer in silence. For her. Never mind how loud my shattered heart screamed. But I would have my revenge. And I'd make it slow.

When I didn't speak yet again, Suri's lips thinned. "Right. Somber Kimber, got it."

She huffed to her feet—dress now tailored to perfection—and motioned towards the mirror.

"So...what do you think?"

I twisted towards the mirror, and my breath snagged. I was a gods' damned vision: smoky eyes, crimson lips, ashen curls tousled about my shoulders. The black gown's silhouette highlighted my curves with a sense of urgency, giving off an old-timey, Polaroid picture vibe, like I was the only woman in the room. Ever. A sight to behold, and yet my groom wouldn't give two shits. He wouldn't know the lengths I'd gone to end up in such a gown. Wouldn't know what I'd sacrificed to ascend the throne nor the insecurities I'd overcome. Neither the people I'd lost nor the home I'd left behind. The nagging nausea in my center reminded me of the sad truth: I wasn't Malachi's prize. My throne was.

"Kim?" Suri broke through. "Are...are you not satisfied? Would you like me to change something? Anything?"

I bit my cheek and wrapped my arms around Suri, squeezing her tight. Tears threatened to flow, but I pushed them down.

"It's perfect. *You* are perfect," I said, my hold remaining firm for a few more seconds. I pulled back and wrapped my hands around her cheeks, placing a quick kiss on her forehead. This was it. My time had run out. With a reassured nod—more for my own encouragement than Suri's—my gem-studded stilettos clicked across the hardwood floor to the door, and I breezed into the spiraling staircase, sights set on the garden.

The halls sat still. Every guest and servant awaited my arrival under the bare oak trees, and I fought against the panic, swapping it for rage instead. Each step proved heavier. My thoughts darkened. Alone I'd come to this world of eternal night, and alone I'd take up my rightful place. While tradition bound me to a counterpart, *I* would rule over Anathema. Malachi might have the upper hand, but I'd see to his suffering. Denounce his rights and assign him the role he seemed so fit to fill: scavenger. Yes, I would tend to his torment personally. For both Lyvias and my mother's sake. They deserved justice. Gods, I could only imagine where they were. What torment they'd been subjected to.

Fucking Nasheesh.

When my heels clicked on ground level, I paused to refocus. Mere minutes stood between me and my future. The Reigning Reaper, Queen, Death incarnate: all...me. Before I could stop it, a sinister laugh spilled from my lips, building until it grew so loud I feared I might never stop. Oh, the horrors Nasheesh had coming. It'd be a masterpiece: his end. He would rue the fucking day he crossed me.

A new sense of purpose overtook me then, and I ushered for the lone doorkeeper to hop to. I swept down the front stairs, wound around the corner, and ambled beneath the rose-covered gates. I knew then, clear as night.

Revenge. *That* would be my reign.

Not only for me and the ones I loved, but for every woman and child afflicted by the crooked men in power who should have been their protectors. Their guardians. But instead, they raped, pillaged, and burned anyone in their path that didn't serve their needs. Fuck. Them.

I snuck about the garden's dark recesses, careful to avoid the already seated crowd's detection, and marveled at the grim fairy tale scene dead ahead. Black ribbons littered the treetops, a red paisley runner—drenched in candlelight courtesy of staggered, ornate candelabras—jutted through the center aisle, ending under a grand, polished bone and silver archway. My girl had outdone herself. I made a mental note to spoil the hell out of Suri the next time I saw her. I was thinking something along the lines of "Personal Advisor to the Queen" and an all-expenses-paid shopping spree at the most prestigious jeweler I could find.

A servant wafted to my side in sudden realization. "Your Highness, are you ready? Shall we start the music?"

"Yes. Just need a moment."

"Certainly." He nodded, but remained in place.

"Alone," I said, and he scampered away, forehead creased.

Cadagon's voice filled my ears as he wafted from the shadows, his tone oddly gentle. "My, my," he said, looking me over. "You are quite a vision, my daughter."

I bit my tongue, nails digging into my palms. It wasn't worth it, fighting him. No point in rehashing his lacking as a father or a role model, little sense in reminding him of all the damage and havoc he'd caused. Not when his death was so close at hand. I'd let my shadows do the talking as they ripped out his shriveled heart.

With a smile that crinkled the corners of his eyes—his throat bobbing with a tense swallow—he removed a silk cover from the ornate wooden box in his hands I hadn't noticed until then. His fingers twiddled about the chest's edges, lips turned up in an expectant grin.

My sights trailed from him to his offering and back again. "What is it?"

"Open it and find out." He extended it. "The locks will obey your hands and yours alone, same as the contents within."

Focusing back on the box, I sent a shadow to explore the lock, and the hinges popped open on contact. I met Cadagon's anticipated gaze, parted the material, and caught my first glimpse at quite possibly the most beautiful pair of blades I'd ever seen nestled in a bed of lace.

"My scythes," I muttered, and ran a finger down the curved, black daggers. Their cool touch sang to me. Red gemstones encrusted the weapon's full lengths; intricate rose vines spiraled along their handles. Had I ordered the blades made personally, I doubted they'd have come out with such vision. They were so familiar, so... me. But how? This man hadn't the slightest clue who I was. He couldn't name my favorite food or movie. Had no idea of the heartbreaks I'd had growing up. He was not a father. He knew nothing. And yet, the blades were perfect.

"And look here." Cadagon pointed to the hilt's base, his eyes literally glowing.

I turned one over in my hands, and my breath caught. Carved deep: a sun, rays of light streaming out. The symbol for Fate. Elysium. Turning over the other, I found a crimson crescent moon. The symbol for Anathema.

"I know how hard it is," Death whispered, placing a hand on my shoulder. "I too offered a great sacrifice to Fate. But this way, you can keep a part of her light with you always. A small reminder when the road gets steep and all you see is darkness."

Warmth pressed behind my eyes. June. She'd be with me always, her light.

The gesture threw me. How incredibly thoughtful of Death. Kind, even. And furthermore, how unsettling. Empathy did not become Cadagon. Or maybe I'd just never seen it there, hidden in his stare. Lost for words, I lifted each blade from their bed, and swung them about. My heart leapt at the crisp slice they made through the air: glorious. "They're perfect..."

"I'm quite pleased to hear it." He handed the empty chest to a passing guard. "I wish for everything involving your big day to be so: perfect. Happy birthday, dear one."

Again, words evaded me. Sitting in the nearest chair, I blocked out the world. Letting my eyes fall shut and lungs relax, I attempted to calm my rapid heartbeat. Shadows crept from my fingers, lacing their way across my new scythes in examination. A giggle returned to me. They were pleased. And I knew exactly whose blood those blades would taste first.

"It's alright, Kimber." Cadagon broke through the silence, pulling my attention back to him. "This is to be your revival, a grand new start to an altogether more balanced future by your hand. Balance I could not restore despite my many attempts. Whoever your groom shall be, you will be the queen of change. Mark my words."

My fury verged on destructive—all remnants of Death's recent benevolence gone in a heartbeat—eager to billow over and devour anyone who stood in its way. Cadagon, a plague upon this realm and the next, had the audacity to spit out yet another lie. The need for change existed because *he* had created unrest! Cooper's vegetative existence, Lyvias's disappearance, my mother's capture, not to mention the shifter massacre: all him! Anathema faced imbalance because he'd chosen himself over his people without fail. So much chaos, and yet his insatiable hunger for destruction yearned for more, yearned to put an end to the one person who'd given him a chance to become more than just a monster. My sweet, patient mother. He'd conspired with Nasheesh and in doing so, had forced my hand.

Amongst Death's incessant lies, he'd spoken one truth. I *would* be the change, the start to a new era where Cadagon would cease to exist. Wrath, delicious and intense, seeped about my veins. I boasted a wide grin, cracked my neck, and snapped at the nearest guard, "I'm ready."

Death offered a parting nod, expression almost pained, and started towards the altar.

Suri's gentle smile greeted me at the aisle's start, her dainty frame tucked behind an ivy wall. "You can do this," she said softly, and smoothed the black veil over my face.

"I have to."

A dark symphony erupted in lamenting song the second I showed my face, and I clutched my blades with white-knuckle force, grateful for what little concealment my veil provided.

Death smirked from atop the bone altar, the centuries' old *Book of Shade* open in his hand. He puffed out his chest and scanned the crowd. "Announcing Miss Kimberly Ann Bradshaw, Princess of Anathema."

In succession, the crowd stood and gawked. Their comments, both well-intentioned and pointed, filled the air as I started a slow march towards uncertainty. Harsh jabs regarding myself dominated the chatter, but I found myself grinning. I knew I looked damn good. Jealous fools, the lot of them.

The hushed undertones, however—the ones centered on Lyvias's absence—those stung. Some proclaimed cowardice while others claimed it for the better, but one comment in specific took the cake for most vicious. They blamed me. Me: who cared more about his disappearance than I could put into words, let alone understand. Insecurities nipped at my heels, but my steps didn't falter. Their opinions were nothing but uneducated stabs, shallow, high society gossip. I knew the truth, and it reflected back at me on the advisor's treasonous face.

At his side, a man made of pure darkness sat, billows of black smoke ebbing and flowing all around him. Malachi. Still cowering behind his shadows, his only visible features were those penetrating emerald eyes, discernible details concealed from any onlookers. Even his bride to be. A rock settled in my center as I launched daggers through my stare. If the asshole had any care, he certainly didn't show it as his attention fell towards the altar. But Nasheesh? He held my gaze with intensity as if my discomfort was the very air he needed to stay alive. Head held high, I passed them, hiked the stairs, and stopped at Death's side.

"You may be seated," Cadagon called to the crowd, giving me a soft glance, and began to read from the book in his hand. "Night's appeasement, the backbone of our society in Anathema, has always been granted through the Reigning Reaper's inherent strength. Their power, stemmed from all four courts, balanced by Fate and Death themselves, sustains our teetering existence over the void, and has since before time began. Today, we honor our newest Reigning Reaper, my daughter, wielder of dual scythes." He focused on me. "Tell me, Kimberly, do you seek to restore and retain balance among your people for the duration of your rule?"

I turned to him, calm and collected, though ferocity itched under my skin. "I do."

"And do you swear to put this great realm and its citizens above yourself in all regards, even should it lead you to Death's door?"

"I do."

"Let it be known amongst the masses," Cadagon boomed, and outstretched his arm. "Your future queen bestows a promise upon you." Again, he turned to me. "Give me your hand."

Cadagon retrieved my rightmost scythe, arranged my open hand next to his, and with one swift stroke, sliced both our palms wide open. While it burned, I didn't wince or inhale, didn't flinch in the slightest, all the while remaining fixed on him. Blood pattered to the carpet in steady drops, hardly distinguishable against its crimson red threads. Red: the same hue as Lyvias's eyes. My heart fell.

"A pact in blood to seal our new leader's fate," he called before his inflamed irises landed back on me. "A pact in blood is binding, as you well know. If you should turn from the promise you make to the void here today, our world's balanced state will cease to exist. By law, you are to make your choice here and now. If you seek the void's path, take Death's hand. But if you should wish a breach in the royal bloodline, leave now. You have only one opportunity to walk away with your life intact."

I stole a glance towards the crowd, towards Nasheesh, and my heart clapped against my ribs, my ears growing hot. This was it: the moment I'd become my true self, for better or worse. With a condescending grin at the crooked advisor—a malicious promise written on my face just for him—I took Death's bloody hand in mine. "I will serve this realm until my dying breath."

Cadagon's clutch on me tightened. "And so it shall be."

Our blood meshed and swirled like it possessed a life entirely its own, and Cadagon released his hold. Beautiful in the strangest way, a gray fog trickled from the puddled blood in my palm and leeched into the open air above in brilliant plumes. Magic: ravenous for a host. It traced a vaporous touch across my scythes, wound itself in my hair and around my limbs. The essence was fucking intoxicating. Addictive. Then, without prompt, the magic crept between my ruby lips, covering my teeth in the dry tang of blood and ash.

My gods, this feeling.

It hit my bloodstream, spider-walked up my spine, and sank into each solitary cell in my body. Death's cheeks turned to chalk, his powers no longer his own. No, they were mine now: the strength, the title, the raw power. I surveyed his crown, a wicked hunger ripe within me. I had to have it. Cadagon assessed me briefly, a woeful glimmer in his stare.

"Now," Death continued, "as is customary in the coronation ceremony, you will make an oath to your counterpart. This is a pledge of allegiance, a promise to rule with a shared responsibility to Anathema's fragile equilibrium, and all who dwell within it." He squared his shoulders and called out, though the asshole already knew my betrothed wouldn't answer. "Sir Lyvias Kraven, warrior of the court of substance, come forth."

I searched the crowd in vain, a shallow hope buried deep inside me. But as I'd assumed, there was no shuffle in the back row or movement towards my position. Only empty, deafening silence. It wasn't long before disapproval reared its ugly head. The guests began to comment. Their whispers intensified, growing louder with each passing second. Discord began to erupt.

"Silence," Cadagon snarled. "This is not the first time Anathema has happened upon such an occurrence, and I bid you all to remember your place!"

More raised voices demanded the king's solution to the supposed atrocity. Questions of rank, status, and orientation in the courts' rotation to the throne began to rile the crowd further.

"An outrage," one called it.

"Blasphemy," said another.

Death raised his hands. "I assure you; we will settle this. As is stipulated in *The Book of Shade*, the next fitting champion is to take the betrothed's place."

A chill crept up my spine as shadows laced through the crowd like vipers, one coming to coil around my ankle. Malachi stood—the coin clinking in his fingers making me damn near murderous as I recalled what he'd done to Cooper—and turned towards the masses, face still concealed.

"I, Malachi Avarti, warrior of the court of power, volunteer to stand in the coward's place," he said, his voice course like sandpaper on dry stone.

"He isn't a coward," I snarled, simultaneously smashing Malachi's shadow under my foot, sending it slithering back to its master.

"Kimber, be calm," Cadagon whispered, jaw tense. He turned to the crowd. "Are there any other warriors in our midst who wish to step forward? Offer themselves as a tribute to the crown—"

"With all due respect, Highness," Nasheesh interjected, an edge in his words. "Such a thing is not customary. *The Book of Shade* clearly states that the next court in rotation is to have the first right, and the demon court is more than happy to oblige. Unless you'd deny us our inherent right?"

Death met my gaze and released a pent-up breath. "Come forward then."

Malachi strutted to the altar, a haughty air about him, and hiked the stairs, the thick darkness around him dancing with visible excitement. He offered a half-ass greeting purely for appearances before facing Cadagon.

I looked him over. A new, severe rage, backed by the full weight of Cadagon's power—no, *my* power—begged to sever flesh from bone. To dig through those shadows, find his neck, and snap it. Instead, I turned to him, and with poison in my voice, I said, "Would you deny your bride a chance to gaze upon the face of her future? Or shall you hide?"

His eyes snapped to me. "This *is* me. My looks should be of no consequence to you."

Arrogant bastard. He was probably ugly as hell under there, and his fragile ego wouldn't let him live it down. I shifted my weight, transferred the fury in my gut to my hands, and clenched them taut around my scythes. Malachi honed in on me, and sudden images fluttered about my mind in rapid succession. Each image proved more disturbed than the last, but all were of my lifeless body. Head on a spike. Severed limb from limb. Impaled. Had...had he made me see those things? But...how? Who the hell was this monster?

"Let the union commence," Cadagon called.

He drawled on with more passages from his book, all centered around partnership, respect, and honor. None of which I'd ever have with Malachi. I let my magic float about me, willing my consciousness forward. It swept across his shadows and burrowed deep, though he didn't appear to notice. Or maybe he didn't care. His energy—thick and vicious—shook me to my core. Twisted my guts. He noticed me then and winked, lowering an unforeseen glamour over his eyes so only I could witness the threat held beneath. Bile seeped into my mouth. Shit.

So it was true.

This was no demon. He was the fucking hybrid. Evil incarnate stood before me. I rattled through my options as panic settled in my bloodstream. I was trapped like a caged animal. Any attempt to stop him would only lead to dire consequences for my mother. And I wasn't about to fuck with that. But if I allowed the ceremony to continue, well, the strength Malachi would inherit through our union might just promote him from hybrid grunt to my equal. Or worse, my superior. Either way, without the coronation's completion, I'd never hold onto to my newfound power. And no power meant no chance in hell I'd beat him. If I was going to put this atrocity in his place, I'd need Death's strength permanently. *My* strength. So I stilled my thrashing heart and tuned out Cadagon as he rattled on about things I could give two shits about. All I could focus on was the sharp thirst for revenge in my gut.

Cadagon tore my scythe from my grip—bringing me back to attention—and snatched my still bloody hand. "Do you agree to this union? To binding your soul to the court of power and sharing your rule with Malachi Avarti?"

I froze, my tongue stuck to the roof of my mouth.

Malachi grew antsy. "Speak up," he hissed low enough for my ears alone.

"Don't you dare order me," I seethed under my breath. The way he spoke, his smug expression: it reminded me of Lyvias's and my first encounter. Before he'd changed and laid claim to my heart. I'd never expected that I'd actually want that cocky vampire by my side in this moment, but he was all I could see. Fuck, this was harder than I'd expected. The silence thickened, the blood in my veins turning to ice.

Again, the crowd roared their opinions.

"Silence," Cadagon demanded again. "Princess, you *must* answer."

"I-I..." Words escaped me as I looked Malachi over once more. Liar. Deceiver. Murderer. No life we'd share would ever be worth living. But I had to. For my people. Yet my mouth refused to cooperate. "Well, I—"

"I object," a loud voice cut through the silence.

Every head spun to face the garden gates. There, drenched in blood, sweat, and dirt, stood Lyvias. The tension in my chest released, warmth pushing behind my eyes.

He'd come for me.

ℭHAPTER 18

HYBRID BLOOD

Lyvias limped forward. "It is my right, and mine alone, to stand by the queen's side."

I abandoned my post, one scythe still clenched in a fist, and ran to him. His face lit up at my approach, and my stomach leapt as those crimson pools locked onto me.

"You came back," I whispered once at his side.

"I'll always come for you," he said, and drug a shaky thumb across my cheek.

His energy zapped through me, and I took in his wounds. A dislocated shoulder, countless open and gushing cuts, a busted lip. I grew murderous as I hoisted his arm over my shoulders. But that would have to wait a little longer. We needed to present ourselves as a united front. To show our people that nothing could break us. Nothing.

Nasheesh shot from his seat. "Sire, this is blasphemous; the ceremony has already begun!"

"What is blasphemous," Lyvias called, limping at my side, "are the lengths you went to keep me from being here today, Nasheesh Avarti. Tell them: how you sought me out in the dead of night, stole me away, and saw to my torture by your own hand."

The guests went from shock to horror to ravenous. Talk of treason abounded. People began to stand, demanding Nasheesh's death, right then and there. Not that I blamed them; I too wanted that. But Cadagon waved a hand, settling them with the power still lingering in him that was yet to be mine.

"Calm yourselves," he demanded, and turned. "Malachi Avarti, step down."

"I-I had no knowledge of this," Malachi lied through his teeth.

But Death snapped once, sealing his mouth, and armed guards emerged from every hidden space about the garden, easily fifteen men strong.

A sinister smile teemed on Cadagon's face. "Guards, see that these traitors remain firmly planted in their seats without any further disruptions. I want them to see their own failing firsthand before they lose their sight completely. Lyvias, Kimberly, please take your rightful places."

Gods, I couldn't wait to see the light fade from their eyes when I snuffed them out like a candle.

"The future queen's coronation is why we gather here," Cadagon continued. "A trial and investigation will be launched in regards to this matter, I promise you, but let us not forget the purpose of this unholy night."

The guests reluctantly sat. My soul thrashed. How I ached to run my blades through both treasonous disasters, but I bit my tongue and faced Lyvias. I found peace in his stare as though he neither saw nor cared about anything else in that moment, and it stilled the thrashing magic in me like a balm on a fresh burn.

Cadagon projected into the crowd. "Royal heirs, take one another's hands and repeat after me. 'Bound in blood and rite, I will lead my people through eternal night.'"

We did what was asked, repeating the words as a solid oath. It dawned on me then that I believed it. We would do just that. "Together," Lyvias mouthed, reading my mind.

"Once again," Death said, "we come to a pact in blood."

I drew my scythe down my left palm—the one untouched by the night's first pact—and did the same across Lyvias's. Our attention never strayed from one another as we clenched our marred hands together. His essence seeped into me, a heady euphoria caressing as it flowed. We were one. Bonded in darkness.

Cadagon addressed the masses again. "By night and balance bestowed to me by Fate herself, I deem this marriage bound. Both of you take a knee."

A servant hurried from the recesses and extended an ornate copper box to Death. From it, Cadagon removed a charred-bone crown, and with a seemingly genuine smile, placed it on Lyvias's head. Cadagon faced me then, removed his own crown, and placed it atop my head.

Settling into my sight line, Death tipped my chin up. "I am so proud of you, my daughter. Now rise, Queen and King of Anathema, and seal your nightly union with a kiss, like your forefathers and mothers before."

This was it. Lyvias's and my blood called to each other then, begging to be nearer still. A strange peace washed over me as chills flushed across my chest. The vision before me stole my breath as Lyvias stepped closer and peeled back my veil. No turning back. He pushed the hair from my face the same way he'd done countless times. When he'd saved me. Healed me. Protected me. My stomach jumped. Like a consuming fire, his lips met mine, burning with firm assuredness. The sensation embedded itself in my being, and I relinquished control, lost in unfettered passion. In that moment, all else fell away, leaving just us. Him. His hands around my waist pulled me closer, need thrashing through his kiss. Together, we would be the change. My partner. My husband.

My king.

Sudden chaos pricked my ears; gasps, scuffled movements, and curses rose from the crowd.

"Intruder!" one screamed.

"Falsifier!" yelled another.

In quick succession, Lyvias's frame dissolved to reveal the truth hidden in plain sight. The heat drained from my cheeks. I stepped back and beheld the man whose arms still encircled me, blinking to clear away the vision before me. But he stayed, unmoving. I swallowed hard. "Cooper?"

"My Queen." He bowed.

Heart crashing against my ribs, I beheld him with brand new eyes, like I'd never truly seen until then. Calm and collected, he cradled my chin in his hand, and the memories tore through me in rapid succession. How he'd torn the hounds limb from limb. The way he'd loved me so gently as he carried me to safety, setting me in the bath. When he'd held off Death to give me the chance to say goodbye to Fate. Calling me Kim and never my full name. His refusal to lay with me that night because of the secrets from his past. Hell, the man literally sucked poison from my veins. *Of course*, it was Coop.

It'd always been him.

His dark sights honed in on me—his eyes now his own: burnt caramel and smoke. And the gentle quirk of his jaw...butterflies erupted in my gut. But...how? Breath laboring, I snagged his sleeve and drew him in close. "What is happening? How are you here? How…just, how?"

Cadagon's voice faded into the background as he addressed the crowd, attempting to calm the forming riot as they screamed for an explanation on where the real Lyvias Kraven was. But I remained locked in place as if my feet had fused to the ground. Cooper wrapped me in his strong arms inked in poisonous flowers, and I buried my face in his chest. Melted into him. The familiar scent of blood and wine carried around him. *His* smell. Not Lyvias's. His. How I hadn't connected the dots sooner... I should have known. A tinge of guilt struck me. While he'd know me anywhere, I'd missed him. Never expected his salvation. Tears pooled, threatening to undo me, but I forced them back down. My knight in shadowed armor. He'd come for me. "Was…was it you all along?"

"Almost," he whispered into my hair, and kissed my brow. His hold tightened as he looked over the destruction around us. "I'll tell you everything, Kim, I promise. But you have to trust me right now. End this madness, Lady Death. You're the only one who can. I'll be here waiting when the ashes settle."

I followed his sight line, and my power surged. Cadagon. Throat tight, I shifted on my feet. "I don't know if I can do this," I said low enough for only Cooper's ears.

He tilted my chin up; his lips devoured me. Sparks raced through every corner of my body, goosebumps rising up as his power brushed mine. When he finally broke our hold, I found violence woven into his grin as he asked, "Together?"

I nodded with a depraved smile of my own. "Together."

Cadagon grabbed my shoulder hard, snapping me back into the moment. "They've gone mad," he snarled. "They refuse to hear reason! I can do nothing!"

But I could. No, *we* could.

I watched in stunned silence as Coop wrapped his hands around mine—blade tight in my grasp—and hurled our combined strength through the air, burying my scythe to the hilt in Death's chest.

White noise tangled in my ears. The once mighty Death locked his sights on me, mouth gaping open, and clutched at the blade. Coop dropped his hold, but me? Mine tightened around the weapon's grip, and Cadagon sunk to his knees. His time had come. I'd signed and sealed his fate, as I'd promised. Removed the filthy smudge from Anathema's history.

The life drained from him the way a firefly's light disappears in the night, his soul hanging on by a thread. The black stains on his fingertips crept through the blade between us and edged under my fingernails. Dropping my hand a second too late, I studied the swirling darkness as it splayed up my wrists and sank in. My top lip arched in sudden satisfaction. Death's timeless spirit had abandoned the old king and claimed me as its new vessel. And my, my, how sweet its clutches.

I turned to behold my people, jaw taut. They'd gone mad. The scene slowed, adrenaline settling into my veins as I beheld the utter chaos. Chairs flung through the air, brawls breaking out along the outskirts. They were killing each other, divided by more than what they'd just witnessed. This had been years coming, and here I was: frozen, consumed by one thing alone. Amongst the thrashing sounds, Cadagon's heartbeat echoed in my ears, each beat slower than the last. From a pitter-patter to an off-beat click. I turned, hands cemented around my blades, and found the strangest of sights. Cadagon's soul splayed out around him; its slithery, charcoal aura pooled at my feet. His familiar presence loomed, smothered. Him, but in his most basic form. My shadows dipped in and out of the dying soul, curious. I stooped to my knees, drug two fingers through the black fog, and silently encouraged Cadagon's spirit to let go, to move on. Ruthless or not, no soul deserved to suffer. One last thump, and his heart went silent, spirit sinking into the soil with a hiss.

Goodbye, Cadagon. May you land where you deserve.

With the scene back in real time, I turned to Cooper. Hands frantically patting his cheeks, I swept a long, dark lock off his face. He was here. He was real. He was…my husband!

But I had no time to question him as my people's panicked cries pierced the night. With my newfound power thumping in my bloodstream, I took in the horror all around me. Shadows tore through the crowd, slicing flesh clear to the bone. Ripping open guards before they could raise their weapons. At the center of it all, Malachi stood motionless. His darkness slaughtered and marred of its own volition. In the madness, he turned and gave me a wink.

Game the fuck on.

An all-consuming laugh tore through me as I pushed my shoulders back, the Reigning Reaper's darkness within burning my eyes. Sights locked on Malachi, I uttered but one word that my power delivered straight to his ears: "Run."

For the first time, his confidence noticeably wavered. And to my surprise, he did as he was told, flitting off into the night like the coward he was. Attention set on the present, I waded into the continued madness and bloodshed, and sent my shadows to devour the lingering ones Malachi had left behind. In mere minutes, one man had caused so much death and destruction. But I was something more now. Something stronger.

I was *Queen*.

Collecting my scythes in one hand, I raised the other to the sky, and the moon flushed red. Thunder cracked. The guests froze mid-motion, their bodies claimed by my invisible chill.

"Get ahold of yourselves, all of you," I hissed, my voice new and silken.

"I warned you about her," Duke Jarlin's voice rang out from the crowd. "I warned you all that she was not fit to lead, but no! You wouldn't even consider my words as truth, and now look."

The traitorous rot in his aura wafted about me, so strong it singed my nose, like sulfur and brimstone. He'd been working with Nasheesh and Malachi. I felt it in my bones. "Duke Jarlin, you've been found guilty of treason."

His eyes widened. "What, you can't just—"

I snapped once, and the demon turned to soot blown on the wind. Excitement tickled my skin, a satisfying shiver running up my spine.

Cooper laced a hand through mine and squeezed once. "You are absolutely terrifying, my Queen."

I offered him a smirk before raising my pinched fingers and addressing my people once more. "Tell me. Is there anyone else present who wishes to question my authority? By all means, do speak up."

Utter silence.

"Nobody?" I asked again. "Not a single, solitary person will question me as Duke Jarlin did? I'm all ears." I swept down the aisle, silent as death. "Good. Return to your homes. Forget what you've seen here today and await my next decree."

Freed from their invisible holds, the guests trailed out the garden gates.

Now to go hunting.

Instinct swept in, and I placed my palms in the garden soil, using its energy to fuel my search of the castle grounds. Hurled through space and time in my mind's eye, I found the advisor first, cocky, anticipated grin and all. Nasheesh. He was in my suite, but he was alone. What a deadly mistake on his part.

"Guards," I called to the two in my midst still breathing. They were before me in seconds. "Take the new king and find the advisor's son by any means necessary, but return him alive." My nails tapped against my blades. "I'd like to have the joy of ending his life myself."

Cooper placed a quick kiss on my cheek, leaning in to whisper, "Give him hell," before setting off with the guards in haste.

My magic spoke to me then: "Tell us where you aim to be, Lady Death, and we shall make it so." With a sharp inhale, I pictured my suite. Wind whipped about me—the whoosh of one thousand bat wings all around—and in a second's time, I found myself there. Nasheesh sat with legs crossed on the edge of my bed. Waiting.

"You," I seethed.

"Came for my head, I presume?"

"I feel it's only fair, don't you, Nassie? I mean, you tortured people I love and plotted the downfall of my entire kingdom, for hell's sake." I stepped closer. "I must say, I'd expected you'd run like the coward you are, not wait around for your end."

"I am many things, but a coward is not one of them." He sneered. "I am also no fool. I know the powers you now possess. If I had run, you'd have tracked me. At my age, I'm beyond such petty cat-and-mouse games."

A lie. I looked him over, a sour tinge on my tongue. "You're hiding something; I can taste it."

"And what would I hide from you, hmm? You've won."

Another lie. "Where is she?"

His eyes darkened. "Why, who dear?"

I fought the urge to sever him in two, my unseen grasp pinning him in place. "You know who. My mother, you idiot."

"Ah yes, her." He tapped his chin, a challenge in his tone. "I've no reason to keep her anymore, given my *obvious* failure. Your marriage, monstrous as it is, is binding on a cosmic level. A downgrade, I'd say, trading a hybrid demon Lord for a filthy Talonborn shifter. But then again, I've never truly understood your ways. Tactless mortal thinking isn't my forte."

A growl clawed its way out. So much talk and yet not a single answer. "You're dodging my question. Tell me where she is or—"

"Or what, you'll kill me?" Nasheesh laughed. "I know the look in your eyes; you're blood hungry. Your father used to get the same way. You've already decided my fate, and nothing I do is going to change that. You've got nothing, Princess."

"Queen." I tilted my head, pressing the pad of my thumb into my scythe. It bit my finger, sharp and satisfying. "I have your son. Tell me where my mother is, or I'll slice off your eyelids and make you watch as I end his life."

"Ha, nice try, but my son can't be killed by mere blade or magic. I think you'll find him to be much more than you bargained for."

More mind games. He aimed to distract me, buy Malachi time no doubt, but I'd had enough. My scythes rattled the nearer I drew to him, their insatiable hunger downright palpable. "I know what you're doing, and it won't work. My guards pursue him as we speak. They will find him, and I *will* kill him."

"You think so, do you?"

"I don't think; I know." My rage whispered to me then. It pressed me to touch skin and read his energy to unearth his secrets. I collected my scythes in one hand, clasped my free hand around Nasheesh's head, and the visions came: moist cave walls, iron-clad tracks. Chaverton Mine, a few miles outside the demon capital. My mom would be there.

"Found her," I smirked. Death's freeze radiated from every pore as I yanked the advisor to his feet and crossed my blades at his throat.

"Any last words?"

"Yes," he spat. "Go to hell."

In a brutal display, I put an end to the false teacher, the one who sought to steal my throne. He thudded at my feet, lifeless and headless. Adrenaline rushed through me. So long I'd wanted to end him, yet my scythes were still thirsty. Unsatisfied. And what kind of person would I be to deny their need? They'd get their fill.

Of hybrid blood.

My newfound abilities sang to me once more, urging me to reach towards the gory mess at my feet. I dipped two fingers in the warm, crimson pool, and the energy took root in me instantly. Malachi's lineage—descended from Nasheesh's—called to me: heartbeat fast, quick breaths, footsteps upon cobblestone...the paths. He'd be there.

A breeze tickled my cheeks, and I found myself before the courtyard gates in a flash. Teeth gritted together, I stalked straight for Malachi's silhouette reflected on the shifter path ahead. The moment he noticed me, he slapped a hand on the shifter plaque and raced towards the parting door which had somehow heeded his call. I stopped in my tracks. How? Those gates only minded Death's will. The door should never have opened for him.

"Stop," I demanded, and cemented Malachi's feet in place.

They stuck, but only for a moment before he broke free. I pursued him with calculated, slow steps. The overbearing essence of wrath hit me and coiled around my brain, tightening like a vice. Suddenly, I was ravenous. Flames erupted in my mouth all at once, and I doubled over. My gums tore, pulsed, and shifted. With a shaky hand, I pressed a finger against my canines and found fangs protruding where smooth teeth once lay. I was becoming what my Death magic needed me to be: bloodthirsty. I could smell him clearer now, hunger settling in my gut.

I would drain him down to the last drop.

"Malachi," I called in a haunting, singsong tone. "There's no sense in running. I can smell a coward a mile away."

Hands tight around my scythes, the thrill of the hunt went wild in my veins. I stalked through the shifter gate to find Malachi motionless in the flame-engulfed street, waiting.

"So the insufferable mortal queen finally finds me," he seethed. A longsword at his side illuminated in the flame's light. "Attack me if you are foolish enough. But I warn you, I am deathless."

"All things die; you are no exception." Like condensing vapor, I appeared at his side and hurled my blades at his throat. But he mirrored my speed and disappeared before my eyes. I growled, searching.

A slow clap sounded from atop the burnt home behind me. "Nice try, but you lack conviction!"

I whipped around, but he remained unseen until I was firmly planted. He phased a foot ahead and swung his sword. Barely dodging, I slipped through time to escape his swing radius. The power he held: it was greater than I'd anticipated. I had to end him. Quick.

"You mock me?" I said, lowering my stance. "Knowing the strength I've claimed? I'm Death, asshole. You're nothing to me."

I stepped forward and struck again, but he evaded, slipping through my grasp.

"I hold knowledge you could only ever dream of, and Cadagon was the embodiment of idiocy, not Death. Same as you." Again, he flashed before me. "*I* am Death!"

Blasphemous! His blade slashed, and I jutted my head back just in time to avoid decapitation, but my arm absorbed the brunt. The hiss of torn flesh echoed, and chills dotted my skin.

Fuck, that one was deep.

Blood ran, but I let it fuel me. Push me. I stood, counting the droplets as they pelted the pavement below, and a murderous air surrounded me. Malachi didn't retreat, but I saw his concern. His pupils shrunk, and he tightened his grip on his sword's hilt. Time to lay my trap.

"You know nothing of strength," I ground out, lowering my stance yet again. "You are a weakling, just like your father whose body lies cold in my wake!" I projected behind him and traced a single finger along his shoulder as I circled to face him. "Oops, did I forget to mention I killed him? Yeah, cut his head clean off. My apologies."

His brow flinched. "Impossible. The pact would never allow it!"

He mirrored my steps and reached for my shoulder in an attempt to bait me. But I'd planned for such. I had him right where I wanted him.

"Gotcha." I spun about, jutted my blades, and hit my mark with precise accuracy. But it wasn't Malachi's flesh I'd pierced. Frozen in time, heartbeat clapping hard against my ribs, I watched the brute remove my scythe buried in his shoulder as if he were simply swatting away a gnat. "Odin."

He settled at the hybrid's side, wrapping his arm around Malachi's hip.

"There you are, my love," Malachi whispered, and leaned in to kiss him. "I was afraid you'd miss the finale."

Odin met my gaze. "Never. I want to see her head land at the true king's feet."

Well, shit.

While I no longer feared death—my powers cemented in me— nothing would keep them from abducting me and torturing me within an inch of my life. I raised my remaining weapon, spinning it about. If my end was at hand, I wouldn't go down without a fight. "Give me your best shot."

Odin's sights sharpened. With a howl, he took his beastly form. His snarl said it all. One of us wasn't walking away from this. On me in a blink, he toppled me to the ground like a rag doll thrown from a car window. My skull cracked hard against the dirt.

Get up! This is not your end!

World spinning, I hopped to my feet and attempted to put some space between us. Damn, he was fast. Malachi's laughter knotted my stomach, but I never let Odin drift from view. Teeth bared, he charged me once more, but this time I slid from his path, leaving a projection of my magic behind. My shadows snaked around his neck and constricted, sinking into every crevice. He crumpled to the ground, whimpering.

"You bitch," Malachi screamed, and he stalked towards me.

My knees buckled. Oh, shit. Odin bit down on my shadows, the weight sinking into my marrow, and every muscle constricted. My power returned to me in a flash, hiding. A vicious wind picked up, sending ash and ember flying. He'd hurt my shadow babies. Wrong fucking move. "You'll pay for that, *pup.*"

I shifted towards the incoming beast, heels planted to hold my own. But it was too late. I lifted my head in time to catch Malachi circling behind, a sinister laugh rattling through him. He snatched my hair in his hand and ripped my head back. The cold sting of a blade nicked my throat.

"You can't kill me," I muttered through clenched teeth.

"You're wrong," Malachi growled into my ear. "You see, your coronation was never fully completed. The ceremony was interrupted. Which means…"

He didn't have to say it. I knew with every fiber of my being. I was still partially mortal. All this, and for what? A few hours as Death? What of my revenge? The vengeance I aimed to deliver? Sobering reality hit me, hard and swift. It was over. I let out a deep sigh, body relaxing in acceptance. I'd lost. "Just do it then. End me."

A feral growl slipped through Malachi, and he jerked my head back farther, a clump of hair falling out by the root. My scalp throbbed as Odin returned to human form and glowered down at me. I didn't give them the luxury of diverting my stare. They'd see my soul slip away, and I hoped they'd choke on it. That it scarred them, and I'd never leave their minds. Oh yeah, I'd haunt these assholes until their dying day.

I met Odin's gaze. "Do it then. Go on. Do it!"

"Easy now," he said, brushing a thumb across my bottom lip. I thrashed at his touch, but Malachi held tight. "We wouldn't want to—"

A thud echoed around us. Odin's eyes grew wide with confusion, words stuck in his throat. Opening his mouth to speak, I landed on the reason: a blade protruded through him, pointed straight towards me. Blood poured from his mouth. He choked, crumpling to the ground in a heap. Dead. Cooper stepped over his lifeless body, removing the dagger from the hound's skull.

"No!" Malachi shrieked from the depths of his soul.

I looked up in time to see the golden edge in his eyes reflect the fading in Odin's, and I made a startling discovery. A piece of the hybrid had just died, irises now gray. As if his life had been linked to Odin's somehow.

"Sorry about your mate," Cooper said nonchalantly as he started towards us. "But I couldn't very well let him live after he attacked my queen, could I?"

"You fucking monster," Malachi wept, and shoved his sword into me harder.

I fought a swallow, knowing damn well it would tear my throat open.

"Let her go," Cooper demanded, "and I'll let you keep your life."

"Filthy Talonborns. Righteous pricks." Malachi spit at his side. "Mate for a mate." He raised the blade above me, bringing it down with full force.

But Cooper proved faster. His dagger swept past my face, finding its home right below Malachi's chin. More blood spilled, this time dousing my hair in thick, warm streams as an iron perfume overtook my senses. Cooper's hand locked onto mine, whirling me to my feet, and stepped between us.

Malachi pawed at his free-hanging jawbone and ripped the dagger free. Still, he muttered, "You can't kill me."

"Shut your lying mouth before I cut out your tongue!" Cooper turned to me and bowed his head. "Lady Death, would you care to do the honors?"

"With pleasure."

My power sang a warning then: "Be weary of the deathless one."

While I had no clue what the hell that meant, I knew one thing with absolute certainty. Deathless or not, nobody could avoid the void's vastness. Its clutches were eternal. I snatched Malachi by his shirt collar, dragging him back towards the gate. He thrashed at my hold, but my shadows willed him into submission.

Heels clicking on the cobblestone path, I looked down over the void below, its emptiness teeming with sounds I'd never heard. My new ears perked at the rising growls, the gnashing of teeth. Based on the fear in Malachi's eyes, he heard it too. And he was shitting himself. He grasped at my hand cemented around his neck with shaky fingers, but he found no purchase. I set him down on the path's edge and crossed my blades over his throat.

"Any last words? Maybe an apology?" I mocked, a wicked grin

spreading up my cheeks.

Foam, like that of an infected animal, teemed around his tongue. "Never."

"May the void show you the same kindness you showed me," I snarled, and sliced him clean open. I reveled in the tear of flesh and bone, the magic within me thrumming. And with a final sigh, I released his body to the unending darkness below, the cry of a hundred beasts lifting to greet their new meal.

CHAPTER 19

MINE

We found my mom shaken and bound in frayed rope, her wrists torn to shreds. But she was alive. Once returned to the castle, I placed her in Suri's personal care to see to her rest and recovery. The look in my mother's eyes: that vacant, shaken shell of the strong woman I'd always known killed me. And so my decision was made. The second she recuperated, I would see to her relocation. No way I was letting her out of my sights again. She'd be untouchable under Anathema's laws and my careful eye. To my surprise, she seemed quite happy with the arrangement, sending guards immediately to retrieve her belongings from the mortal world. Queen energy still flowed through her, it seemed.

With my mom sound asleep, I tended to my own needs: a steaming hot shower that, if it weren't for my self-healing genes, would have melted flesh and bone. I scrubbed until I'd erased all signs of blood, both mine and not. Still, no matter how hard I tried, remnants remained caked under my nails, barely visible against my black-stained fingertips. Cadagon, Odin, Nasheesh, and Malachi: washed down the drain like day-old filth, their memories gone. Much to my surprise, I felt neither regret nor guilt but rather unabashed satisfaction. I'd wiped a damn plague from Anathema's midst.

Cloaked in Suri's most recent creation—a cherry-colored robe strewn in billowed lace sheets—I traipsed about the hall, its reports pointing straight to Cooper on the main staircase. I rounded the corner, and my feet stuck in place. There he stood—statuesque in his perfectly tailored, pinstriped suit—long locks swept over one shoulder; his stare cemented on Cadagon's portrait still hanging in plain view. Too many emotions to count simmered under my skin.

Face flushed, I dared that first step towards the answers I sought. "So care to explain what the hell just happened?"

"Come with me," he said softly, and reached for my hand. "I want to show you something."

I took a moment to process, but relinquished, laced my fingers through his, and followed his lead to the north wing staircase. The wing denied to me since my arrival. The hall of the Reigning Reaper. We wound about halls and corridors and entered doors I had never seen, let alone stepped through. Cadagon had sealed it all away from anyone but himself, yet Coop navigated them with ease.

"How do you know where you're going?" I called ahead.

"I know a lot more than you think I do, Kim." At the back most corner of a personal study cloaked in dust, he forced open a rickety door which led into a narrow staircase. "Almost there."

When we reached the top, he laid his shoulder against a corroded iron gate. Its rusty hinges squealed at his first couple of shoves, but come the third, the gate gave out and granted us access to a wide deck tucked below the castle's tallest tower. Coop strolled out, rested his elbows on a waist-high, stone wall dotted in archaic telescopes, and

I found my place at his side. I scoured the castle grounds below, its beauty matched by none, and I caught my breath. Stunning.

Cooper made his way to the tallest tower roof, its ledge barely reachable if not for his towering height.

"The kingdom's astronomers once used this place to study the void's shifting patterns when the last severe imbalance came about. This," he said, grasping the tower's gutter and hoisting himself up, "is the best view in Anathema. Here, give me your hand." He noticed my hesitation and chuckled. "Come on, I don't bite. Well, maybe a little."

"A vampire joke? Seriously?" I crossed the deck and stared up at him, reluctant. But I inevitably gave in, and he hoisted me up as if I were a mere fabric sheet, the corded muscles in his arms accentuating the thick-lined tattoos coiling up to his neck. "Holy shit, you're strong."

"Perks of being a pureblood." He winked.

"Pureblood, huh? So what, you think you're hot shit or something?"

His grin widened. "I might not be wearing Lyvias's face anymore, but I can still hear your heartbeat, Kim. It tells me you certainly think I am."

A breathy laugh seeped through me, warmth spreading in my cheeks. Gods, he was hot. I'd always known it, but damn. My stomach somersaulted as he helped me navigate the safest roof shingles to step on, his hand finding its place around my waist. Where he touched, my skin tingled the same as when Lyvias had done so, and I fought the urge to pull him closer. To see how other bits of skin might react to his touch. His lips. His tongue.

Bad Kim! Focus! Answers first, then you can devour him.

At the far side, he sat and patted the space next to him, an expectant shimmer in his eye. I sat and cast my sights to the horizon. My kingdom sprawled out amongst blanketed darkness. Each court teetered on thin stilts made of starlight, their gates and paths suspended above the endless black. An incredible, unbelievable sight, and yet there it lay, plain as night. Without a doubt, the most beautiful thing I'd ever beheld, in either Anathema or the mortal world.

Amongst all the courts, the shifter realm gave me the most pause. Its countless waterfalls spilled over defined borders and dissipated into the nothingness like water flowing over a counter top. While most streams seeped at a constant rate, the rightmost one roared in constant chaos thanks to the court's sure lean to the right. The imbalance, it was visible to the naked eye: undeniable.

I cleared my throat, refocusing. "Is this your first time in Anathema? Or..."

His lips pursed. "No, I've visited. Always in disguise of course. But I always knew I'd return one day to fulfill my duties."

My gut fell. Was that all I was? A responsibility? "Duties. Right."

He turned and tucked a stray hair behind my ear, his eyes dropping to my lips. "I know what you're thinking, and no. You were never a duty to me. You've always been the reward."

My chest tightened, sights set on the studded shine in his smile. I should have been livid, furious, *enraged*. He'd lied to me. I'd believed I'd never see him again. That my sacrifice to Fate meant a life without him. After everything, the disguise, the secrets he'd kept, and *still*, emphatic trust danced between us. This man, the hold he had on me, it defied reason. And I loved every damn second of it. All the while, he'd been there. And Lyvias, well, I'd shared so much with him, allowed myself to care for him. Holy shit. I'd almost fucked my best friend without even knowing it!

He raised an eyebrow. "What?"

"That night...that's why you stopped me, right?" My cheeks flushed.

"Yes," he said, trailing his thumb along my jawline. "I wasn't about to be inside you and not have you scream *my* name."

An anxious laugh slipped through me. "It wasn't that you didn't want me then?"

"Don't tell me you question my feelings for you, Kim. You're smarter than that."

Two sharp fangs peeked behind his lips, and I almost asked if they'd been his all along or if he'd grown a fondness for them after wearing Lyvias's face for so long. Flashes of those teeth sinking deep into my skin made the space between my legs throb. Weep. But the need didn't outweigh the heavy question rattling in my skull. "How is this possible? You, being here with me. I gave you up. You were my sacrifice to Fate."

"Was I? Or were your attempts to rescue me the sacrifice?"

My body tensed. That *had* been the wording of Fate's and my deal, yes. Clever. A loophole in the blood pact. "Did you and June...did you plan this?"

"In a way." He leaned back and sighed. "It wasn't easy, reaching her. We both knew your survival was all that mattered. If you'd kept hunting for ways to save me, then you'd never have seen the plot against you. Your stubbornness would have been your downfall," he said, bumping my shoulder playfully.

June's face covered in light trickled across my mind, heart surging at the thought. She'd loved me as I'd loved her, despite the old gods' attempt to sever us. So much so, she'd given me the most selfless gift: a chance. To love again. To trust. To find joy after loss. I squeezed my eyes shut, holding back tears. My sweet ray of sun. "You did this together?"

"We all did, yes. For you."

"Because you love me," I stated. It wasn't a question. Not anymore.

He smiled wide. "Always."

Words escaped me. Every silent assurance spanning our years together crashed in. While he hadn't said it out loud, he'd expressed his feelings for me over and over again. Each time he'd told me I was beautiful, talented, and capable. When he'd woken up early to grab me coffee, sure to add my two Splendas and whole milk just how I liked it. Punches he'd thrown to defend my honor.

His brow creased. "Do you not feel the same?"

"I...I do." I ran a hand over my face. "But you lied to me. Why? Why pose as Lyvias and not just tell me the truth?"

His face fell. "Lying to you is the hardest thing I've ever done. I hated every second of it. But we had to, for your safety. Death assured me it was the only way."

The floodgates of fury opened wide in my soul, my magic raging. Cadagon? My enemy, the one we'd sought to kill. They'd worked together? My hands shook. "You were working with that monster? Why in the hell would you do that?"

"He wasn't what you think, Kim."

I yanked my hand from his, raised it in dismissal, and denied the dark desire to seal his lips. "After what he did to you, your people, you're going to defend him?"

"I can prove his innocence." He reached for my hand again. "But first, can you hear me out? Let me tell you what I have to share? I can explain everything if you let me."

I said nothing and frantically searched his face for any red flags or acute warning. My shadows coasted across his skin, probing, and he let them. When they returned, they confirmed his innocence. After a few beats, I breathed out the remnants of anger. If anyone deserved my patience, it was him.

"Fine," I said, sharp. "But for old time's sake. The verdict is still out on your guilt, got it?"

A smirk teemed at his cheeks. "More than fair."

"Well, go on then. Tell me everything."

"Right," he said with a nod. "Well, I'll start at the beginning then. When I was young, your mom saved me. My mother knew what was coming for the shifters the night of the massacre, for the purebloods in specific. The chaos started, and she saw your mom fleeing into the woods to hide you away. She begged her to take me too. So she did. She brought me to the mortal world with you, hid me. I'm alive today because of her."

I shuffled. "What happened to your mom then?"

He paused in thought for a moment. "The flames got to her. At least that's what I've been told. She went back to save my father and never came out again."

The memory of my mother confronting Cadagon overtook me. How Death was alerted to a missing pureblood, my mother's harsh words about the friend she had found, burnt and broken. I set a hand on Coop's and squeezed. "I'm so sorry."

"It was a long time ago," he said, though his rigid shoulders told me it was anything but old news.

"Your mom, back in the mortal world?"

"Not my real mom, no." He shook his head. "She was a shifter your mom tracked down after everything. Her name is Clarava. She taught me what she could, about how to keep my shifting in check, but pureblood energy is hard to teach when you don't possess it yourself. Mostly, I think your mom just didn't want me to be alone."

I had always wondered how Coop had ended up so different—both in appearance and personality—from his mom. It made sense. "If you're a pureblood, that means…"

"Breathe easy, I hail from the Talonborn line." He squeezed my hand. "The Bloodbanes were at fault for the massacre. They tried to wipe my line from existence, leaving them with all the power. Cadagon sought to stop it."

"By killing and banishing all the shifters?" I scoffed. "That's lunacy."

"None of it was his fault."

I squinted up at him. "But I saw it the day I read the realm. He conspired with a demon to ensure all the shifters had been wiped out like he'd ordered."

His expression hardened. "It's not what it looked like. But that part is not mine to share."

Nails pressed into my palms, I sucked in a deep breath. "If it wasn't how it seemed, then why didn't Cadagon tell me the truth? Explain it all?"

Coop busied himself in his suit pocket, removed a wax sealed envelope, and extended it to me. "He did."

I grasped the letter, hindrance at my fingertips. The sincerity, the honesty I found in Coop's expression unsettled me. Even my shadows stilled. For the first time since I'd arrived, I questioned myself and what I'd known about Cadagon. Who he was. My composure faltered, toes curling, and my stomach knotted. I peeled back the corner and exposed the dead king's words.

My dearest daughter,

If you are reading this, it means you've succeeded in ending me. Contrary to what you may believe, this was always my plan: to die by your hand. Please know how sorry I am for the way I treated you, my dear, but I needed you to believe I was at fault—

"No." I crunched the letter to my chest and sobbed, entirely overwhelmed. My magic danced about the tear stains on the page. If I'd been wrong…if Cadagon had held honor above all in his mind until death, and I'd killed him, then—fuck. My breath caught in my throat. Did that make me the real monster in this story? I shook my head, rocking myself back and forth. "No, I'm not ready for this."

Coop wrapped his arms around me. "You don't have to be. He'll be there, when you're ready."

"I was so cruel to him," I whimpered.

He grasped my face, turning it towards him. "You freed him. He knew you were ready, knew you'd be the leader Anathema needed. He wanted this."

I let his words be the truth I settled on. How long I let the grief overtake me, I couldn't be certain. But Cooper remained patient, holding me close. While I hungered for the answers surely included in Death's parting letter, I hadn't the stomach for it. Not yet. And so I willed my body into submission, forcing Cadagon from my mind. I'd had enough death, enough turmoil, enough chaotic truths revealed for one day. In that moment, I needed something different. Something kind. A moment of peace.

Tucking the letter in my pocket, I pressed into Cooper's arms, resting my head against his chest, and lost myself in his gentle heartbeat. "Thank you."

He kissed my head. "For what?"

"For always being there for me. Even as Lyvias, you were still *you*." I sat up straight. "Wait, was that you all along?"

He shook his head, a playful bit of violence in his eyes.

"When did you do it? Kill Lyvias?"

A vengeful smirk overcame him, eyes hooded. "The night I saw him disrespect you on the castle stairs. Nobody calls my woman a cancer and fucking lives."

"Wait, you saw that? How?"

He stiffened and shuffled nervously. "If I tell you, will you promise not to murder me?"

"I will promise no such thing."

"Okay, okay, I'm...I'm Poe."

I slapped his arm hard enough to get a satisfying *oof* from him. I'd loved the hell out of that strange little bird, thought nature had chosen me or some shit, just to find out it'd been him all along. "You were in my room! Saw me undress, you creep!"

"Not true!" He spun and crossed his legs. "Seriously, think about it. Do you ever remember me around when those moments came about? *Really* think."

I thought long and hard, but as he'd said, I drew a blank. He'd always flitted off into the woods, only present when I could pay him full attention. I'd never given his flighty escapes much thought, but now it made sense. "Fine," I sighed, and leaned against him. "Dude... you ate worms."

"Yeah, not my best look." He snickered. "But to be honest, they weren't half bad once you got used to them. Earthy flavor. Lots of protein. Plus, it made you happy."

"Nasty!"

We laughed together, like old times and yet altogether new. I was comfortable here—hidden in his arms—in ways I'd never considered I could be. My best friend, my partner. But there was one thing I'd yet to claim him as.

My lover.

In the low light of night, I studied him, unable to resist any longer. I grabbed his face, my thumbs gently caressing his sharp cheekbones.

"What?" he whispered.

"Want to know something?"

His face softened. "I don't know, do I?"

"How about I give you a hint?"

I brought my lips to his, but paused an inch shy. The electricity built as I gazed into his eyes. He leaned closer, the spark between us igniting, and I allowed the moment to take hold. I kissed him as if my life depended on it, like he was the very air in my lungs. My hands twisted through his hair; I relinquished control for the first time in so long. Truly let go, with no reservations or doubts. Just him, and the unarguable safety he'd always gifted me. Comfort in every possible way.

I climbed onto his lap, parting my legs to settle. His growl rushed through me as his hand slipped into my silk bottoms, thumb brushing my most sensitive spot. Every inch of me reacted, goosebumps raised at his touch. Without a second thought, I slid down his body, unzipping his pants, but his hand clasped over mine.

"You don't have to do that," he said breathily. "I just want you."

But I wasn't about to stop. While other wicked men had sucked the pleasure out of such acts in the past, this man was not them. Cooper had proven himself trustworthy. Had loved me through every fucked-up instance, and I aimed to reward him for that. My hands went back to work on his pants. "Let me show you how much I love you."

His lips quirked up. "If you insist, my Queen."

Shimmying his bottoms off his tight ass, the thick length that burst forth made me pause. I'd seen him—all of him—before, but not like this. Not with sober, hungry eyes. I took him into my mouth slowly, driving him into the back of my throat. The sweet taste tickled my taste buds, nails latching onto his hip bones. He moaned deep, encouraging me as I grasped the base of his length, shoving him farther in, tongue swirling on his head.

"Good fucking girl," he praised, hands knotting in my hair.

And that, well, that was all it took. Ravenous, I devoured him. Hand pumping, I felt him begin to climb. His muscles tensed under my wandering tongue as I kissed and sucked and bit.

He grasped my chin, lifting it. "Enough. I want to come inside you, woman."

With that, he flipped me on my back, ripping his coat and shirt off with haste, exposing the tattoos cascading across his smooth skin. I stared in wonder. Fuck, he was stunning. His fangs found their place at my neck. No warning, all gentleness gone, he sank his teeth into me, and I came on contact.

"Holy. Fucking. Shit," I whispered, body spasming in my climax's wake.

"You ain't seen nothing yet, Lady Death." Sights darkened, he ripped my clothes off piece by piece until I lay there, bare before him. "You are perfection. You are *mine*."

"And you are mine," I breathed, reaching to pump him. His head rolled back with pleasure. Dropping down, he slid his tongue against my swollen clit, nipping until I came. Again. *Fuck*, he was good. I forced him upward to meet my gaze. "I want you inside me."

At that, he flipped me to my stomach, lifting my hips. "What my queen wants, she gets."

With one large thrust, his thickness filled me to the brim, and I cried out. I'd never felt so complete, so full, so uncontrollably in want. No, need. Pushing back against him, I met each thrust, eager to please. His hands slipped around to cradle my breasts, fingers pinching my nipples as he continued barreling into me, hard. Those gentle touches mirrored by his less than gentle hips had me climbing for the third time.

"There," I sighed heavily, savoring the rush his hard length gifted me. "Right there, don't stop."

He pulled out suddenly, leaving me empty and panting. "Is this what you want?" he teased, smacking his dick against my ass.

"Yes, don't stop." My lungs labored, the fire inside raging so hot I couldn't see straight.

A deep chuckle rattled through him. "I didn't hear a 'please.'"

"Please," I begged, all semblance of control and dominance drained from my body. "Please, Cooper, fuck me."

"Gods," he snarled, and shoved into me with full force.

We climbed together, our bodies working effortlessly in tandem until he edged me once again, cutting off my pleasure.

"Why!" I cried out.

He grabbed me by the waist, man-handling me onto my back. "Because I want to see that pretty face when you scream my name, Kimber."

At the sound of my name on his tongue, I took control, shoving him deep.

His brow crinkled, mouth gaping as he looked down, watching his thickness sink in and out of me, over and over. And I knew I had him: hook, line, and sinker. But he had me too, his thumb working my clit as he found that perfect rhythm. Wrapping my arms around his neck, I whispered, "I love you, Cooper Rollins. I am yours."

His pleasured groan echoed out against the castle walls, my own rising to meet it. Our eyes locked, and we crashed over the edge.

Together.

EPILOGUE

THREE WEEKS LATER

I flipped the tattered letter in my hands, Cooper placing a single kiss on my cheek. He didn't utter a word, but then again, he didn't have to. Everything he had to say was written right there in his kind eyes. It would be okay. I was ready now. With a nod, I stepped out onto our bedroom balcony. What was to come could be avoided no longer. Not with the rising unrest spilling out from the once silent void beneath our kingdom. A deep breath, and I peeled back the crumpled edge, revealing Death's words.

My shadows shifted inside, and before I could process what was happening, my inner power had already locked onto the astral. Landing on my feet in the very same place I'd met Fate during our time together—sky shrouded in violent, violet clouds—I found him. Hands behind his back, he greeted me with a warm smile.

"Kimber," Cadagon said, voice shaky. "You came."

Tears welled as I took him in. "I'm sorry it took me so long… Dad."

The word destroyed him, a sob slipping out, and warm tears rolled down my cheeks. Lost for words, he lifted a hand and flicked it through the air. The wax-sealed paper in my clutches obeyed his command, fluttering to him in the breeze. He knew I hadn't read it. How, I wasn't sure, but he did. Rummaging in his robe pocket, he removed a pair of glasses, pushing them to the brim of his nose, and cleared his throat.

My dearest daughter,

If you are reading this, it means you've succeeded in ending me. Contrary to what you may believe, this was always my plan: to die by your hand. Please know how sorry I am for the way I treated you, my dear, but I needed you to believe I was at fault. That I was the one who'd caused the imbalance within Anathema, because in essence, I did…just not in the way you'd always presumed. It all started when your mother fled, her reign incomplete. I don't blame her for her decision, not in the slightest. She made the right choice. But it did put Anathema's law into effect, ensuring a second shifter would have their just inheritance of the throne. And so, you were promised to Copernicus Talonborn, 'Coop' as you so interestingly call him. Unbeknownst to me, Nasheesh grew envious of both the throne and the role you two would play in the future. What happened in the shifter realm all those years ago was directly stemmed from that jealousy. He sought my heir's throne, your throne, but knew it would be no simple task. Until

I saw Nasheesh amongst the chaos that night, blood dripping from his hands and seething like the beast he was, I had no idea of the promises he'd made and the consequences if he weren't to deliver on them. You see, he had always possessed a strange ability which allowed him to commune with the Void herself, and he held sway over Anathema because of it. Throughout the years, he'd convinced himself that the Void wished for a reset, a new monarchy, when in fact all she craved was restored balance. But that route didn't lead him to the crown. So he turned the courts against one another and encouraged a thirst for power within the Bloodbanes. He bred hatred, constructed a cult he later convinced that I was the personal enemy of. He thought if he pushed the imbalance to a certain level, the Void would heed his desire for new rulers and choose his bloodline to do so. Together, the cult pushed the world farther out of balance, using ancient rituals to cast the shifter realm into eternal darkness. They were the cause of the massacre that fateful night, seeking to sacrifice anyone they could. My forces sought them out, but by the time I grew keen to Nasheesh's plan, it was already too late. I meant to end him, sought his life reaped, and yet I couldn't. As I drew my blade, he muttered two words that stopped me in my tracks.

Cadagon met my gaze, shoulders shaking.

"Kimberly Ann." He knew where you were hidden, claimed he had forces on the ready to strike you down. And so I made the best and worst decision of my life, a pact in blood. His and his own son's immunity, and my personal assistance in his scheme for

your safety: the one who remains the sole hope for the people of Anathema. And so, bound by blood, I needed you to hate me. I needed you to end me, to break the pact and become queen without my shadow looming above you. Only then could Nasheesh's sins be brought to light, wiped clean from our world. Now, I know your heart. Had you believed I had even a speck of light still in me, you'd have spared my life, sought an alternate path. Cooper, he knew it too, which is why he was willing to not only lay in that coffin to convince you to return to Anathema, but to seduce the real enemy into getting close enough that we might strike. Little did I know just how far Nasheesh was willing to go: binding Malachi to sacrificial magic in an attempt to denounce our bloodline. To steal Death's gift bestowed on our family. And while Cooper posed as Lyvias—whose loyalties had always laid with the void cult—I become the villain you needed me to be while he got inside information into Malachi and Nasheesh's plans. You must know, we both hated every moment of it: lying to you as we did. But this, Kim, was the only way. You'd never have let me go if not. And that, my dear one, would have been your end: a fate I simply couldn't bear. So please do not fault him. And do not regret your choice; stand firm on it! For you will change everything. I know this with more conviction than I've ever known a thing, because you changed me. If you can do that, you can do anything. I love you, Kimber. Even death itself can never change that.

Sincerely, Your Father

I ran to him, buried my face in his chest, and sobbed. Then, as quickly as he had arrived, he was gone. Through his sacrifice, his love would be with me forevermore.

ACKNOWLEDGEMENTS

First and foremost, I want to thank The Universe for constant guidance, encouragement, and opportunities to grow and learn. It's been a long road to get here, but I know I didn't make it this far on my own.

Justin, love of my life, you are *incomparable*. Your love is the very reason I write. Every kiss in the moonlight, every time you've shown up for me, defended me, every tear you've wiped away has kept me here. Thank you for being my light in the darkness. Know I will find you in every lifetime with the intention to know you better and love you deeper than the last. Not even death can keep us apart. Thank you for being you, baby.

Now, I'm going to use the age-old cliché: it takes a village to raise a book. And boy did I have a kind and gracious community backing me the entire way to publication!

Cassie: my best friend, soul sister, and phenomenal copyeditor. The tears we've shed, the panic attacks we've weathered, and the years we've grown alongside one another all led to this point. Thank you for never giving up on me or this dream, even in those hard moments when I wanted to. *Death Shall Bow*—and me—is what it is today because of your unwavering support. I'll never be able to thank you enough for believing in me and always being there to remind me who I am. I love you, woman.

Gramma, your love and support know no bounds, and simply put, *I* wouldn't be here today without you, let alone this book. I'll always strive to capture even a fraction of the fierce compassion you've gifted me into every story I write. Papa, thank you for teaching me what it means to dedicate yourself to the things and people you care about as you have dedicated yourself to the well-being of this family your entire life. I have the best grandparents a person could ever ask for; and I, again, thank The Universe for giving us each other.

To my mama, thank you for always cheering me on and reminding me that when I put my heart into something, anything is possible. You are one amazing woman, and I am so lucky to call you my friend and mom. Dad, thank you for teaching me that with hard work and determination dreams can become reality. Without your help and encouragement, I would have given up on this dream a long time ago. I'm so glad I didn't. <3 And to my little sis, thank you for teaching me what it means to fight for what you want. Your determination is a constant inspiration.

Thank you to my incredible and wise aunt, Connie, for all the late-night cry sessions and celebratory crystal shop dates. The positive energy you sent me throughout this process never went unnoticed. To my all-around amazing cousin, Kristen, I can't wait to hold YOUR book in my hands one day and scream, "MY COUSIN WROTE THAT." Your enthusiasm for this book carried me through when I lost the path, and for that I am forever grateful!

And now, my bookish village. Thank you to my exceptional editor and friend, Maria. Your vision, insight, and knowledge took this book to new heights I hadn't imagined were possible. I am forever in your debt. To my Scream Queen Witchy Tia, Eunice, and Harper, there aren't words to express how thankful I am for everything you've done to help me along the way. I appreciate you more than you'll ever know! And to the rest of my spooky book club babes: you kept me sane, laughing, and showered me with more support than I thought possible. Here's to many more years of celebrating our mutual love of books in Spooky Tomes and Tombstones. *whispers* Reader, join the discord if you haven't already. We have fun there! ;)